COVER THE BONES

A DETECTIVE MARK TURPIN CRIME THRILLER

RACHEL AMPHLETT

SAXON
PUBLISHING

Cover the Bones © 2023 Rachel Amphlett

The moral rights of the author have been asserted.

All rights reserved.

This is a work of fiction. While the locations in this book are a mixture of real and imagined, the characters are totally fictitious. Any resemblance to actual people living or dead is entirely coincidental.

CHAPTER ONE

South-east of Didcot

Derek Andrews scratched at his greying beard and squinted against the bright afternoon sunshine.

The wide field had been planted with barley until recently, stubble remaining in the tractor wheel ruts under his boots and grain scattered where it had escaped capture.

A cloudless blue sky cradling a late-summer sun warmed his back while he peered up at the fifty-metre-high steel electricity pylon beside him. The static charge from the structure was tangible, tickling the fine hairs on his bare arms.

Keeping a wary eye on the archaeological magnetometer hanging from canvas straps over his shoulders, he reached around to tug at the collar of his polo shirt to stop it sticking to the back of his neck. Adjusting the bandanna that covered his head and provided some protection from the sun's glare, he lowered his gaze to his notebook, checked the grid references on the screen in front of him, and grunted under his breath.

'Fancy a quick drink after work, love?'

He glanced over his shoulder at the voice and smiled as Michelle wandered between the series of tiny yellow flags that poked out from the dirt, her skin bronzed after the previous week's outdoor work.

'Who else is going?' he said, jutting out his hip to take the weight of the magnetometer while he waited for her.

'Gerry said he might – he isn't planning on heading back to Reading until tomorrow. Tim, too – and I think Helen might come along. She said she was going to phone her other half and see if he can sort out the kids' dinner. I figured at least that way we could relax while we share the updates from the weekend.' Michelle stopped next to him and raised a hand to shield her eyes from the sun as she peered at the field boundary. 'You'd have thought they'd have done this when they finalised the planning application instead of leaving it until the last minute.'

Derek turned his attention to where she looked, running his gaze over the line of heavy plant machinery churning up the soil in the adjacent field. A wide ditch had been carved into the earth over there, the pale grey clay and chalk-heavy soil cast to one side in gigantic piles that baked in the August heat.

'It was probably too wet in March to get conclusive

results. That's why they opted for a drone survey instead back then, I suppose.' He swallowed, his tongue scoring the top of his mouth, and he nodded his thanks as Michelle handed him a bottle of water. 'Anyway, it does us a favour, doesn't it? Helps us top up the coffers before winter sets in.'

'True. So, what about that pint?'

'I think I could be persuaded,' he said, grinning. He took a swig of the water, then swiped the back of his hand across his mouth. 'Where're they planning on going?'

'Probably the one in the village.' Michelle shrugged. 'It's the nearest, so more convenient for everyone.'

'Okay.' Derek held out the water bottle. 'Thanks.'

'Put it in your satchel, just in case. I don't mind driving home after the pub if you want more than one, either. I've got an article for the local newspaper to finish writing tonight if I'm going to meet their deadline.'

'I'd best get a move on, then. How's it going over there?'

He jerked his chin to where a group of four young archaeologists knelt beside one of the pylons behind his position, their voices just audible over the sweeping calls of larks that swooped and ducked over the field.

'That anomaly on the readings Tim noticed turned out to be a handful of seventeenth-century nails.' She wrinkled her nose. 'There were a couple of musket balls nearby, but that was all – nothing to worry about.'

'I'm not worried,' he grinned. 'I'll bet he's disappointed though.'

Michelle rolled her eyes. 'You should never have told him

about the Saxon tribe that was based around here. He's got his hopes up now.'

'Don't tell Bill that – he'll never forgive us if we find something significant now. It'll completely cock up his project schedule.'

'True. How much longer are you going to be?'

'Not long.' He pointed towards the thick line of trees a few metres away. 'The cables are going to go under the stream that forms the boundary beneath those, so I'll map the area beside it before I call it a day. I can pick up the cable route from the other side in the morning.'

'Okay. See you in a bit.'

She threw a wave over her shoulder and turned away, her long strides easily covering the ground between him and the small group.

Derek turned back to the magnetometer screen, rolled his shoulders to take the weight of the straps, and checked the grid settings.

Satisfied he hadn't strayed from his bearings while chatting with his wife, he looped the headphones over his ears, his brow furrowing in concentration.

He set off at a brisk pace, keeping time with the constant *beep* emitted by the machine, easing into the familiar routine.

When the National Grid had announced that their nationwide beautification project would extend to other parts of the UK, he and Michelle had kept a weather eye on the contracts awarded to construction companies, pouncing on the opportunity to bid for the second phase of archaeological surveys.

They had narrowly missed out to a competitor from Milton Keynes for the first phase, but their local presence won over the contracts manager for this final check ahead of the cable route being carved through the countryside south of Didcot. Once that was done, the pylons would be torn down, returning the view of the horizon to one not seen since the 1930s.

Derek sighed with relief when he reached the trees.

A mixture of oak and alder provided welcome shade, light dappling on thick foliage that swayed above his head as he paused beside a blackthorn bush.

The thread-like path that lay beyond the brambles was rarely used, according to the farmer whose land bordered the stream, despite it having an access point that emerged beside a twisting B road half a mile away.

Taking a deep breath, relishing the coolness under the trees, he paused at the sound of water bubbling along at a leisurely gait beyond his position.

He could sense the history here, and, despite his words to Michelle, he appreciated Tim's excitement.

Named after a Saxon chieftain, Hacca's Brook wound its way between here and the Thames, carving a path through the landscape over centuries. The stream had witnessed the waxing and waning of the Roman invasion, the English Civil War and more, and yet here it was, almost forgotten beneath a tangle of fallen branches and leaf litter.

He found an opening to the path overgrown with long

grass and stinging nettles, a pale blue butterfly rising into the air as he kicked a rough track through and lowered the magnetometer once more.

He would complete the required grid layout this afternoon, and, if anything gave him cause for concern, he would flag it and return with the metal detector in the morning.

His heart rate increased as he worked, the thrill of the chase kicking in as he began to sweep the ground.

Yes, Bill McFarlane would be frustrated if they did find something of archaeological significance, but surely the site manager would be swayed by the publicity. If only...

The machine chimed, and Derek's gaze snapped to the screen.

He froze on the spot.

Something was down there.

He glanced over his shoulder.

The path had curved to the right, following the watercourse, but in his trancelike state, he had drifted off to the left by accident, scuffing against the longer grass without noticing.

Derek cursed loudly. If any of his post-graduate assistants had done the same thing, he would have berated them for sloppiness, but...

This was how the big finds were made.

The ones that made headlines.

By accident.

Swinging the magnetometer away from his body, he used

the toe of his boot to gently prise away an errant bramble, and stooped to take a closer look.

The ground was undisturbed, lush grass carpeting the area so the indentation the specialist equipment had identified was years old, rather than recent.

He couldn't make out any signs of animal disturbance, and there were no tracks in the thin mud at the fringes of the path either.

Gently, he unclipped the straps and lay the magnetometer on the path a few metres behind the target area, then fished a trowel from his satchel and dropped to a crouch.

After making a series of well-practised cuts to the earth, he lifted out a section of the grass and felt around in the soil. Whatever had caused the alert on the machine was close to the surface, he was sure.

Clenching his jaw, he used the trowel to scrape away a little more of the clay soil, its texture damp now that the sun-dried top layer had been removed, and pushed back the dirt with his fingers.

He blinked in surprise.

A pale green material, similar to that of his polo shirt, emerged from the small indentation he'd created. A strip of cotton perhaps, firmly stuck under the rest of the soil that still covered the area he'd swept with the magnetometer.

He followed the direction of the material to the left, farther away from the stream and into the thicket of brambles that separated his position from the arable field.

Frowning, Derek reached out and pulled back a tangle of ivy.

He lurched backwards with a startled cry.

Reaching up between a sapling's tentative roots, its pale grey skeletal fingers clawing from the earth, was a hand.

CHAPTER TWO

Detective Sergeant Mark Turpin rolled up the sleeves of his pale blue shirt and peered over the top of the pool car.

Beyond the hedgerow that lined the narrow potholed lane, a weather-beaten and dusty collection of machinery had been abandoned in the middle of a barren field, the grubby yellow paintwork of excavators, dump trucks and bulldozers at odds with the lush greenery that bordered the landscape.

The drivers stood beside their vehicles, heads lowered and hands in pockets while they scuffed at stones, occasionally pausing to glance over their shoulders towards a line of trees half a mile away from Mark's position, then turning back to their colleagues, the occasional shake of a head replacing words that were left unsaid.

Above their heads, a steady line of electricity pylons

marched across the field, weaving their way past a pair of enormous barns before disappearing from view.

Mark turned his attention to the vehicles lining the lane, running his eyes over the liveried patrol cars belonging to Thames Valley Police as uniformed officers turned back traffic and created a detour away from the crime scene.

He sighed, aimed his key fob at his borrowed vehicle and walked towards a young constable at the outer cordon.

The blue and white crime scene tape that was stretched between a signposted public footpath and a sycamore trunk lifted in the breeze as he approached, the cool air providing welcome relief from the sweltering heat that had baked the countryside these past two weeks.

'Afternoon, Sarge.' The constable – Knowles, according to the name badge over his left pocket – held out a clipboard and a pen. 'Word just came back – they reckon it's female, probably buried within the past couple of decades or so.'

'Christ.' Mark wrinkled his nose. 'Definitely not a historical find, then?'

Knowles shook his head. 'One of the archaeologists confirmed the clothing's too modern. What's left of it, anyway.'

'Is DC West along there?'

'Yes, Sarge – she got here twenty minutes ago.'

Voices filled the air while he signed his name on the log sheet – shouted instructions tinged with panic from the construction site mixing with the more practised tones of three crime scene investigators. He watched while they unloaded equipment from a nondescript white van parked beside a five-bar wooden gate on the opposite side of the lane, then turned back to Knowles and handed him the clipboard. 'New to the area, aren't you?'

'Yes, Sarge. I finished training six weeks ago.' The constable noted the time beside Mark's signature and held up the blue and white tape that blocked access to the public footpath. 'Follow it along about four hundred metres – you'll find the inner cordon after that bend you can see from here. There's a spot there where you can get suited up.'

'Thank you. And Knowles – keep those details about the victim to yourself for now, all right? Speculation about the circumstances won't help her, or her family.'

The young constable's cheeks flushed. 'Absolutely, Sarge.'

Mark ducked under the tape and hurried along the dirt path.

It was cracked in places down the middle where the sun had broken through the tree canopy and baked the surface, but a thin layer of mud clung to the verges on each side.

To his right, a ribbon of water twisted and edged its way beneath the trees, sunlight sparkling on the surface as the brook bubbled over rocks and fallen branches.

A thick swathe of long grass filled the left side of the path, insects buzzing past his face as he picked up his pace.

There was nothing to suggest the path was well-used before the discovery of the woman's body.

How long had she lain there?

And why?

'Sarge.'

Detective Constable January West raised her hand in greeting as he rounded the bend, her hair gathered up under a hood attached to the white protective suit she wore.

She excused herself from the group of three similarly clad figures she'd been talking with and made her way over to him, pausing at the second barrier of crime scene tape.

Peering past her, he nodded in greeting to the Home Office pathologist, Gillian Appleworth, who was standing beside the grave site and talking to two colleagues.

'Hell of a way to start the week, Jan. What do you know so far?' he asked, wobbling to keep his balance on the uneven ground while he tugged plastic booties over his shoes and then took the sealed bag she held out to him. 'Thanks.'

'As soon as Gillian got here she called in a forensic archaeologist and an anthropologist – we can't risk excavating the grave until they've got a full record of what's here.' She paused while he dragged the protective suit over his suit trousers and zipped it up to his neck. 'It's not ancient, that's for sure, and given the sort of clothing that they've uncovered so far, they think it's female. Off the record, of course, until they get the remains out of there and back to the lab.'

Mark pulled the hood up over his hair, snapped gloves over his hands, and entered the crime scene.

'Jasper's got a demarcated route set along this side.' Jan pointed to a series of pegs set into the dirt to the right of the path as she led the way. 'We can get to within a metre or so of the grave along here. They can't risk us getting any closer at the moment – they're still searching the ground either side of it for evidence.'

He followed her mutely, eyeing the pile of stinging nettles and brambles that had been cut away and laid farther up the path, away from where Jasper Smith stood next to a mound of earth, his head bowed while he watched his team work.

Beside the grave, three CSI technicians grappled with a temporary white tent, ready to place it over the gaping hole and protect it from the elements.

Jasper took a step back as Mark and Jan approached, lowered his tablet computer and scratched his head. 'I'll never get used to wearing these suits in this heat.'

'Then I'll try not to keep you from your work for too long.' Mark jerked his chin at the grave. 'Jan mentioned the grave was well-hidden.'

'Considering it's not even a metre deep, yes.'

Mark craned his neck to see the overgrown path snaking between the trees alongside the stream, narrowing as it headed east from their position.

The route seemed forgotten, abandoned – just as Jan had said.

'Dug in a hurry, perhaps,' he said, turning back to the CSI lead. 'So, was this footpath used more often at one time, I wonder?'

'There's an old faded wooden signpost at the far end that's pretty rotten and some of these trees blocking the path have been here a while.' Jasper shuffled in his protective suit until Mark could see his tablet screen, then flicked through the photographs. 'The grave itself is shallow but sheltered under the trees, so over time the leaf litter built up and covered it even more. If the project survey team hadn't been assessing the area for the cable route, the grave might never have been discovered. Add to the fact that the path looks more or less abandoned – you can see the vegetation's grown over it as well. I looked at the route on a satellite image – it doesn't link up to any of the more popular walking routes nearby, either.'

'There aren't that many houses around here,' Jan said. She pointed through the thick foliage to the field where the construction vehicles and their drivers idled. 'The farmer that owns this land told uniform he never used the path, which goes some way to explain why none of the hedgerows have been cut back this side, and the land on the other side of the stream is privately owned. Again, the family that live there say they keep a small flock of sheep in the field, and never use the path – in fact, they were surprised to hear it was through here. The wife said she thought the field was just bordered by the stream.'

Mark grimaced as the images on the screen changed to close-ups of the contents of the grave, the twisted skeleton visible amongst the soft dirt and knotted tree roots as the specialists worked methodically to uncover its final resting place.

'We'll speak to the other property owners in the area as soon as we can, then.' He shivered and turned his gaze from the screen to watch the work in progress. 'Who's the tall bloke at the far end, Jasper?'

'Robert Kerridge – he's the forensic anthropologist that Gillian called as soon as she realised what we've got here, and the man crouching in the trench at the moment is Hayden Bridges, a forensic archaeologist from Banbury.'

'Kennedy's going to have a heart attack when he sees what they charge.'

The CSI lead grimaced. 'I hope they both live up to their reputations, then.'

Beside Mark, Jan used the heel of her hand to wipe away a bead of sweat between her eyebrows, the protective suit crackling with the movement. 'Do you want to speak to the project archaeologist who found her, Sarge?'

'Might as well – and then we're going to have to speak to Kennedy about wrangling some extra manpower to start going through the missing persons database as soon as we have more information about her.' He sighed. 'Whoever she is, she was someone's daughter, perhaps someone's mother. We owe it to them to find out what happened to her, and why she ended up here.'

CHAPTER THREE

Jan scrunched up the discarded protective suit and stuffed it into a biohazard bin outside the cordoned-off grave site.

Over her shoulder, she could hear the gruff tones of the forensic anthropologist assigned to the find as he barked orders to the other experts. She turned to watch while Gillian's archaeology expert calmly explained that it would take at least another hour or more to assess the grave before they could begin the gentle process of removing the remains.

A breeze shivered through the sycamore trees above her and she lifted her chin to catch it against her face, relishing the coolness across her skin after the brutal reality of the crime scene.

Raking a hand through her hair, she fell into step behind Turpin as he led the way back to the lane with his phone to his ear, bringing Detective Inspector Ewan Kennedy up to date, and giving him the bad news about what was going to happen to his overtime budget.

'Christ, the boys…' she muttered, then pulled her phone from her bag and quickly typed a message to her husband Scott about what he might find in the freezer for their twins' dinner.

That done, she paused on the footpath while Turpin strode on ahead.

The low voices around the graveside had receded the minute she'd passed the bend in the path, and the knowledge that the lane was only a few hundred metres away from where she stood did nothing to ease the sense of eeriness that descended around her.

Apart from the gentle flow of the stream as it wound its way past, she could hear nothing beyond the tangled hedgerow leading to the field where the construction team waited.

She couldn't even see their dirt-streaked yellow vehicles.

On the opposite side of the stream, dark green ivy strangled thick oak trunks, the space between them cluttered with tall ferns that blocked out any indication that another field stretched beyond.

Jan shuddered, and hurried to catch up with Turpin.

He ended his phone call as she drew near and shoved his phone back into his shirt pocket.

'What's the name of the bloke who found her?'

'Derek Andrews. Runs the company with his wife, Michelle, who's also on site this week.'

'Do you know where he is?'

'Sam Owens did the initial interview with him when we got here. I'll ask him. Hopefully they haven't been sent home yet.' Jan smiled in thanks as Knowles lifted the crime scene tape above their heads, then paused to scuff the worst of the dirt from her shoes. 'Where's Sam, Ian?'

Knowles pulled his radio from his vest and jerked his chin towards the neighbouring field. 'I'll call him for you. He managed to corral the archaeology team into a corner of the site car park while we were taking statements earlier. I think he was just waiting for the nod to let them go.'

'Tell him to hang fire,' said Turpin. 'I want a word first.'

'Will do, Sarge.'

Moments later, Jan walked through an open metal gate and into the field that bordered the footpath.

A thick-set man in his fifties wearing dirty safety boots hovered beside one of the uniformed constables. He checked off the names of those who passed, and she recognised the logo of the private security company emblazoned across the left-hand side of his hi-vis vest.

His face was glum as he watched the police hovering outside the three temporary cabins that bordered the gravel car park in a rough U-shape, and Jan noticed the weary smile he gave to one of the construction workers as he passed by.

Sam Owens raised his hand in greeting and excused himself before crossing to where Jan and Turpin waited.

'Ian said you wanted a word with the bloke who found the body,' he said, and pointed to the cabin on the far right-hand side of the car park. 'They're all in there at the moment.'

Jan frowned as she eyed the powder-coated aluminium sides of the rectangular dirt-spattered building. 'How the hell did they all fit in that?'

'There were only six of them on the site today – they just use that Portakabin for keeping their equipment secure at night. And the coffee machine.' Sam shrugged. 'I figured they'd be more amenable to hanging around if I asked them to wait in there rather than out here.'

'Any complaints?' Turpin asked.

'None, Sarge. Michelle Andrews said they're used to being patient in their line of work. I think they're using the time to log the results from today's finds.' His smile faded. 'The historical ones, I mean.'

'Introduce us, then.'

'This way, Sarge.'

Jan noticed the door to the Portakabin was already open, as was the single-paned window facing out onto the site car park, no doubt in an attempt to allow a modicum of air to pass through the tiny office space where the archaeologists worked.

A set of three metal steps led up to the door, and someone peered out through the window at them as she and Turpin drew closer.

Sam rapped his knuckles against the door and waved them inside.

Six faces turned to them, a mixture of inquisitiveness and apprehension in their eyes.

Two rectangular trestle tables took up most of the space inside the cabin, set up along the middle of the room and covered in small bags similar to the evidence bags Jan kept in the car for emergencies. Inside those, she noticed small shards of pottery, lead musket balls, and a rust-covered coin nearest to where she stood.

At the far edges, the archaeological team had set up their laptop computers, the hum of the machines' fans whirring in the background like errant flies.

Around the tables, shelving units sagged with paperwork and thick well-thumbed reference books, and towards the back she spotted a small refrigerator with a coffee machine on top, the aroma of burnt beans tinging the air.

'Everyone, this is Detective Sergeant Mark Turpin, and Detective Constable Jan West,' said Sam. 'They have some questions they'd like to ask you.'

Jan watched as a man in his early sixties pushed back his chair, the legs scraping across the linoleum floor.

His brow furrowed, crinkling weather-beaten skin and exposing a weariness in his eyes.

'I'm Derek Andrews,' he said, moving around the table with his hand outstretched. 'I'm the one who found the grave.'

'Thanks for waiting for us while we got our bearings.' Turpin shook the man's hand and then turned his attention to the other members of the man's team. 'Thanks to all of you. I realise it's turning into a longer day than you'd have liked.'

A woman standing beside the window with shoulder-length dark hair held up her hands and shook her head. 'Don't apologise. We've used the time to catch up on work that would've kept us here over the weekend. Besides, we know you've got your own processes you have to follow.'

'Do you know who she is?' blurted one of the younger men at the far end of the table.

'Tim...' The woman rolled her eyes at him, then turned back to Turpin. 'Sorry...'

'It's all right. No, we don't know who she is. Do you?'

Tim's eyebrows shot up. 'No. Of course not. I've never been here before...'

'Okay, well let us have a word with Derek and then we'll want to speak to each of you,' said Turpin, his tone calm. 'Just a formality, that's all. Once we've done that, you can head off for the day.'

Jan watched as the young man relaxed back into his seat at her colleague's words, and bit back a smile.

Derek rolled up his shirt sleeves and jerked his head towards the door. 'It's probably cooling down a bit out there now. Do you want to have a chat outside?'

He led them back down the stairs, and Jan nodded her thanks to Sam as he wandered back to his position next to the security gate before she followed Turpin and the archaeologist around the side of the Portakabin.

As soon as the man reached the shade afforded by the building and the one beside it, he pulled a packet of cigarettes from his shirt pocket.

Jan noticed Turpin pause at the corner of the cabin and angle his head away from the first trail of smoke that Derek exhaled with a heavy sigh, attempting to protect his damaged larynx. She extracted her notebook and a pen from her handbag, giving her colleague a moment to recover.

'Sorry,' said Derek, lowering his hand and angling the cigarette away from them. 'Michelle's trying to make me quit, but after today…'

'Had you been along that footpath prior to today's survey?' said Turpin and loosened his tie.

'No. No need to – we'd mapped the rest of the cable route across this field over the course of the past day or so, and they won't reach that stream until the middle of next week with the excavator. It gives us a bit of time to gather anything we find before they make a start.'

Turpin brushed past Jan and walked to the back of the cabins, staring out across the field before turning back to Derek. 'Seems strange to me that they'd leave it this late to survey the field. Surely they would've done that prior to the construction work starting?'

'They did, in March.' Derek took another surreptitious drag on the cigarette and blew the smoke away from the DS. 'Weather conditions were bloody awful back then, though, and they didn't want to find themselves in a position where a big find had been missed. They're behind schedule as it is.'

'Would they have used the same surveying equipment as you back then?'

'To a certain degree, yes.'

'And working to the same scope of work, with the same coordinates?'

'Yes.'

'And yet they missed the grave.'

Derek gave a sad smile. 'Unfortunately, as with any equipment, it has its limitations when the ground is waterlogged. And if your victim isn't wearing any jewellery for instance, then that would make it even harder to pinpoint her grave at that time.' He sighed. 'As it was, I only found her because I was tired and wandered off course from the GPS coordinates I'd set. A rookie mistake on my part, but if I hadn't then she might not have been found until construction work started there. If at all.'

Jan shivered at the thought of one of the enormous bulldozers smashing through the woman's remains, scattering her within one of the piles of backfill that littered a corner of the field away from the Portakabins.

'Okay, I think that's it for now,' said Turpin. 'We'll have someone liaise with you to let you know if we need anything else, but here's my card.'

'Do you have any idea who she is?' Derek asked, his eyes troubled.

Jan shook her head. 'Not yet. It's still too early in the investigation.'

'When you do...' The archaeologist blinked, then stubbed out his cigarette and shoved his hands in his jeans pockets. 'Would you let us know? We'd like to do something for her family if she has one... I don't know what. But something to let them know we care.'

CHAPTER FOUR

The landscape was being claimed by a humid dusk by the time Mark and Jan finished interviewing the rest of the archaeology team and sent them on their way.

As Mark watched the last of the team's cars leave the parking area beside the security gate, he inhaled the fresh air laced with the thick scent of honeysuckle and elderflower in the hedgerow, turning to face the other temporary cabins set out in a small semi-circle around him.

Swallows swooped and glided across the field behind them, chasing the midges and flies that Mark found he was constantly waving away from his face, the birds' incessant chatter a white noise under the voices of the various uniformed officers and plain-clothed experts who roamed the construction site.

At the sound of heavy boots on gravel, he turned to see a

thick-set man in his forties approaching with the force of a bull.

High-visibility vest flapping under his arms, his brow furrowed as he stormed from the direction of the farthest cabin, he stopped in front of Mark and glared at him.

'Have you finished yet? I saw the archaeologists leaving.'

'We'll be a while yet, Mr…?'

'Bill McFarlane. I'm the site manager.'

'Ah, yes.' Mark glanced over his shoulder as Jan approached, then back. 'We were hoping to speak with you. Got a minute?'

'I've got a project meeting with the owners in fifteen minutes. One of them's calling in from New York.'

'And I'm managing a murder investigation. Shall we?'

Mark gestured to the man's site office, then followed in his wake as McFarlane spun on his heel and stalked towards it.

The site manager waited on the top step, holding the door open for them, then crossed to a well-worn chair at the head of a chipped oblong table and slouched, worry lines etched around his eyes.

'I'll apologise if I came over abrupt out there,' he said, his accent north of his current location. 'Derek probably told you we're running behind schedule, and now this… My company has to pay the client for any delays, you see. They're going to be wrangling about this one for years.'

'I can't help that.' Mark pulled out a chair for Jan, then took the one beside her. 'Until I have some answers about what a body is doing buried next to that stream and my crime scene investigators tell me they're releasing the site, there'll be no more work going on anywhere near it. By anyone. So, in the meantime, and given that your meeting is starting in, what, ten minutes now, shall we get on?'

McFarlane gave a resigned shrug, and Mark pressed on.

'How long have you been based at this site?'

'I've been back and forth here for the past two years. This set-up you see here was established a year ago. There weren't as many people back then, of course. We're expecting thirty more next week when the cabling engineers catch up with us.'

'Where do you stay while you're here? Your accent...'

'Carlisle.' McFarlane jerked his chin towards the door. 'The company puts me up at one of the big motels near the dual carriageway on the other side of town.'

'And you've always stayed there while you've been working on this project?'

'Yes. I presume they get a discount rate or something. There're plenty of blokes like me running sites around the country, especially with this latest project roll-out.'

'You said you've been back and forth from this site for two years. Who else was here with you?'

'Surveyors, soil testing contractors, that sort of thing.' McFarlane pointed to a large 3D image that had been printed out and plastered along the length of one wall. 'They do all the computer modelling for the cable route before we even start. That helps with correcting any oversight with regard to land acquisition as well, to try to give the legal teams time to renegotiate.'

'Do you recall ever seeing anyone near the woodlands at the far end of the field during that time?'

'No, can't say that I did. Like I said, I'm usually busy with meetings. Putting out fires most of the time,' McFarlane replied, a note of weariness in his voice. 'That, and arguing for more budget. Speaking of which…'

He broke off and pointed at the computer screen in the corner, and Mark checked his watch.

'All right. We'll let you get on.' He slid a business card across the table to the site manager. 'If you do remember something that could help us, my email and direct phone number are on there.'

The man ignored the card, and instead pushed his chair back.

Mark took the hint, followed Jan out of the cabin and paused in the middle of the gravel car park.

He watched as McFarlane slammed shut the door. Moments later, the man's muffled voice sounded through the thin walls of the cabin as his video conference began.

'What do you think, Sarge?' Jan asked as he turned away and walked with her towards the gates. 'Something's bothering you about him, isn't it?'

He waited until they'd passed the new uniformed constable on sentry duty and were walking up the lane towards their cars before answering.

'Out of all the people we've spoken to this afternoon, McFarlane's the only one who's had access to the site since this project was approved,' he said. He paused next to Jan's car while she retrieved her keys from her bag. 'And yet, he says he didn't see anything.'

His colleague wrinkled her nose. 'Well, I suppose if he's here, he's working, and he seems to spend most of his time in that pokey little office of his. I doubt he's ever had much time to stare out of the window.'

Mark moved to one side as a plain white van passed them, raising his hand in greeting to another member of Jasper's team he recognised, then turned back to Jan.

'As soon as you get a chance, have someone back at the station run a background check on Bill McFarlane. Just in case.'

CHAPTER FIVE

The musical singsong of finches and blackbirds accompanied Mark the next morning while he walked along the fringes of the nature reserve at Barton Fields.

His gaze travelled to the already dry grasslands to his right, the lush greenery from earlier that year turned to yellow and brown, and withered from the assault laid on by a series of hot summer days.

Poppies and cornflowers peppered the grasses, and the pungent fragrance of St John's Wort mixed with a heady pollen that tickled the back of his throat. Butterflies and bees fluttered and hovered over the low hedging to his left, lost in their work and oblivious to him as he passed by.

He had found sanctuary here in the past year, exploring the seventeen-acre site and watching as various environmental groups tended the ponds and different habitats that dotted the area through the seasons as they encouraged wildlife to thrive.

The small mongrel at the end of the lead he held zig-zagged from one side of the path to the other, his nose to the ground while he sought out fresh scents, and for a moment Mark could imagine he was simply one of the many dog walkers out for an early-morning stroll before the forecast heatwave took hold.

Then his phone buzzed in his trouser pocket, and he tugged at the lead while he fished it out to read the message.

'Hang on, Hamish.'

On my way – be about 15 minutes.

'Okay, mate. Let's go.' Mark pulled Hamish away from a straggly-looking vine at the base of a willow and set off towards the far end of the reserve.

He nodded to a passing pair of female joggers, then turned left when the path forked.

The sound of water gushing and tumbling through the sluice gates reached him before he saw the weir, and he kept the lead short while he crossed the narrow metal bridge above it, unwilling to let Hamish wander too far despite the safety fencing on each side.

He held up his hand in greeting to the man standing outside the lock-keeper's cottage.

In reply, the man raised the coffee mug in his hand and called out. 'Morning, Mark. Working today?'

'I'm about to head in.'

'Would you let your Lucy know I saw Beatrice Williams

and her husband pass through here early this morning on their way back to Rugby? Beatrice was raving about the sketch Lucy did for her.'

'I will, thanks.'

Not for the first time, Mark marvelled at how well his girlfriend's new venture had panned out that year. The towpath was often crowded with visiting narrowboats, and Lucy had turned her artistic skills to offering commissions, providing a permanent reminder of people's time on the water.

Three boats were moored up to the towpath after the lock, all painted in the bright colours and insignia of an Oxford-based rental company and the curtains still drawn in two of them.

A fine mist rose from the water as it warmed and Mark inhaled the fresh air, savouring the last few moments of peace.

No doubt the incident room would be bedlam now that a major crime investigation was underway, and he reckoned a few late nights and long days faced him.

Hamish emitted an excited yip when their narrowboat came into view, and Mark smiled at the figure standing on the gunwale.

Crouching down, he released the dog from the lead and watched as he shot off along the path, his stubby tail pointing upwards as he propelled himself towards the visitor.

'He'd better not be muddy,' Jan called out.

Moments later, Mark caught up with Hamish and gave a sheepish grin as he looked at the paw prints on his colleague's trouser hems.

'It's dry, at least.'

'Very funny.'

A mass of curls emerged from the cabin, and then Lucy appeared carrying two travel mugs and a hessian tote bag.

'I figured you could both do with one of these,' she said, handing a coffee to Jan. 'And there are sandwiches and muesli bars in the bag to keep you going. I'd imagine you're not going to get a chance to get anything yourselves by the sounds of it.'

'Saves me feeding him, too – thanks.' Jan grinned at Mark and then sidestepped from Hamish who was trying to weave around her legs. 'Get off, you daft dog. You'll have me in the river at this rate.'

'Give me thirty seconds to change my shoes and we'll go,' said Mark, then squeezed Lucy's arm as he passed her on his way into the cabin. 'And thanks for the caffeine. I knew you were a keeper.'

'Oi.'

Ten minutes later, he and Jan reached the far end of the meadow bordering the river and slipped past a metal gate that prevented unwanted vehicles churning up the grass.

Jan pointed to a blue hatchback close to the car park exit and then handed him her coffee as she pulled keys from her pocket. 'I pulled the short straw last night. This was all they had available on the roster.'

'I'm sure Tracy does it on purpose. What did Alex get?'

'The Audi.'

'I knew it. I'll bet Caroline got the new Focus, didn't she?'

Mark dropped the tote bag into the passenger footwell, slid the two coffees into the mug holders between the seats and settled in for the short ride to Abingdon police station.

He checked his watch as Jan crossed the bridge over the river and followed the road through Market Place. 'Okay, so let's see what Kennedy's got for us in the briefing in case there are any updates from Gillian or Jasper, and then I thought we could contact the contractor that carried out the original site survey in March.'

'I'm not sure whether Bill McFarlane was more horrified by the news a grave had been uncovered, or by the thought his site might get shut down.' Jan slowed as she approached a roundabout. 'Especially given he's already behind schedule. Oh, and I heard from Caroline late last night – there's nothing on the system about him, so he's in the clear as far as that's concerned.'

'It's a long shot contacting the original surveyors, but they might be able to shed some more light on that path and whether it was being used back then.' Mark paused while Jan buzzed down her window and swiped her security card across a panel fixed to a metal post outside the police station's car park. 'What if—'

'Is that Kennedy? What's he doing?'

Mark frowned as the security gates swept open and DI Ewan Kennedy strode towards them, his hand raised in the air.

Jan stopped next to him, and Kennedy bent down, resting his forearm on the sill.

'Forget the briefing. I need you back at the crime scene, pronto.'

'Why's that, guv?' Mark raised an eyebrow at Jan, who shook her head in reply, her brow creased.

Kennedy exhaled, and Mark's stomach flipped, a sixth sense anticipating his superior's response before the DI held up his phone and showed them the text message from Jasper.

'Because they've just found another grave.'

CHAPTER SIX

Jan reached the construction site in under twenty minutes, taking full advantage of the car's handling and the blue lights and siren Turpin had switched on the moment they left the car park.

Wrenching the handbrake, she shoved her handbag under the passenger seat out of sight and aimed the key fob over her shoulder as she hurried after him and signed into the crime scene.

Once that was done, a weary-looking constable lifted the cordon tape, and Jan recalled the number of times that she had carried out the same role in the early stages of her career.

She gave him a sympathetic smile, then turned her focus to the path once more.

'What the fuck has been going on around here?' muttered Turpin as he stomped ahead of her. 'One was bad enough.'

She didn't have an answer for him, her own thoughts tumbling over one another while she followed.

Jasper was waiting for them at the second cordon, red-rimmed eyes peering over his mask as he fought back a yawn. 'Gillian left half an hour ago, but Robert Kerridge and Hayden Bridges are here and can answer any preliminary questions you've got.' He paused while they ducked under the tape, then pointed to where the larger group of suit-clad CSIs worked. 'The second grave we found is farther back, and possibly the older of the two.'

'Weren't they dug at the same time?' asked Turpin, gesturing to Jan to walk ahead of him.

'No, we don't think so.' Jasper pointed to the first grave where two of his team crouched inside, scraping away at the remaining layers of dirt. 'We're continuing to look for trace evidence in this one where the woman's remains were found yesterday but look at the edges. See how they're rough and uneven? We think this one was dug in a hurry. Come and look at the other grave.'

The CSI lead pointed them to the demarcated path his team had laid out, and led them deeper into the copse of trees, away from the footpath.

Ferns and stubby brambles smacked against Jan's legs, and she paused to stoop and pull away a tangle of thorns that stuck to her protective suit, cursing under her breath.

When she caught up with Turpin and Jasper, they were standing beside a trench that was deeper than the first.

She watched as two suited figures worked at the far end of

it, one with a tablet computer held up to take photographs while the other maintained a running commentary into a mobile phone – all the beginnings of a thorough report that would be handed over to the investigation team.

Jan swallowed, readying herself. Although she had dealt with plenty of deceased victims in her time as a police officer, she knew she would never become immune to the horrors one human could inflict on another.

One of Jasper's team nodded to them as they approached and stepped aside, a pencil hovering above the sketch of the gravesite he'd been making.

'Robert, Hayden – you'll remember DS Turpin and DC West from yesterday,' said Jasper by way of introduction.

The taller of the two men standing beside the skeletal remains straightened, his bushy eyebrows knotted together. 'Ah, the police. You got here at last, then?'

Jan recognised the gruff voice of Robert Kerridge behind the mask and saw Turpin glare at the anthropologist.

'You can come closer,' the man continued. 'It won't bite. Not any more.'

Turpin raised an eyebrow at Jasper. 'Is that okay with you?'

'You're fine if you keep within the two pegs there. We haven't finished around the other sides yet, and probably won't until these two have finished and the remains have been safely removed. You may as well see it in situ to help with context.'

Jan moved until she was beside Turpin, and then they both approached the uncovered grave.

'Shit.' Turpin emitted a sad sigh.

Inside, the body of an adult had been arranged in such a way that it was obvious to Jan that prior to the victim being buried, both a tibia and a femur were broken, splintered halfway up each bone where the killer had had to bend them in order to fit the body into the hole.

'Do we know the sex?' said Jan. 'I mean, I realise it's hard while it's still in there, but...'

'Female. Again,' said Kerridge. He shifted, then stood with one foot raised on the lip of the grave and glanced over his shoulder. 'I wonder what she did to deserve this.'

Jan clenched her teeth and resisted the urge to pitch the anthropologist back into the grave at his words, but bit back her frustration as Turpin met her gaze and gave a slight shake of his head.

'If the killer had waited a few hours, he wouldn't have had to break her bones, either,' Kerridge continued, oblivious to the effect his words were having on his audience. 'The rigor mortis would have passed, and he would have been able to easily bend her body into the shape of this grave.'

There was a brief pause while Turpin absorbed the information, and then he turned to Jasper. 'You said there was something different about how this grave was dug?'

'Yes. Remember on the last grave how the edges were ragged and uneven? If you look at this one, there are straighter lines, and each section appears to have been dug at eight-inch spaces.'

'He used a shovel for this one,' said Jan, realisation dawning. 'He was better prepared.'

'That's what we're thinking.'

'Which one was buried first?' said Turpin. 'This one, or the one back there?'

The other suited figure turned around from his work and held up his hand before Robert could venture a guess. 'If I may? We'll need to get the remains back to the lab and do a comparative analysis with the other victim that was found, but based on the soil samples taken since yesterday, the landscape around here is quite acidic, which means that we can see a higher degradation in bone mass in the skeleton that has been in the ground the longest.'

'How sure are you, Hayden?'

'I'll confirm with the test results, but looking at the area surrounding this victim, there is more evidence to suggest that this body has been here longer than the other. For example, you can see how the remnants of clothing have rotted away more than the other one. I'll be sure to check how much of that can be attributed to its position under the tree canopy and how much sunlight can be expected to come through here over the seasons, but it's my view this one is the older grave.'

'Will you be able to tell us if the victims are of a similar age?' Jan asked.

Kerridge stood a little straighter as their attention turned back to him. 'I won't be able to give you an exact age, but I'm confident that I'll be able to narrow it down to within a decade.'

'That would help,' said Turpin. 'Often in cases like this, we get told juvenile, middle-aged, or old age.'

'I'm sure I can do better than that for you.'

Jasper turned his attention to Hayden. 'Would you mind if I interrupted your work for a moment so you could show the detectives what you discovered about the first grave we found?'

'Of course, no problem.'

They stood aside to let the archaeologist climb from the trench, and then he led the way along the footpath to where two of his team still worked. He paused beside the grave and pointed at a twisted pile of tree roots inside it while his colleagues crouched at the earth around it and carefully clipped away some small branches.

'Whoever dug this grave came back and planted this birch sapling. As it grew, the roots became entangled between the legs of our victim, which is why it took us so long to remove the remains yesterday.'

Mark itched at the side of his nose through his mask. 'Why come back and plant a tree?'

'To help conceal the grave,' said Hayden. 'This one is shallower than the first one. The sides are uneven…'

'Indicating whoever did this was in a hurry, like we thought.'

Jan lifted her gaze from the grave at the sound of dogs barking and spun on her heel to face the footpath.

'Shit,' said Turpin. 'Who the hell let dog walkers come through here? Surely they can see the cordon's still in place.'

'The cordon *is* still in place.' Jasper grimaced. 'That's the cadaver dogs.'

Jan paled. 'You think there could be more graves here?'

'I'm not sure what to think at the moment, detective.'

CHAPTER SEVEN

When Mark walked into the incident room mid-morning, there was a crowd starting to gather around Ewan Kennedy while he paced the carpet at the far end.

Despite the air conditioning filtering through the suspended ceiling tiles, a cloying stuffiness remained due to the sheer number of uniformed and plain-clothed officers and all the associated computer equipment brought in to deal with a major crime.

An intangible energy crackled in the atmosphere, and Mark could sense the adrenalin in his colleagues as they moved as one towards a large whiteboard fixed to the wall, wheeling chairs across to where Kennedy waited.

The DI paused in his pacing, and waved Mark and Jan towards the group, his blue eyes troubled.

'Just in time,' he said. 'We were about to discuss the statements taken from local landowners and residents.'

Mark led the way over, gestured to the last remaining chair, and waited until Jan had settled before he pulled his notebook from his backpack and dropped the bag to his feet. 'The cadaver dogs turned up just before we left,' he said. 'Jasper and the forensic archaeologist have drawn up a grid and they're working through it over the course of today while Robert Kerridge and his team arrange to remove the second victim.'

A murmur swept through the team at his words until Kennedy called them to attention.

'I'll call him for an update after the briefing.' The DI turned and gestured to a large map pinned to the wall beside the whiteboard. 'My thanks to uniform, who have conducted interviews with both the landowners and residents of these two villages closest to our crime scene. Residents were specifically asked if they were aware of any missing persons within the last thirty years. First-hand accounts, rumours – anything. To date, no one has ventured any information that ties in with who our two victims may be. Hopefully, once Gillian and Kerridge have carried out the post mortem tomorrow morning, we'll have more information about the first body discovered yesterday.'

Kennedy turned his attention to DC Alex McClellan who was leaning against one of the printers beside the wall. 'I'd like you to make a start by going through historical investigations of murders on the system. On the basis that the two graves are close together, I want you to look for patterns of multiple murders. I know of at least three individuals from within our policing area that have been put away for life in the past twenty years, who we weren't sure had confessed to all of their crimes. Once we have that list, we'll be able to compare that to our victims' profiles once we have them and see if they fit a historical pattern.'

'What if the victims were killed by someone who we haven't known about until now?' said a voice from the front. 'Someone who's gone undetected all this time, I mean.'

Mark recognised it as DC Caroline Roberts, and a chill travelled across his shoulders at her question.

'Don't think it hasn't crossed my mind,' Kennedy replied. 'We all know there have been plenty of high-profile killers who've made the national headlines once they were caught because nobody realised what they were doing and, given the number of unsolved murders on our own system, we know it's a possibility.' He turned his gaze to the rest of the team. 'That's why I'm insisting on a total media blackout about this case and our progress until we know what we're dealing with. Is that understood?'

A rumble of agreement met his words, and he gave a curt nod.

'Right, next.' He held up the sheaf of statements. 'We've got no one recalling a man or woman going missing in the area from these, but it's likely some of these residents are new to the area – they might not have been around a decade or so ago. Caroline, I'd like you to lead a team to work out who's moved into the area within the last ten years, and who relocated. That way, when we know more about our victims' ages we have a list of potential witnesses to speak further to about missing people. We might have more information about our victims that'll jog people's memories by then.'

Mark saw Caroline nod before she lowered her gaze to her notebook, and was grateful she took on the task without complaint.

No one liked being relegated to a desk during a murder investigation but it was an essential part of the process, and her work would be vital to the team's progress.

Kennedy's attention turned to him. 'Mark, I want you and Jan to continue with your plans to interview the archaeological expert who surveyed the site in March. Tracy's set up a video conference call for you with them in half an hour. I'd also like you both to attend the post mortem tomorrow morning for the first victim. Gillian phoned earlier – she's going to have Robert Kerridge there as well in order to get his opinion on the anthropological nature of the remains, given that there's not much for her to go on.'

'Will do, guv. What's the latest with regard to the clothing remnants that were found in the first grave?'

'Jasper's assistant Gareth signed everything into evidence with the lab and given the look on his face when I saw him earlier, they've already got a backlog. We won't be hearing from them for a while.'

A collective groan emanated from the assembled officers.

'Did they find any jewellery or anything else in the grave?' asked Jan. 'We left before they finished yesterday.'

'Nothing,' said Kennedy. 'Which makes me think that whoever killed her stripped her of her belongings so she couldn't be identified.' He paused and ran a hand over thinning hair. 'It'll certainly slow us down. Let's hope they have more for us once the second body's removed this afternoon.'

The DI dismissed the team, and Mark wandered back to his desk, dropping his notebook next to his keyboard before taking his mobile phone from his pocket and checking the screen.

There were no messages from Jasper yet.

'No news is good news,' said Jan as she pulled out her chair beside him and sank into it. She placed the tote bag Lucy had given to them between the desks and passed him one of the sandwiches. 'Eat that, then we'll have that video call with the surveyor.'

'Sounds like a plan.' Mark logged into his computer and navigated his way through his emails while he devoured the food.

He quickly deleted anything that resembled a round-robin type message, figuring that if something was urgent one of his colleagues would tell him, and narrowed the list down to six that could be delegated elsewhere and three he would return to later regarding an older case that had been closed two weeks ago.

Alex walked over, pausing at Jan's elbow and handing her

a pair of single-page documents. 'This is the roster that got issued before the briefing. Thought you might want a copy each. Me and Caroline are working this weekend with you.'

'Thanks,' said Jan, giving one to Mark and running her eyes down the list. 'I'd better ask Scott to do the school run next week by the look of this.'

'I can cover for you if you get stuck.' Mark finished his sandwich and pulled a paper tissue from a box on the desk before wiping his fingers. He watched Alex take a seat beside Caroline and frowned. 'Have either of you taken a look at how many missing people have been reported in our area in the past decade?'

'Yes.' Caroline peered over her computer screen from her desk opposite Jan's, tucked a strand of hair behind her ear, and sighed. 'The depressing thing is, thousands have gone missing every year.'

'And we have no idea what happened to any of them,' Alex added with a groan. 'So this is going to take us forever.'

CHAPTER EIGHT

Mark cricked his neck and paused at the threshold to the box-like meeting room.

He ran his gaze over the computer screen and camera that had been set up on a desk spanning the width of the space, took a swig of coffee, and watched while Tracy made some final adjustments to the video conferencing software.

One of the recessed lights in the ceiling tiles flickered in the corner of his vision, and he reached out to flip the switch beside the door before crossing over to the single window and opening the blinds to compensate for the sudden darkness.

Tracy turned from her work and blinked. 'You won't be able to see the screen properly.'

'As long as he can see us, that's all that matters,' he said, dropping his empty takeaway cup into a bin under the desk. 'Better than getting a headache.'

'I'll get onto maintenance. I emailed them a week ago about the lights in here, and the one in the kitchenette.'

Mark winked. 'I could get a ladder…'

'And cause me no end of grief with the health and safety paperwork if you topple off? No thanks.' Tracy grinned as Jan appeared, and pointed at the computer. 'Right, you're all set. Just click the link when you're ready to start.'

'What's the name of the bloke we're talking to?' said Jan, crossing to the desk and dropping a pile of folders onto it.

'Marcus Draper. He owns and manages the survey company – he's bringing along Simon Hollis who was working with him on site.'

'Okay, thanks.' Mark checked his watch. 'Might as well log on and wait for them to turn up.'

Tracy paused at the door. 'I'm on extension two oh three if there are any issues. I'll check back in an hour or so.'

'Ta.'

Seconds later, the connection made, Mark looked up from his notebook to see a man in his early sixties with straw-like hair peering back at him.

Behind him, there was a row of bookshelves that teemed with leather-bound tomes and paperback books with cracked spines, all displaying titles that covered various periods of history and sociology.

'Dr Draper, thanks for speaking with us at short notice,' said Jan, making the introductions.

'Not at all. Anything we can do to help.' Draper glanced to his left as a younger man eased into the seat beside him. 'This is my research assistant, Simon Hollis. Simon was assisting on site and with the development of the survey report afterwards.'

'As my colleague said, thanks for your time this afternoon.' Mark inched closer to the screen, pen poised. 'Before we begin, I have to insist that this conversation remains confidential given the nature of what we're about to discuss. My inspector has imposed a full media blackout on this investigation, which we are expecting everyone to adhere to. Is that going to be a problem for either of you?'

Both men shook their heads.

'Not at all,' said Hollis.

'Okay, good. You may be aware that during the course of a final archaeological survey on site yesterday, the remains of a woman were discovered in a copse of woodland beside a stream known locally as Hacca's Brook,' Mark continued. 'The body was discovered in a shallow grave, and a sapling had been planted close by to help obscure it.'

'We were contacted by a DC Alex McClellan yesterday and provided a statement,' said Draper.

'Which we appreciate, thank you. What you won't know is that a second body was discovered this morning.'

Both men reeled back from the camera and looked at each other in shock.

'Another body?' Draper managed, running his hand over his jaw. 'Where?'

'A few metres from the original grave. What we're trying to do today is to understand why those weren't discovered when you carried out the previous survey.'

'We used a drone back then,' Hollis explained. 'Although all the vegetation had died back somewhat, our scope of work was to look for larger structures or changes in the landscape – anything that would have given cause for immediate concern. Once the drone mapping had been completed, we carried out a light detection and ranging survey, which we use to pick up any anomalies along the cable route. The output from that assists the client's engineering team in determining the final route as well – they'll have then created a 3D image of the entire path it's going to take.'

He paused while Draper unfolded a well-used map, the paper crackling over the microphone as the man wrestled it into a more manageable shape, and then both men peered at it.

Draper jabbed his finger to the page. 'Your colleague gave us the coordinates where the first body was found yesterday, and it's actually several metres from our survey area in March. I've gone back through the photographs we took at site during that time, and you can see the wooded area in the background of those. Despite the time of year it looked very overgrown with bracken, brambles and suchlike.'

'Could we get copies of those photographs?' Mark asked. 'Including the ones that didn't make it into your final report.'

'Of course. We'll email those to you.'

'Was anybody else working with you on site at the time?'

'We had two teams of three,' said Draper. 'But Simon and I were the only ones working near that woodland area. I'll send you a list of personnel – Simon here is a full-time member of staff, but the six working that day were all contractors that I bring in when I need extra manpower.'

'Were any of you familiar with the area prior to being awarded the contract for the survey?'

'No, not as far as I know. We're based in Milton Keynes and the closest contractor to the site lives in Banbury. Once we were awarded the contract, we spent two weeks conducting additional pre-survey research to get a better understanding of the history of the place, particularly with regard to previous Saxon and Roman finds.'

Jan edged a little closer to the screen. 'Did you experience any issues with the locals while you were working on site?'

'Not that I recall,' said Hollis. 'I do remember we had some interested people stopping by to talk with us, but that was only when we were by the gates next to our vehicles and setting up. I don't remember anybody approaching us while we were actually working in the fields.'

Mark drummed his fingers on the desk. 'When you tendered for the work, what sort of information were you given by way of existing knowledge of the site title ownership, Land Registry documents, things like that?'

'All of that,' said Draper. 'Along with documentation about best practice dealing with landowners to each side of the land acquired specifically for the project, rights of way and access to the site.'

'So, did you go anywhere near those woods or that stream?' said Jan.

'No – like Dr Draper said, we didn't need to,' Hollis

replied. 'All of our work was done remotely using the drone. It's a quicker process that way and served to demonstrate that the chosen route was still viable.'

'From a historical and archaeological point of view there was nothing large enough to raise concern to stop the construction works,' added Draper. 'I'm sure if you speak to the current archaeological team on site, you'll find that they're only preserving smaller finds and recording them for future reference. I doubt very much that they'll find anything of huge archaeological significance – they're simply doing a checks and balances exercise so someone on site can tick a box.'

Mark ran a hand over his jaw. 'Unfortunately, Dr Draper, it's proving to be a lot more complicated than that.'

CHAPTER NINE

The following morning, Mark peered through the car windscreen at the two-storey building in front of him, its contents at odds with the bright sunshine that streamed across the dashboard.

As he climbed out, he peered across the car park to the constant stream of traffic that circled the busy city hospital's road system, suppliers' vans and trucks mingling with ambulances that peeled away from the queuing cars at speed, sirens blaring.

Everywhere he looked, there were temporary buildings wedged into cramped spaces or construction works underway and he wondered how much more expansion would be needed to cope with the demands of the local population.

'Shall we?' Jan nudged his elbow before dropping the car keys into a side pocket of her handbag.

'Might as well get it over with.'

He led the way across the asphalt to a set of double doors with darkened privacy glass, grateful that his colleague didn't say anything further. Each of them was lost in thought, trying to counter the discomfort of watching a post mortem with the knowledge that they desperately needed information about the victims.

Opening one of the doors for Jan, he was struck by the coolness of the small reception area, goosebumps prickling his forearms as he crossed to where a tall thin man in his twenties worked behind a battered desk.

'Morning, Clive.'

Gillian Appleworth's assistant peered up at him, a permanent melancholy in his eyes.

'Detectives Turpin and West. I'd say it was a pleasure to see you, but...'

'We're a bit late, sorry. Traffic on the ring road—'

'No matter. Gillian hasn't started yet. She's been giving Dr Kerridge an orientation briefing. He hasn't graced our laboratory before.'

Mark caught Jan's eye and looked away, but not before a smile threatened. He couldn't tell whether Clive was being facetious or genuinely in awe of the forensic anthropologist.

They were saved from commenting at the sound of a door opening at the far end of a corridor to their right, and Mark saw Gillian advancing towards them, her grey eyes sparkling.

'You're here. Good. Robert is getting ready so if you'll

follow me, we'll find you some coveralls to pop on and then we'll make a start, shall we?'

'You're in a good mood in the circumstances,' said Mark, falling into step beside her as she led the way towards the locker rooms.

'Am I? Well, I suppose I am, yes. I mean, it's not every day I get to work alongside an academic of Robert's repute, is it?' Gillian said breathlessly. She paused beside the first door they reached and fished out a sealed bag from a wicker basket beside the door, then frowned. 'You will be on your best behaviour, won't you?'

'He promises,' Jan said, then lowered her voice. 'What's so special about this Dr Kerridge, then? To be honest, I thought he was a pretentious git on site yesterday, especially the way he insinuated it was the victim's fault she ended up there.'

'Well, I suppose he can come across as brusque when he's busy.' Gillian shrugged. 'We all can from time to time, can't we? But Robert, well, he's had success in cases like this in the past and we're very lucky to have him. He only moved down here four years ago. He made his reputation on a notorious case in Northamptonshire just before he relocated. Have you read his book?'

'No,' said Mark and Jan in unison.

He shot his colleague a quick look, then turned his attention back to Gillian and took the sealed coveralls from her. 'We'd best suit up and reacquaint ourselves with Dr Kerridge, hadn't we?'

'Come on through when you're ready. We'll make a start on the preliminaries while you're getting changed.'

Mark watched Gillian walk away, a bounce in her step, and shook his head.

'Anyone would think Kerridge was a saint, the way she's acting,' Jan murmured.

'This is going to be interesting, that's for sure.'

CHAPTER TEN

Jan tucked her hair under the protective bonnet that she had unwrapped with the blue coveralls and scowled at her reflection in the mirror.

After dabbing some menthol gel under her nose, she placed her personal belongings in one of the lockers and scuffed out into the corridor.

Turpin was waiting for her, matching plastic bootees covering his shoes while he peered at a noticeboard filled with dog-eared posters and safety messages.

He managed a small smile when he heard her approaching, and inclined his head towards the door at the end. 'Come on then. Coffee afterwards?'

'Yes. As long as it's takeaway. I can't face sitting in a café with all of those food smells after one of these. Never have.'

'Deal.'

He gave the door a shove, and she walked into the mortuary.

A hushed silence hung in the cool air, and as she cast her gaze across the stainless steel shelving units and tables that filled the walls, her eyes fell upon the knives and saws gleaming under the bright lights suspended from the ceiling.

Gillian had her head bowed over the remains of the woman, while Robert Kerridge stood with his arms across his chest, watching her every move, his head cocked to one side.

The pathologist paused in her work as the door swung shut behind Turpin and looked up, a ferocious-looking scalpel in her hand.

'Good, you're here.' Kerridge beckoned to them imperiously. 'Come on over, then. You won't see anything from there, will you? I thought you were here to learn.'

Jan gritted her teeth and padded across to the gurney, resisting the urge to take a deep intake of breath.

The victim's features were indecipherable, lost to time and nature.

What remained of her hair was streaked with grey, remnants of a deeper colour akin to a dark brown sticking out in patches at the sides of her skull.

Her eye sockets glared at the ceiling tiles, accusatory in their emptiness, her jaw open in a silent scream. A skeletal hand was brought up to her chest, clawing at exposed ribs while the other arched crab-like at her side over the stainless steel table as if attempting to find purchase on the smooth surface.

After the initial shock, Jan noticed that there was very little skin or muscle, and realised why the anthropologist's presence was necessary.

There was hardly anything left for Gillian to assess from a pathology perspective.

'Where on earth do you start?' Jan murmured.

The pathologist gestured to the remains. 'Each bone has been photographed and documented, and I've had X-rays taken of some of these as well.'

Turpin frowned. 'Some of the bones are missing.'

'We're examining those under the microscopes over there,' Gillian explained. 'I've managed to extract samples of mitochondrial DNA from them – that's all that's left, given there's no skin, cartilage or other soft tissue remaining.'

'Will that be enough for familial comparisons if we get that far?'

'Hopefully. If you can trace who she is, and a direct family member can provide a DNA sample, then it should work.' Gillian turned back to the victim's skeleton. 'Of course, we also have some teeth to work with, although I'll need to consult an odontologist—'

'I'd offer to take on that analysis myself,' Kerridge interrupted, his voice braying within the enclosed room, 'but unfortunately my current workload means I'm over-committed as it is. You were lucky I was able to attend today.'

'Indeed,' Gillian murmured. She gently prised open the skull's jaw. 'You can see here that our victim has had quite a lot of dentistry, although some of these fillings are worn down. Again, I'll consult with the odontologist, but it's my view she didn't visit a dentist for a number of years prior to her death.'

'If she'd gone missing, she might not have had access to healthcare,' said Jan.

'That's very true.'

'What about cause of death, Gillian?' Turpin's brow furrowed as he circled the gurney and paused at the skeleton's shoulder.

'Ah, well, that's a little easier.' The pathologist closed the jaw, then gently turned the skull. 'My preliminary findings include what appears to be a blunt trauma wound, just behind her left ear.' Gillian brushed the strands of hair away from the skeleton, tracing a thin crack with her little finger. 'This is what I mean. There's no indication that this is caused by rodents or other carnivores, especially as her head remained buried all this time. Only her fingers were gnawed at, and something – perhaps a fox, or crows – managed to pierce the abdominal cavity.'

Jan shivered. 'What—'

'And it's my view that this was the strike that killed her,' said Kerridge, nudging Gillian to one side. He took the skull in his hands as he warmed to his subject. 'It's the only wound to the head, and certainly peri mortem – that is, it didn't occur when she was dropped into the grave. Nor is it an old wound. No, this is definitely what did for her.'

'What about her age? Anything that could help us with that?'

Jan heard the note of desperation in her voice, and clamped her mouth shut.

Gillian gave a slight shake of her head. 'We'll run some more tests on the samples we've taken before we can say for definite—'

'Actually, I think I can help there.' Kerridge straightened from his examination of the skull. 'Based on my observations, I'm confident we're looking at a middle-aged woman. Definitely not a youngster.'

He chuckled under his breath as he turned back to his work, and Turpin frowned.

'Middle-aged? How can you be so sure?' He looked at Gillian, whose grey eyes bore into his, then back to Kerridge. 'I mean, sorry – not that I'm doubting your expertise, but—'

'Quite simply, detective, it's all in the bones.' Kerridge seemed nonplussed at Turpin's question, and Jan watched as the anthropologist strode around the table to the victim's legs. He paused and looked across to Gillian. 'Didn't the archaeology chap – what's his name?'

'Hayden Bridges.'

'Right, him. He mentioned the land around the south-west of Didcot is acidic in nature, with pockets of chalky soil.' Kerridge gently lifted the femur from the gurney and turned it between his fingers. 'See here. The bones have become demineralised. That's the effect of the acidic soil. If the grave site had been dug in one of the chalkier areas around the town, the bones would be less worn. As it is, I would posit that she's been lying undiscovered for at least four years, maybe longer.'

'Middle-aged,' Turpin mused. 'That would make her, what, forty to fifty years old when she was killed?'

Kerridge puffed out his chest. 'The true anthropological term refers to the ages of thirty-five to fifty.'

'Any other signs of injury?'

'Just an old break to the humerus bone, here,' said the anthropologist. He used his little finger to trace a jagged line across the victim's upper arm. 'I'd posit that this was sustained a few months before she died, looking at the way the healing process has been interrupted.'

'What about the other victim?' said Jan. 'Any similarities between the two?'

'Too early to say, I'm afraid.' Kerridge gave a dismissive wave towards Gillian. 'We're still waiting to receive the remains from the site, although I gave them my authority to proceed late yesterday. I don't know what's holding them up.'

'Jasper phoned an hour ago to say it's taking longer than anticipated,' Gillian said. 'I'm sorry, but the softer condition of the soil in the second location is making it difficult to extract the bones. They can't rush these things.'

'Understood.' Turpin held up his hand as Kerridge opened his mouth to speak. 'We don't want to take up much more of your time, so could you let us know about the clothes she was wearing? We only had the remains of a cotton shirt and what looks like a brown skirt in evidence.'

'She's was wearing shoes when she was buried but Jasper didn't want to risk removing those on site for fear of damaging the skeleton,' Kerridge said, and jerked his thumb over his shoulder. 'We had a hell of a time getting them off. They're over there, bagged up to go across to the lab this afternoon, along with the underwear.'

'Here,' said Gillian, crossing to a laptop computer on a table at the side of the room. 'I've taken photographs of the manufacturer's name that's embossed on the sole of one of the shoes. I saved a copy for you.' She gave a slight shrug, and passed a memory stick to Jan. 'You might be able to glean more information from that.'

'In the meantime, Detective Sergeant Turpin, you can tell your DI that he can expect my full report first thing tomorrow,' Kerridge added, his voice booming across the room from the examination table. 'We wouldn't want to keep our investigators waiting, would we, Gillian?'

The pathologist met Jan's gaze, then called over her shoulder. 'Indeed we wouldn't.'

'Thanks.' Jan took the memory stick, then lowered her voice. 'Good luck.'

She smiled at Gillian's surreptitious wink, then hurried from the mortuary after Turpin.

Fifteen minutes later, with a fresh waft of perfume on her wrists thanks to the miniature bottle she kept for such emergencies in her handbag, Jan walked through the front door and found Turpin leaning against a low brick wall with his phone to his ear.

'Anything urgent?' she said, shielding her eyes from the bright sun and basking in its warmth. She sniffed her wrist, trying to lose the remnant memory of the mortuary.

'No, just a message from Caroline to say Kennedy wants a debrief as soon as we're done here.'

Jan fluffed the ends of her hair over her shirt collar and jangled the car keys in her hand, a lightness in her step now that she was out in the fresh air with sunlight on her shoulders.

'Well, Kerridge certainly seems to know his stuff,' she said when they reached the car, slipping on her seatbelt as Turpin settled into the passenger seat. 'His report about the first victim might give us a lead or two after all.'

Her colleague scowled. 'I'll bet he has a portrait of himself in his living room.'

'Now, now.' Jan laughed and twisted the key in the ignition, then pointed the car towards the police station.

CHAPTER ELEVEN

Ewan Kennedy looked up from the plastic cover-bound report he was reading when Mark knocked on his office door an hour later, his eyes weary.

'How did it go?' he asked, waving Mark towards a chair in front of his desk. 'Was Gillian able to shed any light?'

Turning the chair so he could stretch out his long legs, Mark loosened his tie and sighed. 'Robert Kerridge was assisting with the PM, and reckons we're looking at a middle-aged victim between thirty-five and fifty, buried about four years ago, maybe longer.'

'Christ.' Kennedy slapped shut the report and tossed it onto a pile of others in a tier of three trays. He rested his forearms on the desk. 'Caroline was in here earlier. Do you know we have over seventeen hundred missing persons reports entered into the system—'

'That's not so—'

'Every *year*.' Kennedy slumped in his seat. 'Every year, Mark. Thirteen per cent are found safe and receive the help they need. Everyone else…'

He held up his hands, splaying his fingers as if completing a magic trick, where all that was left was thin air.

'We can start with the missing people last seen closest to the graves,' said Mark, trying not to let his own frustration colour his words. 'Work our way outwards until we—'

'Get lucky?' Cocking an eyebrow, Kennedy peered past Mark's shoulder at movement near the door. 'Come on in, Jan. We were just talking about the post mortem findings.'

'Such as they were.' Jan closed the door and sank into the chair beside Mark. 'I mean, trying to find out who she is, let alone who murdered her…'

Kennedy reached out and wiggled his computer mouse to wake up his screen and stared at it, brow furrowed. 'I've got wall-to-wall meetings at Kidlington all day tomorrow. I suggest you run the morning briefing in my absence, Mark. What time is the second post mortem?'

'Gillian phoned a moment ago to say she can't get Kerridge to assist,' said Jan. 'Apparently he's got commitments up north for the next two days but given the circumstances, she's bringing in another anthropologist from Bristol. She knows we're desperate for a breakthrough so she didn't want to delay while waiting for Kerridge to be available.'

'I'll owe her a drink after this, then,' said Kennedy, not unkindly.

'She did mention that.'

The DI clicked across his computer screen and pushed his reading glasses up his nose. 'Okay, according to the latest updates to HOLMES2 while you've been out, Jasper and the archaeology expert are still at the crime scene working on the removal of the second victim's remains. The cadaver dogs are due back there this afternoon – Jasper wanted to let his team work through the undergrowth first, rather than let anyone else disturb potential trace evidence.'

He flicked to another update. 'Caroline and Alex have almost finished drawing up the list of missing persons within our LPA, organised by date last seen.'

'What about the National Missing Persons Helpline, guv?' said Jan.

'I called them first thing this morning,' Kennedy replied, his eyes still on his screen. 'They're on standby to receive a note of any identifying markings that Gillian finds on our two victims as well as a note of any evidence that might indicate who these people are so that they can assess that against their database.'

'What are the chances they'll find out who our victims are before we do?' said Mark.

Kennedy shrugged. 'It'll depend whether our victims' disappearances were reported to us, or just the helpline. You know what it can be like – sometimes those looking for missing persons don't want to get the police involved.'

The detective inspector clasped his hands beside his keyboard, lost in thought for a moment. Eventually he gave a slight nod.

'All right, this is how we'll proceed in the morning. I'm inclined to agree with you, Mark. In the absence of any identifiable features on our first victim – apart from the possible crack in her skull that might've been the killing blow – make a start with missing persons closest to the grave site. Until Gillian and her experts can tell us otherwise, or we have evidence to the contrary, we'll work on the premise that this is a local problem, rather than a killer travelling into the area.'

'Do you think the two victims might be related, guv?' said Jan, raising her gaze from her notebook.

Kennedy sighed. 'I don't know – not until Gillian can confirm or discount that by way of DNA testing.'

'My gut feeling tells me they're not related,' said Mark, tugging at his ear lobe. 'Just based on Jasper's findings that the graves were dug at different times, and in different ways.'

'Good point,' Jan conceded.

'Let's keep an open mind about all of this,' said Kennedy, pushing his computer keyboard away as his desk phone started ringing. He looked at the screen and frowned. 'That's the Chief Super – I'm going to have to take this.'

'We'll let you get on, guv.' Jan pushed back her chair. 'See you sometime tomorrow.'

She opened the door, pausing on the threshold for Mark, who gave Kennedy a steely gaze as the DI reached out for his phone.

'We'll find out who they are and who put them there, guv,' he said. 'One way or another.'

CHAPTER TWELVE

The next morning, Mark pedalled his mountain bike across the meadow away from the narrowboat, a renewed energy in his chest.

He jumped off to negotiate the gate in the far corner of the grassy expanse, then remounted and joined the stream of traffic heading into Abingdon.

Kennedy's assertion that he should run the morning briefing weighed heavily on weary shoulders, the responsibility of leading such a large team at the beginning of a major crime investigation not lost on him.

Part of him relished the challenge. The other hoped that it wasn't an indication that a promotion was in the wind, and he would lose the right to make such an integral contribution to a case and instead be side-lined to a management role.

He wasn't ready for it.

He didn't want it.

Not now.

He changed gear and increased his speed to catch up with a motorcyclist to negotiate the narrow bridge over the River Thames, rather than risk being pushed into the gutter by one of the tradesman's vans that nudged too close to the back of his bike for his liking, and took a left turn as soon as he could to cut around the backstreets to the police station.

By the time he reached St Helen Street and zipped past his favourite pub, his shoulders had relaxed a little and he picked up his pace.

Four cabin cruisers were moored on the opposite side of the river, and he caught sight of a man in his sixties wrestling with fishing rods and a tackle box while two teenagers on the towpath ignored him, faces lowered to their phones.

Mark shook his head, a rueful smile forming before he followed the road around to the right, the scene serving as a reminder he should call his daughters as soon as he got a chance. His ex-wife, Debbie, had taken them to St Helier to visit their grandmother and returned late yesterday. According to the loose arrangements they had in place, it was his turn to have them next weekend, and his heart sank at the realisation that he would have to postpone.

Ten minutes later, he braked to a standstill at the back door to the police station, and after placing the mountain bike in one of the stands, he swiped his security card and jogged up two flights of stairs to the men's locker room.

A quick shower, a change of clothes, and then he walked

into the incident room with his shirt sleeves rolled up, and squared his shoulders in anticipation.

He nodded to Alex who was standing next to the printer, the young detective constable battling with a stack of statements that had to be scanned and saved into HOLMES2, before crossing to his desk and eyeing the blinking light that was a portent of the number of voicemail messages waiting for him.

Caroline was at her desk, munching her way through a bowl of muesli and held up her spoon in greeting to him.

'Morning, Sarge.'

'Morning. Anything interesting on the emails overnight?'

'One from Dr Kerridge with his report,' she said, lowering her bowl to the desk. She reached out for her mouse and clicked. 'I've put that into the system and circulated it, and there's a copy on your desk there – if you can find it amongst all of the messages piling up.'

'Okay, thanks.' He sighed, and listened to the first of the voicemails.

Five minutes later, he crossed the room to where the whiteboard had been rolled next to a semi-circle of chairs. Running his eyes over the notes to date, he fought down a rising sense of panic at the lack of information.

A vibration in his pocket preceded the trill of his mobile phone, and seeing Gillian's number on the screen, he answered it rather than let it go to voicemail.

'Tell me you're having a better morning than I am,' he said.

'Not quite. I've just had word from the team over at the crime scene, and I'm not going to get the second victim's post mortem done today. The ground is so damn dry and hard after the past couple of weeks' weather, it's taking them longer to remove the remains than they thought it would.'

Mark ran a hand through his hair and bit back a groan. 'When do they think they'll get the body released?'

'Later this afternoon,' said Gillian. 'Too late to do the post mortem I'm afraid, but they can't rush – it's the same process as it would be with any archaeological excavation. If they try to work too quickly, they could damage the skeleton, not to mention lose any trace evidence that might be remaining.'

'I understand. Could you give me a call once you know what time tomorrow you're going to do the PM? I'm covering for Kennedy today, so this number is probably the best one to catch me on.'

'I will. Hope your day improves.'

'So do I.' He choked out a laugh and ended the call, then turned to see that most of his colleagues had now arrived.

The briefing room was filled with the sounds of people calling to each other with frantic updates, the coffee machine working overtime, and everywhere he looked there were administrative staff rushing back and forth between desks.

'Of all the times for him to be asked to go to Headquarters,' he murmured. Checking his watch, Mark raised his voice over the throng. 'Let's get this briefing started, then. If I could have everyone's attention please.'

As one, phone calls were finished, conversations paused,

and the team converged on the available space around the whiteboard.

Jan handed him a copy of that morning's agenda generated from the HOLMES2 database and a glass of water, then took a seat beside PC Nathan Willis.

'Thanks, everybody.' Mark took a sip, then placed the glass on a table beside the whiteboard and ran his eyes down the page. 'DI Kennedy is having to attend meetings at Kidlington for most of today, and sends his apologies. I'll be deputising as SIO in his absence, with Jan acting as my deputy. All other incident room management roles remain unchanged.'

He rapped his knuckles against the photographs from the crime scene, and began by giving his colleagues a review of the post mortem findings from the day before. 'Based on Dr Kerridge's opinion that the first victim is middle-aged, that is between the ages of thirty-five and fifty, Caroline, I'd like you to divide up the list of missing persons you've collated into groups of six, starting with those people who were closest to our crime scene when they were last seen. Start with those who have been gone for over three years, because Kerridge reckoned the environmental indicators mean that the bones have been in the ground for at least that long, and quite possibly longer.'

The detective constable flicked through a stapled sheaf of paperwork and tapped her pen against her lips while she worked. 'Okay, by my estimation that gives us sixty-three people. That takes us back to nineteen ninety. Do you want me to go back any further than that? The way Kerridge was talking in his report, he doesn't think we'd have much by way of a skeleton beyond thirty years ago due to the acidic soil where it was found.'

'Hold fire for now. Sixty-three is enough to be getting on with. Can you sort them by proximity to the grave site?'

She nodded. 'If you can give me an hour after the briefing, Sarge, that should leave me enough time to finesse the information and divvy it out amongst us.'

'So, everyone – you heard Caroline. Ten o'clock, be at her desk for your assigned missing persons.' Mark gestured to the enlarged map of the area south-west of Didcot. 'We'll work in increasing circles away from the crime scene and speak to family members and friends to ask if they have any knowledge of this particular wooded area, or the two villages either side of it. At present, we cannot tell them that we have an unidentified body, only that new information has come to light that we're investigating, is that understood?'

A rumble of agreement filled the room.

'Jan and I will be out on the road too, so if you do find out something that can't wait until this afternoon's briefing, phone me.' Mark turned and picked up one of the felt whiteboard pens and scrawled his mobile number above one of the photographs. 'Listen out for village gossip too while you're out and about. What is it about that woodland that might've attracted our killer? Why dig the two graves there? Is the location significant to the killer, or to the victims?'

Silence descended as heads bowed to open notebooks, and

then the scratching of pens on paper filled the space while he paused to take another sip of water.

'Where's Tom?' he said, craning his neck to see over the assembled officers.

A paw of a hand rose from the back row, and Sergeant Tom Wilcox rose to his feet.

'Tom, plain clothes today for you. Alex has organised an appointment at the prison on the other side of Witney and I want you to accompany him, please.' Mark paused to check his notes. 'You'll be formally interviewing one of HM prisons' guests about his victims from eight years ago to find out if we missed a couple.'

'Will do.'

Mark nodded, grateful that the uniformed sergeant accepted the task with no fuss.

Reinterviewing a convicted killer to ask for help was an unenviable job, but he couldn't think of anyone more experienced to accompany Alex, especially as Tom was one of the officers who worked on the original case.

'Okay, everyone – thanks for your time. We'll reconvene at four-thirty this afternoon.'

As chairs scraped back and the team dispersed back to their desks or out of the door to continue house-to-house enquiries, Jan wandered over to where Mark stood and gave a slight smile.

'Well done. Kennedy would've been pleased with that.'

'Thanks. Let's just hope we have some results for him by the time he gets back here later today.'

CHAPTER THIRTEEN

Mark stood on the pavement with his hands in his pockets, peering up at a pockmarked red tiled facia.

The southern fringes of Didcot comprised long sweeping roads lined with semi-detached houses before reluctantly giving way to countryside, and he had no doubt that soon the fields beyond the gardens would be claimed by urban sprawl.

The lower half of the semi-detached house in front of him had been rendered once, although its grubby off-white façade was evidence of neglect for a number of years since, and moss was beginning to claim the roof shingles.

Someone had attempted to at least mow the lawn recently, perhaps a shade too short given the yellow dry patches that pitted the front garden, but weeds stuck up through the gravelled driveway, intent on staking a claim for the front tyres of a battered two-door hatchback parked on concrete pavers.

Whatever the homeowners had used to try to coax the turf back to life was pungent, though, and he resisted the urge to hold his hand over his mouth and nose as his colleague joined him.

'This is it. Number fourteen.' Jan peered at her phone screen. 'David and Gloria Marston.'

'When did their daughter go missing?'

'The twelfth of August, five years ago.' She tucked her phone back into her bag and wrinkled her nose. 'This doesn't get any easier, does it?'

'No.' He frowned, eyeing the chipped paintwork peeling from the front door. 'Do you think they use that, or the one beside the driveway?'

'Side door. There's a boot scraper next to it.'

'Tradesmen's entrance it is, then.'

He led the way down the driveway, keeping to the gravel, his shoes sinking into the uneven stony surface as he glanced up at an upstairs window.

The net curtain twitched, a muffled shout resonated beyond the walls, and then the door next to the driveway swung inwards before he could reach up for the bell.

'Have you found her?'

A woman in her seventies stood on the doorstep, rheumy blue eyes boring into his. Behind her, he could see the gloomy interior of a kitchen, a round wooden table taking up most of the space.

Despite the warm weather, she clutched a thin cardigan around her shoulders, her chin jutting out while she waited for his answer.

'Mrs Marston? I'm DS Mark Turpin, and this is my colleague DC Jan West. Would you mind if we came inside?'

'Is this about Helen?'

A man's voice carried from inside, and then he joined his wife. Several inches taller than her with thick white hair stained nicotine-yellow in places, he placed a hand on her forearm and gently pulled her away from the door.

Guiding her to a matching chair beside the table, he glanced over his shoulder.

'Come in, then. Shut the door, else you'll let the flies in with you. They were spreading muck on the fields again this morning.'

That explains the smell.

Mark tucked his warrant card back in his pocket and gestured to Jan to go ahead of him before climbing the two shallow steps into the kitchen.

'Tea?'

'No, thank you.'

'Have you found her?'

The woman found her voice again, twisting in her seat to face them, a forlorn hope in her eyes.

'I'm sorry, I can't say at this time.' Mark hated himself for the words, but refused to give them hope. It was simply too early in the investigation, and false hope would be cruel.

'Would you mind if we asked you some questions about your daughter?'

'Her name is Helen.'

'Helen,' he repeated, then indicated the spare chair beside her. 'May I?'

'Both of you – sit yourselves down,' said David, a weariness entering his voice. 'We've told your lot everything we know. And that missing persons crowd. You know, the charity. Still hasn't brought her back, has it?'

'There were newspaper reports and everything when she went missing,' Gloria added, lowering her gaze to a knot in the wooden table and tracing her finger across the whorls. 'No one does that now. Someone phones us once a year—'

'On the twelfth, to let us know they haven't given up on her,' David added. He sniffed, and wiped at his eyes with the back of his hand. 'That's something, I suppose.'

Mark caught movement out of the corner of his eye, and saw Jan removing her notebook from her bag. He nodded his thanks, then turned back to the couple.

'Would you mind telling me what happened, the day Helen disappeared?'

David took a deep breath, steeling himself for another recounting.

'It was the divorce. I always said Aaron was trouble,' Gloria spat before he could begin. 'He was useless when she went missing, as well. Went to pieces.'

'He couldn't help it, love.' Her husband crouched beside her, clutching her hand in his. 'It didn't help that those people on social media started a rumour that it was him who killed her.'

'What was his alibi?' said Mark.

'He was in Penzance, away for business.' David lifted his gaze, patted his wife's hand, and then rose with a groan. He crossed to the sink, turning his back to the window overlooking the moth-eaten lawn. 'He was nowhere near here when she disappeared.'

'They didn't have children, did they?'

'No, thank God. The divorce was bitter enough, without kids being involved as well.'

Mark waited while the other man lowered his head, his heart aching for a father who had no idea where his daughter had gone or what had happened to her.

He dropped his hands to his lap, clenching his fist at the thought of what he would be like if Anna or Louise disappeared without a trace.

'You wanted to know what happened that day,' David said eventually. He pushed himself away from the sink as if setting himself adrift, and collapsed into the chair on his wife's other side, reaching out for her hand once more. 'Helen was staying here with us while the divorce was finalised. She'd been here about, oh, six weeks I suppose. The house in Harwell had been sold – they were just waiting for the exchange and completion dates to be set, and Aaron was living there.'

'She couldn't bear to be around him by then,' Gloria sniffed. 'It's where… it's where…'

'He cheated on her,' said David, eyes blazing. 'In their house.'

'I'm sorry to hear that,' Mark said. 'Was she happy here?'

'Yes.' The retort was vehement. 'It's why she came back.'

'She used to love going for walks across the fields to the old railway line,' said Gloria, pulling a paper tissue from her cardigan pocket and dabbing her nose. 'We're only a couple of streets across from the footpath, you see. And it's beautiful in the summer.'

'She said it gave her thinking time,' David added. 'We'd have dinner together – in here – around about seven, and then she'd wander off while it was still light.'

'Did anyone go with her?'

'Sometimes.' He jerked his thumb over his shoulder towards the window. 'Marion, over the road, used to have a couple of spaniels and they'd walk them together.'

'But not that day?'

'No.' Another deep breath. 'Not that day.'

'Did Helen always take the same route?'

'I think so, yes. We used to walk it when she was little. The path goes around the back of the houses on the next street, past the flood ponds, then you can take a shortcut up to the old railway line. From there, we used to walk back along to Loyd Road, then home. If you go the other way along the line, you get to the Hagbourne villages eventually.'

Mark frowned. 'Did she ever go there? The villages, I mean.'

'Maybe. Not with Marion – the dogs would only ever walk

so far back then.' A sad smile crossed Gloria's face. 'And Marion likes her routine so I doubt very much she would've gone that way.'

'There were one or two times Helen came back late – in a taxi,' David mused, his gaze drifting to a discarded newspaper lying open at the classified advertisements. 'I think on those occasions she might've ended up at the pub in the village, and decided not to walk back because it would've been dark, I suppose.'

'Do you know if she might've been meeting anyone there?'

'No, she never said anything.'

'What about friends in the area? Did she socialise locally?'

'Not really,' said Gloria. 'All of hers and Aaron's friends were Wantage way – that, and some of their neighbours they were more friendly with in Harwell. I never heard her talk of anyone causing her any bother, either.'

'I have to ask, did Helen ever break her arm, just below her shoulder?'

'No.' She looked at her husband. 'Not that I know of, anyway.' The woman dabbed at her eyes again, releasing a loud sigh before speaking once more. 'I know in my heart that she won't be coming back, but I'd do anything to find her. Anything to know what happened, and where she is.'

David patted her hand, and then turned his attention to Mark. 'We just want to bring her home, detective. That's all.'

CHAPTER FOURTEEN

Mark rubbed his neck and kicked a small jagged pebble into the grass verge beside a recently painted metal gate.

Beyond the waist-high fence, a fifteenth-century almshouse bordered an immaculate lawn, the building's covered walkway offering welcome shade to its visitors.

He raised his hand to an elderly man on a bench seat beside the door to the main hallway, receiving a wave of a walking stick in response, then turned his attention to the modern block of flats a few metres away along West St Helen Street.

'Ready?' Jan hurried across the narrow road towards him, flicking her hair from her eyes. 'Sorry – took me a while to find a parking space.'

'No problem.' He glanced at his phone. 'Okay, so we're

meeting Carly Evans, flat one. Her daughter, Tara, went missing four years ago aged twenty-eight.'

He saw his colleague square her shoulders as they walked along the sun-baked pavement towards the building's driveway entrance, and gave her a gentle nudge.

'Are you all right? You've been a bit quiet since we left the Marstons.'

'I'm okay.' She paused beside a red brick pillar as a black four-door car eased out of the car park in front of the flats, then sighed. 'I just feel for them. I can't imagine what I'd be like if one of my kids went missing without a trace.'

'Yeah. Me too.'

Following her across an asphalt concourse towards the main entranceway, he pressed the button for flat one on the security panel next to the door.

He didn't have to wait long before a wavering voice answered.

'Hello?'

'Mrs Evans? It's Detective Sergeant Mark Turpin. I called earlier.'

'Come in. My front door's the first one on your right.'

She was waiting for them on the threshold – a shadow of a woman, underweight and worn down by time and worry despite the brightly coloured clothes she wore.

When Mark shook her hand, he was reminded of a cat he'd had as a kid, the thick fur masking the bony skeleton underneath as the animal withered away with age.

'Thanks for agreeing to speak with us today, Mrs Evans,'

he said, following her and Jan along a narrow carpeted corridor and into a sparsely decorated living room that faced the road.

The space didn't appear to get any sunshine at all through the day and a gloominess claimed the surroundings, aided by thick net curtains that distorted the view through the front window.

'It's not good news, is it?' the woman said. She gave an involuntary shiver. 'It never is.'

'Would you like to sit down, Mrs Evans?' Jan indicated one of the brown suede armchairs opposite a television, and took a seat on a sofa under the window.

'Carly. Please.'

'Thank you.' Jan clasped her hands in her lap. 'I'm sorry. We don't have any news about your daughter at the present time, but we would like to ask you some questions, if that's all right?'

'Process of elimination? Is that the right term?'

Mark watched as Carly picked up a cheap glass tumbler from a side table next to the chair, and took a gulp of amber liquid.

She caught him looking, and gave an unapologetic shrug as she lowered the glass. 'It's past midday and I've got two detectives in my home about to tell me my daughter's never coming home. I think I'm allowed something to soften the blow, don't you?'

'I'm not judging you, Carly.'

'Like hell you are.'

The venom in her voice took him by surprise, and then he saw the tears in her eyes.

She wiped at her cheeks. 'I'm sorry. It's just... no one cares any more. It's been four years with no news. Part of me wants to leave... to go somewhere no one knows me, and then I wonder... what would Tara do if she came back and couldn't find me?'

Jan gestured to three photographs lining the windowsill. 'Is that your daughter?'

'Yes. That one on the left was taken when she graduated from Leeds University.' Carly sniffed. 'Then you've got her backpacking in Ecuador – she worked hard at uni and was offered a job with a biomedical lab near Harwell. That four-week trip was her way of rewarding herself. The last one, that one on the right... I took that when we were on holiday together in Tenerife the summer before she... before she...'

Carly's face crumpled, and she took a gasping breath. 'She disappeared three days after we got back here.'

'I know this is extremely difficult for you,' said Jan, 'and I'm sorry we have to ask these questions. Could you tell us about the day Tara went missing?'

The woman nodded, staring at the worn carpet at her feet. 'She was renting a one-bedroom flat the other side of town, off the Radley Road. Loved her independence, she did. We were going to meet up for lunch on the Wednesday – she had a meeting in Oxford and said she'd call in on the way back to the office, so we could go to the pub around the corner from here next to the river, and have a bite to eat.' She paused, dabbing at her eyes with her sleeve. 'When it got to quarter past one, I tried to phone her, thinking she must've got stuck in traffic. Usually she's five minutes early – I always tease her, telling her she's got that "fear of missing out" thing they're always going on about. There was no answer, so I thought perhaps she was still driving, or that there wasn't enough signal—'

'Did her phone go to voicemail, or...'

'No, the automatic message said her phone was switched off.' Carly frowned. 'Maybe the battery had gone dead, then. Which was strange, because if she was driving, it would've been plugged in to charge.'

'When did you realise something was wrong?' Mark prompted.

'I tried her again five minutes later. Then, I wondered perhaps I was mistaken and that I was supposed to meet her at the pub, not here.' Carly stopped, looked at the glass tumbler, then tore her gaze away. 'When I got there, they hadn't seen her, and I couldn't see her car parked on any of the side streets, so I came home. There was still no answer on her phone, and that's when I started to get scared. I thought maybe she'd been in an accident or something, but I couldn't find anything on the traffic news online.'

'When did you report her missing?' said Jan.

'After I phoned her office and they said she wasn't there, either. It was about two o'clock by then. The man I spoke to – her manager, Jason – said he'd phone the client she was meeting with, but he rang back a couple of minutes later to say their receptionist had seen her drive out of their car park at twelve-thirty. I phoned your lot as soon as he finished talking.'

'Was Tara seeing anyone at the time?'

'Not to my knowledge, no.'

'Would she have told you if she was?'

'Oh yes. We didn't have any secrets.' Carly looked at each of them in earnest. 'Ever since her dad walked out on me when she was eight years old, we've been really close.'

'And if she was in trouble, about anything at all, would she have spoken to you about it?'

'I'm sure she would, yes.'

'Carly, I have to ask you something that could have a bearing on the case we're investigating, and I'm sorry if it causes distress,' Mark said. 'Did Tara ever break her arm, here?'

He tapped his upper arm as he spoke.

The woman paled.

Hands fluttering to her mouth, she blinked back fresh tears. 'You've found a body, haven't you?'

'We can't confirm if it's your daughter at the present time.' He swallowed, fighting the tightness in his throat, and instead concentrating on the information he desperately needed. 'We're following a process of elimination at the moment.'

'O-okay.' Carly exhaled, her hands moving to her chest, and Jan crossed the room to her.

'Can I get you a glass of water?' she said, crouching beside the woman's armchair.

'No, no – I'm fine.' She gave a slight shake of her head,

then seemed to steel herself as she faced Mark once more. 'You wanted to know if she'd ever broken her arm... she hadn't, no. I always said she was invincible, that nothing could hurt her...'

He looked away as Carly leaned into the chair, covering her eyes with her forearm while Jan patted her hand.

'I'm so sorry that I haven't got any news to give you some comfort,' he said eventually when her sobs quietened.

'I know she's gone, I know she's not coming back.' The woman gulped in air, withdrawing her hand from under Jan's and rising to her feet. She crossed to the window as Jan straightened, peering through the net curtains. 'I stand here most days, imagining her appearing at the gate there, ringing the bell to be let in, to tell me she's all right, she's just been on one of her big trips somewhere.'

She turned back to the room, crestfallen. 'And then I tell myself she's gone forever. That she's never coming back. And the worst thing is, I don't know why.'

CHAPTER FIFTEEN

Jan clasped her hands around the tepid mug of tea and took a moment to savour the warm breeze coming through the open back door.

She could smell the sweet scent of the clematis on the trellis above the kitchen window, and somewhere amongst its flowers a bee worked tirelessly.

The sound of her eleven-year-old twin boys playing the latest console game filtered through from the living room, a concoction of explosions, music and laughter lifting her spirits a little.

Just for a moment, she could push away the memory of the two graves, of two women whose lives had been brutally cut short, and two families who never knew what had happened to them.

Then her thoughts turned to all the families who were still

searching, still holding out hope, or expecting the worst but unable to mourn.

'Are you okay?'

She blinked at the sound of her husband's voice, willing herself back to the present, and nodded.

'I'm okay. Just thinking.'

'So... any preferences?'

She put down her mug of tea and peered over Scott's shoulder.

'I like the green,' she said. 'It's calming.'

He wrinkled his nose and leaned back in his chair, turning the paint chart over. 'It might be too dark for the living room. What about this one?'

'Grey? I don't know. We'd have the same problem, wouldn't we?'

'I can lighten it.'

'I'm not sure.' She yawned. 'God, sorry. Can we do this tomorrow? Or next week?'

Scott smiled and folded up the chart, sliding it across the kitchen table to join a pile of trade brochures. 'Or maybe we just leave it until your mind's on home, not those poor women, hmm?'

'Sorry.'

He pushed his chair back before leaning over and brushing his lips against her hair. 'Don't be. I'll check the boys are okay, and then we can sit outside with a glass of wine if you like. It's going to be light for another hour yet.'

Jan groaned as a fresh burst of laughter emanated from the

front room. 'They're going to be a pain in the arse to get back into a routine after this summer, what with starting at a new school as well. I'm sure Luke reckoned that leaving primary school was it as far as his education went.'

Her husband laughed. 'Well, at least now they've made it into the boys' school, we won't have to listen to duelling trombones for much longer.'

'Hallelujah. Let's just hope they don't want to take up drums instead of piano.'

She pushed herself out of her chair as he disappeared out along the hallway, and rinsed out her mug while gazing out over the patch of lawn beyond the patio.

Scott and the twins had spent their afternoon mowing and weeding, evidenced by the trail of dirt across the paving stones to the back door.

A line of well-worn battered shoes were lined up on the step, ready for whatever chores her husband had in mind for them the next day, and she blinked at a familiar tug to her chest.

What would she do if one of them went missing?

How on earth would she cope, let alone look after the ones who were left?

Gritting her teeth, she resolved she would return the two unidentified victims to their families.

Somehow.

She exhaled, placed the mug on the draining rack and turned to the refrigerator, pulling out a half-full bottle of Chablis.

'Okay, I've told them they can have another half an hour and then it's television off.' Scott reappeared and reached into a cupboard beside her, picking up a pair of wine glasses before making his way to the back door. 'Come on, before they find you and try to make you change my mind.'

Jan grinned, slipped on a pair of flip-flops and followed him outside.

A heady scent of lavender greeted her as they settled into the chairs beside a wrought-iron table, and while Scott filled their glasses she closed her eyes for a moment, savouring the normality of hearing laughter from the neighbours' gardens and the light rumble of a passenger jet crossing the sky in the distance.

'Cheers, you.'

She opened her eyes and took the glass from Scott, clinking it against his before taking a sip. 'Only the one for me, mind – I'm on call.'

Scott checked over his shoulder to make sure neither of the twins was within earshot, then turned back to her. 'I take it today was as stressful as you thought it would be?'

'There are so many of them.' Jan gave a slight shake of her head. 'I mean, I knew there were, but until you start talking to the families, one after the other, all with similar stories, all that pent-up grief and anger...'

A shuddering breath snatched away her words, and she took another sip of wine before putting down her glass and wiping her eyes.

He reached out and squeezed her hand, saying nothing for a moment.

'I don't know how they cope,' she managed eventually.

'Did any of them give you any indication that your victims might be one of those missing from the area?'

'Not conclusively. It's like Kennedy said to everyone in the briefing when we got back this afternoon – we just have to keep them in mind as we get more information from the second post mortem.'

'You're going to that tomorrow?'

'Yeah.' She sighed. 'God, what a week.'

CHAPTER SIXTEEN

Mark pulled on a pair of protective trousers, securing them at the waist with a practised twist of the cord into a bow and then shrugged the matching long-sleeved shirt over his shoulders.

Jan would be doing the same next door in a matching locker room, preparing herself for another visit to Gillian's morgue.

It had been a long time since he'd had to attend two post mortems within the space of forty-eight hours, but he was reluctant to delegate the work in case he heard or saw something that would give him a vital connection between the two victims' deaths.

Jan had been quiet in the car on the way over, meeting him in the police station car park that morning before the drive up the A34 into Oxford. She hadn't spoken until they'd reached the Headington exit, and that was only to reply to his query about how the boys were enjoying the last week of their summer holidays.

She seemed distant, contemplative, since they'd made a start on the missing persons interviews, and he resolved to take her out for a drink after work one night this week to make sure she was all right.

He sighed, folded up his jacket and placed it with his wallet and keys in one of the empty lockers, and then opened the door into the corridor.

His colleague was already pacing the polished tiled floor, her hair covered by a plastic blue bonnet that matched his, her brow furrowed.

'I was thinking – do you fancy a drink after work later?' he said as they made their way towards the heavy wooden doors at the end of the corridor, the air cooling around them as they drew nearer.

'Maybe another day.' Jan shot him a small smile. 'I wouldn't mind getting back by six tonight so Scott can get to football practice.'

'Oh. Okay. Good stuff.'

She paused with her hand on the door and turned to him. 'Another night would be good, though – thanks.'

'Let me know when.' He raised an eyebrow. 'I'm worried about you.'

'I'm all right.' That slight smile again. 'Just thinking about all those missing people, and no one knowing what's happened to them.'

'I understand. I'm always here, you know, whenever you need to get it off your chest.'

'Thanks, Sarge.'

Jan fastened a mask across her mouth and nose, then, giving the door a shove, led the way into the morgue.

Immediately, Mark picked up on the charged atmosphere in the room.

Gillian stood beside a slightly shorter woman at the far end of the examination table, near the second victim's feet, and looked up as they entered.

'DS Turpin, DC West, I'd like you to meet Dr Angela Powell, the anthropologist from Bristol I was telling you about,' she said by way of greeting.

'I'd shake your hands, but...'

Powell held up her gloved hands, already covered in – well, Mark didn't want to think what the stains were to her fingers.

Instead, he grimaced behind his mask.

'In the circumstances, that's not a problem,' he said. 'Sorry we're late – we're being bombarded with information from all sides at the moment.'

'Hopefully that's a good thing,' said Gillian, her tone light as she turned back to her work.

While Jan made her way to the victim's feet, Mark circled around the back of the two women who had their heads bowed while they examined the victim's skull and neck, catching only partial words amongst their murmured conversation.

They spoke in earnest while they worked, a tangible excitement between them, and he shook his head in wonder.

Knowing better than to interrupt Gillian's thought processes, he joined Jan at the far end of the table where clothing remnants were laid out.

'Any jewellery?' he murmured.

'Nothing,' she replied, waving a gloved hand across the items. 'This cream-coloured stuff looks like it might've been wool, and there's a pair of lace-up shoes here.'

He paused, frowning, and pointed to two foot-shaped inlays. 'What are these? Insoles from the shoes?'

'Orthotics,' Gillian called over. 'We found them inside the shoes.'

'Any maker's markings?'

'Not that we could see. The lab might be able to find something once they've cleaned them up.' Powell straightened as she spoke. 'Often those can be bought in pharmacies and the like – they're bulk-produced so I doubt we'll find anything unless our victim went to a podiatrist and had them specially made.'

Mark bit back his frustration, and watched as Jan carefully turned over a plastic evidence bag containing a second item of clothing.

'Underwear,' she murmured, placing it back on the table and patting her hand on it. 'Bra and knickers.'

The next bag was bulging with its contents.

'Looks like a coat,' said Jan, peering through the plastic. 'Heavy, too.'

'Buried in a colder month, perhaps,' he mused, then turned his attention back to the other two women at a surprised cry from Powell.

'What is it?'

'There's a distinct fracture to the hyoid bone,' she said.

He walked over to where they stood, Jan in his wake. 'Meaning?'

'Damage to her neck,' said Gillian.

'It's an indication that she may well have been strangled,' Powell added. 'Which is interesting, because there's also evidence of blunt trauma to the base of her skull here.'

Mark watched as the anthropologist moved to one side so he could see and gently turned the victim's head to the left.

'See here? This cracking suggests that she was hit with something heavy. That alone would've been enough to kill most people.'

'But not her?'

'She may have still been breathing. Perhaps your killer wanted to make sure she was dead before placing her in the grave, hence the strangulation damage we can see here.'

'A merciful killer, perhaps? I mean, by not burying her alive.'

Jan grimaced. 'I'm not sure whether that could be considered merciful, Sarge.'

Mark immediately regretted his words, but Gillian nodded.

'You've got a fair point. Whoever did this could've simply knocked her out and buried her. She would've suffocated eventually.'

He shuddered. 'The strike to the back of the head – that's the same as the first victim that was found. The later murder, I mean.'

'Were there any signs of strangulation in that one?' Powell asked.

Gillian shook her head, frown lines appearing above grey eyes. 'Not that Kerridge pointed out, which makes me wonder if the killer had perfected his method by then.'

'Anything else you can tell us about her?' said Mark. 'Apart from how she was killed? Anything that might help us find out who she is?'

'There might be something.' Powell curled a forefinger at him, beckoning him closer, then prised open the victim's jaw.

Gillian reached up and pulled a large lamp on a bracket until it shone into the cavity, and moved aside so Jan could join him.

'There are a number of missing teeth,' Powell said, running her little finger over the inside of the jaw. 'And see here? The jaw bone has receded in places. This indicates to me that either she lost the teeth early in her life and the gums have worn down over time – or she wore dentures.'

Mark frowned. 'Dentures? So this victim is much older than the other one?'

'How old did Kerridge say the first victim was?' Powell glanced over her shoulder to where Gillian stood.

'Thirty-five to fifty. Middle-aged range.'

'Hmm.' Powell rearranged the jaw, and moved away from the examination table, her hands on her hips. 'Well, this one's definitely older. The striation in the bones, for a start. There's all the indication of bone disease there – osteoporosis in the hip joint on the right-hand side, and a general demineralisation in the humerus and tibia bones.'

'Robert suggested that the demineralisation was caused by the environmental effects of where the bodies were found,' Gillian mused, moving closer and running her gaze over the skeleton. 'The soil to the south-west of Hagbourne is acidic in places with chalky deposits.'

Powell said nothing for a moment, pacing the length of the table while she poked and prodded at different bones and muttered under her breath.

Eventually, she paused next to the feet and raised her eyes to them.

'I'll run some additional tests to make sure, but I'm of the opinion this victim was old-aged when she died. The bones are lighter, you see – that leads me to stick with my original opinion that they're of a lower mass.'

'Are you saying that our killer doesn't target a particular age group, but has been more indiscriminate?' said Mark, confused. 'Or are we looking for two killers?'

In reply, Powell turned to Gillian.

'The first victim – the one Robert assessed. Do you think I could take a look?'

CHAPTER SEVENTEEN

Ewan Kennedy ran a hand over his eyes, then put his reading glasses back on and glared at the whiteboard.

Late afternoon, and the incident room bore the tired evidence of an investigative team scrambling for answers.

The distinct smell of a laser printer working overtime mingled with a mixture of sweat and various body sprays, the odours so strong that Mark coughed to clear his throat after providing his update for the afternoon briefing, and then stifled a yawn.

As he looked around at his colleagues, he could see the fatigue in their faces and in the way they slumped in their chairs or against nearby desks as the realisation took hold that there was going to be no quick breakthrough.

He clutched a tepid takeout coffee in his left hand while he balanced his notebook on his knee and jotted down the additional notes Kennedy had added at the beginning of the briefing, anything to avoid the DI's impatient glare being directed at him next. He drained the coffee, placed the cup on the carpet beside his chair and waited for Kennedy's answer.

'So you're saying that Gillian wants me to ask the coroner to authorise a second post mortem on victim number one?' Kennedy said eventually. 'Forty-eight hours after she and an anthropologist carried out the first one?'

'Yes, guv.' Mark sat forward in the hard plastic seat, his arms resting on his knees and forcing himself not to tap his foot with impatience.

He fully understood the pathologist's insistence that the proper paperwork be obtained before the first body was re-examined but it didn't mean he wanted to wait long for it to take place either.

'And you think this second expert – Powell – has got a point?'

'She made a very convincing case about the age of the second victim, guv. I think we need to be sure about the first one to try to understand if there's a connection between the two skeletons and the killer's habits, and Gillian can't proceed without the coroner's approval. We don't want the CPS tripping us up over this if – when – we get this to court.'

'I know, I know.' The DI held up his hands in surrender. 'All right, where's Grant?'

'Here, guv.'

A uniformed constable craned his neck over his colleagues, raising his hand.

'Get onto the coroner's office now while I'm finishing this briefing and request an urgent review,' Kennedy ordered. 'We need Gillian's new expert to do this tomorrow, otherwise we're going to lose access to her as well. Let him know it's imperative to this investigation.'

'Onto it, guv.'

The DI nodded, then turned his attention back to the rest of the team. 'Right – what else have you got for me?'

Alex raised his hand and sat straighter. 'The total number of interviews carried out yesterday with families of existing missing persons between the ages of thirty-five and fifty came to forty-two,' he said. He cleared his throat as he turned the page in his notebook. 'We were hoping to complete a further twenty-one today, but only managed sixteen due to some of those taking longer than anticipated. I'll work with a couple of officers to make sure all of those statements are entered into HOLMES2 before the end of today. That way, we can finish the interviews tomorrow morning. After that, we should be able to start looking for similarities between the original statements and any new information gleaned from the interviews to help narrow down who our victims might be.'

'That's good work.' Kennedy crossed his arms and stared at the ceiling tiles for a moment. 'If we could find a common thread, something that hasn't been noticed before over the years, at least that will give us a lead to follow up while we're waiting on the definitive information from Gillian. Does anything from the statements taken to date lead you to think that any of the families that have been reinterviewed may have something to do with their loved ones' disappearances?'

Murmured conversations rippled through the gathered staff at his words, and he raised his voice.

'It's something that has to be considered – and while we're reviewing all of the original statements and speaking to people, we have to keep an open mind. Yes, we have the remains of two victims – but there may be more. There have been plenty of other cases up and down the country over the years where someone has being killed by someone they know and then reported as going missing. And killers get complacent over time.'

Mark watched with interest as Kennedy perched on a desk beside the whiteboard and ran his gaze over the team.

'Look, this is going to be one of the hardest cases some of you have ever worked on,' the DI continued. 'However, it also presents us with an opportunity. An opportunity to reduce that list of missing persons and find some answers for their friends and families. All I'm asking is that while you're going about your tasks, you listen and watch. Those of you who haven't worked a cold case before have a steep learning curve ahead of you. Not only will witnesses' memories have become distorted over the years, any guilty party has also had time to perfect their story. They may even believe that it's true after all this time.'

'So, guv, basically what you're saying is – don't trust anybody,' Caroline called out.

A smattering of nervous laughter filtered through the incident room, and Kennedy snorted.

'At the risk of sounding like a cynical bastard, yes. That's exactly what I'm saying.'

The humour quickly faded, and Mark leaned back in his chair, biting his lip.

What Kennedy had said rang true.

Time and again, murder victims' loved ones were responsible for their deaths.

A momentary lapse of reason.

A temper, lost in a split second over a minor misdemeanour.

A hidden rage, kept behind closed doors for years, until…

But two bodies, buried in close proximity to each other?

Mark scratched his jaw and then raised his voice. 'Based on that then, our victims could be mother and daughter. If Angela Powell is right about the victim in the second grave site being older than the one Kerridge examined, that is.'

'I don't know what to think, but that's certainly a possibility and an angle we'll have to consider when we correlate all of the new statements with the new information from the post mortem. And we're certainly not going to get DNA testing results back on those remains for at least a week to check for familial links.' Kennedy's eyes narrowed as PC Wickes returned and hovered at the fringes of the group. 'Yes, Grant?'

'The coroner's office agreed with the proposed second post mortem, guv. They've emailed through the authorisation.'

'Thanks. Mark – give Gillian a call and tell her to get on with it.'

'Will do, guv.'

Kennedy shot a final glance over his shoulder at the whiteboard, then turned his attention back to them. 'That's it for today. Next briefing will be at eight o'clock tomorrow.'

CHAPTER EIGHTEEN

Mark twisted the top off of a cold bottle of beer and raised his hand to one of the neighbouring boat owners before dropping the cap into a metal bin outside the cabin door.

Resting his arms on the narrowboat's roof, he gazed along the length of it towards the bridge spanning the River Thames, the sound of traffic diminishing as a pink glow teased at the horizon beyond the trees lining the farthest reaches of the tow path.

He rubbed his eyes, then took a gulp of the amber ale.

Lucy had taken one look at him when he'd reached the narrowboat at half past six, put her pencil and sketchbook to one side, and told him to shower while she went and collected a Chinese takeaway for dinner.

He hadn't the energy to disagree with her, stumbling down the cabin steps in his fatigue while she'd set off across the meadow to the restaurant up the road from the Old Gaol.

Now his stomach rumbled, and he ran his hand through his wet hair and watched as Hamish ran to the end of the narrowboat's roof and barked at a figure crossing the bridge in the distance, curls billowing as she hurried.

'She won't hear you from there, you daft mutt.' Mark clicked his fingers to get the dog's attention. 'Come on – come and lie down here before you annoy the neighbours.'

Hamish reluctantly trotted across the roof to where he stood, then lay with his feet pointing towards the gate at the far end of the water meadow, his nose in the air.

As Mark ran his hand over the dog's fur, he took another sip of beer and tried to let some of the stress ease away, compartmentalising the murder enquiry to the recesses of his mind just a little so he could enjoy the evening ahead.

Since purchasing the boat last year, he and Lucy had made it a home, slowly reducing the glare from the new fittings and turning the vessel into something more welcoming.

Her artistic flair was evident everywhere, from the hanging baskets beside the cabin entrance, to the wind chimes that tinkled above the side hatches. The interior was the same – modern design now softened with throws, comfortable seating and a large master bedroom that was airy and light.

He chuckled and patted Hamish.

Ten months on since moving in together, and he was as content as he'd been in a long time.

Old wounds were healing, past traumas fading to memory,

and as he glanced over his shoulder at a splash from the other side of the riverbank, spotting the telltale bow wave from a vole, he realised for the first time that he was learning to relax.

It was the only way to cope with the job.

Hamish gave a small yip of excitement, launched himself from the roof onto the deck and then tore across the meadow with his stubby tail wagging as Lucy appeared.

Stretching his legs, Mark slid onto the deck and ducked his head as he lowered himself into the galley.

He drained his beer, fetched two fresh bottles from the refrigerator and twisted off the caps as Lucy's voice carried from the towpath.

'If you trip me up, there'll be no food for any of us. Go on – shoo.'

The scratching of paws on the stern deck pre-empted a dark brown streak of fur that tore past Mark and landed in a dog bed lined with old blankets, panting.

'That bloody animal.' Lucy's face belied her words, a smile on her lips as she walked down the steps and handed him a warm paper carry bag. 'Anyone would think he was starving, the way he carries on.'

Mark kissed her, then handed her a beer before reaching into a cupboard above the refrigerator and pulling out two plates. 'I suppose because he used to live rough, he's always made a point of scrounging food whenever he gets a chance.'

'Yeah, but you would've thought after living with you when you arrived, and now with us since we bought the boat, he'd have calmed down.' She shook her head at Hamish, who had recovered from his skirmish and was now sitting beside the dining table, eyes alert and waiting.

Fetching cutlery from a drawer, Lucy laid the table while Mark spooned out noodles and mushroom rice from the foil containers and brought them over, handing her a laden plate before sinking into the chair opposite her with a contented sigh.

'Cheers,' he said, clinking his beer bottle against hers. 'Thanks for getting this.'

'You didn't look like you were going to stay awake much longer, so I figured this was quicker than cooking.'

Their conversation waned as they started to eat and Mark savoured the flavours from the chow mein while watching a pair of ducks paddle past the window.

'I take it this is going to be a difficult one?' Lucy said eventually, pausing to drink, her fork aloft. 'You've been preoccupied – more so than usual when there's an investigation.'

He swallowed, put his fork down and ran his thumb over the condensation running down the beer bottle. 'Cold cases are always difficult. There's just so much evidence lost to time, and – putting it mildly – very little to go on, except a few clothing remnants. Everything else has just…'

Wrinkling her nose, Lucy held up a hand. 'I get the idea. Do you think you'll get a breakthrough from all the interviews you're doing?'

'I don't know.' He shrugged. 'I mean, we've got to do them – there are just so many. It could be days before we find out something useful, and in the meantime you can bet the media are going to start pushing for answers. All Kennedy and the media team have told them so far is that human remains have been found.'

He picked up his fork and took another mouthful of noodles. 'And he had a phone call from the site manager just before I left, demanding when they can continue work.'

'What did Kennedy say?'

'It's not repeatable in present company.'

She laughed, then – a loud guffaw that made him smile, remembering why he loved her so much.

The peace was shattered by the trill of his mobile phone, his heart sinking as he pushed back his chair and crossed to where it was charging on the desk halfway along the cabin.

'Who is it?' said Lucy.

'Gillian. I'd better take this.' He dropped back into his seat and raised an eyebrow at her while she nibbled on a spring roll. 'Evening, Gillian. Everything all right?'

'It was, until about five minutes ago.'

Mark frowned at the noises in the background. 'Are you still at work?'

'We figured that as Angela was still here when the coroner's approval came through that we might as well make a start on the second PM,' said the pathologist without rancour. 'To be honest, I'm as intrigued as you about this one. Anyway, I need you to come over to the lab.'

'What, now?'

'Yes. It's urgent. There's something you need to see.'

Mark looked forlornly at the spring rolls and remaining chow mein on his plate, then at Hamish.

The little dog wagged his tail, his tongue hanging out.

Mark sighed, then lowered his plate to the floor before passing his half-finished beer to Lucy.

'Are you still there?' Gillian's familiar bark burst from the mobile phone as Hamish launched himself at the free food.

'I'm on my way.'

CHAPTER NINETEEN

'What did she say?'

'She didn't elaborate – she just said to get over there, and that it was urgent.'

Mark grabbed hold of the passenger armrest as Jan powered her car away from the slip road and across the junction into Oxford from the A34, gritting his teeth and hoping she had her foot hovering above the brake pedal just in case.

Instead, his colleague accelerated and shot through a traffic light as it turned red, her jaw set while she changed gear.

'She'd probably appreciate it if we got there in one piece too, West.'

Jan choked out a laugh, but slowed as they entered a thirty mile an hour speed limit, then exhaled.

'All right. What do we *think* they've found?'

'I don't know.' Mark turned his attention to the large semi-detached houses either side of the leafy avenue, purple and blue streaking the sky now as the summer night drew closer. 'Maybe they've got DNA back, and the two victims are related?'

'No, too early for DNA results. Those are taking two weeks minimum at the moment, and that's only because the lab brought on three new analysts in May.'

'I don't know then. I guess we'll have to find out.'

Gillian was pacing the corridor beyond the reception area when they arrived, her mask pulled down to her throat and a frown pinching at her eyes.

'Good, you're here. I was beginning to wonder…'

'What can you tell us?' Jan asked breathlessly.

'It's better that you see for yourselves. Can you get gowned up, and I'll see you in there? Angela is just making some final notes so she can explain everything to you. I'm sure you're going to have questions.'

Mark saw the sideways glance his colleague gave him, then nodded. 'Okay. See you in ten.'

Gillian managed a small smile. 'Make it quicker if you can. She charges by the hour, and this is going on Kennedy's budget.'

With that, she turned on her heel and marched back through the double doors leading into the morgue.

Jan snorted. 'What were you having for dinner?'

'Chinese. You?'

'Spag bol. Luke's favourite. Needless to say, he and Harry were already finishing mine when I left.' She sighed, hitched her bag over her shoulder and leaned against the women's locker room door before smiling. 'I'm guessing Hamish got yours.'

Six minutes later, both of them were back in the familiar surroundings of the morgue, staring at the remains of the first victim laid out on a stainless steel examination table at the far end of the room.

Behind Mark, the second victim's skeleton lay where Angela and Gillian had been studying it earlier that day, a stark reminder that he and the rest of Kennedy's team had too many questions, and that somewhere, two families needed answers.

The anthropologist nodded in greeting, and then gestured to the first victim. 'Well, I won't keep you in any more suspense – we've all had a long day, and I'm sure you have families to get home to as well. I've completed my examination, and I'll explain my findings, if I may? Then if you have any questions about what I've found, I can answer those.'

'Sounds good, thanks.' Mark folded his arms across his chest.

He noticed that Gillian took a step back from the table, allowing them space to follow Powell around it as she provided a running commentary.

'You'll recall from earlier today that I felt that our second victim shows signs of ageing, particularly in the teeth and remnant jawline, and the degradation in her bones.' Angela paused, and picked up a humerus, drawing her little finger over the ridges and striations. 'This first woman's bones are similar. Now, I can see what Dr Kerridge was thinking – the acidic soil content and placement of the remains near the stream would certainly cause damage to the bones, and likely contributed to the lack of organic material found. However, *low* bone mass can also lead to this sort of detrimental effect in the preservation of remains. Less bone means the skeleton can decay more easily.'

Mark rubbed at his jaw, his insides churning while he listened.

'With this victim, we have an added implication,' Angela continued. Oblivious to his discomfort, she beckoned both of them towards the victim's pelvis. 'See here? In the hip joint there's even more degradation – you can see the thinning of the bone for yourselves.'

'What causes that?' asked Jan, peering closer.

'Bone diseases, severe malnutrition, cancer – things like that. In this case, I'd suggest your victim was suffering from advanced osteoporosis, which would go some way to explain the old injuries we can see to her arm here.'

'That looks like an old break,' said Mark.

'You're correct, detective.' Angela nodded, evidently pleased with his observation. 'It's healed over time – I'd posit that this injury healed a year or so before she died, but along with the weaknesses evident in her hip, I'm inclined to think this is an older person, rather than a young person suffering from osteoporosis. I'd also suggest she wasn't receiving any treatment for it, or the right treatment for it, at the time she was killed.'

The anthropologist turned to Gillian. 'Have you got that copy of Dr Kerridge's report please?'

'Here.' Turning to the table behind her, Gillian handed it over.

Mark took one look at the coloured sticky notes protruding from every other page and bit back a groan.

Angela flicked through the pages until she found a note near the end and nodded, turning it around so he and Jan could read it.

'His osteological profile isn't right. You've seen these markings in the bones.' She sighed. 'We call it pseudo-pathology. The archaeological and anthropological evidence has been misinterpreted. I think Dr Kerridge misinterpreted the first body as being middle-aged, not old-aged and being in the ground *longer* based on bone degradation rather than recognising it as being age-related degeneration. In fact, the bodies are *older* and were in the ground for *less* time.'

Mark looked at the skeleton laid out on the gurney. 'She's over fifty?'

'Oh yes. Much more. In fact, I'd be willing to say both victims were in their seventies when they died, perhaps a little older.'

'So, what you're telling us is that Kerridge cocked up.' He heard the heat in his voice, unable to contain his frustration. 'He told us the victim's age was younger than she really is.'

Angela's gaze moved to Gillian, then back. 'I'm afraid it's beyond my professional remit to comment on Dr Kerridge's professional approach.'

'Off the record?'

'I think Dr Kerridge is mistaken in his views. I think you're looking for a killer who is targeting older victims.'

Mark turned to Jan. 'We need to get onto Kennedy and let him know. I'll meet you by the car.'

'Wait!'

Angela stepped forward, blocking his exit. 'You don't understand.'

'I think I do. Kerridge cocked up. And we've spent the past three days looking for the wrong missing persons.'

'No, I mean... Yes, there's that...' Angela took a deep breath. 'There's also the fact that the deterioration in the bones suggests that not only are the victims older, but that they were buried more recently.'

Mark swallowed, his heart lurching. 'How recently?'

'Based on my experience, and what Hayden Bridges states in the archaeological report about the burial site, I'd say those bodies have been in the ground no more than two years. Perhaps less than that.'

'Christ,' said Jan, her eyes widening. 'This isn't a cold case any more, is it? Our killer could still be active.'

CHAPTER TWENTY

Ears ringing, Mark lowered his mobile phone, raised his gaze to the night sky and exhaled.

Kennedy's reaction to Angela Powell's findings had closely echoed his own, but with more swearing.

A lot more swearing.

Finally, the DI had told him to go home and be in early the next morning for a full debrief with the whole team, and then he'd promptly hung up.

An ambulance siren sounded from the opposite side of the hospital grounds, streaking away into the city until it was lost amongst the remnant traffic noises of late evening commuters.

Tucking his phone into his pocket, he made his way back to the morgue's reception doors and pressed the intercom.

A rattle trembled through the speaker before Gillian's voice carried to where he stood.

'We're in my office.'

Pushing open the door at the sound of the security mechanism giving way, he made sure it closed behind him then took the metal stairs to the left of the reception desk, his footsteps bouncing off the plaster walls on either side.

He followed a long corridor along the front of the building, its windows overlooking the car park below.

Only two cars remained now – Jan's, and the pathologist's.

Angela had left while he was talking to Kennedy, raising a hand in guilty farewell as she'd hurried towards a two-door sports car before exiting the car park at speed.

Somehow, he felt that she had the right idea.

After delivering news like that, who could blame her?

As instructed, Gillian was in her office at the end of the corridor, the only light coming from a lamp over her desk.

Jan was sitting in one of the visitor chairs, her jacket draped over the back of it. She glanced over her shoulder as he walked in.

'How did it go?'

'I thought he was going to have a coronary.'

Gillian grimaced. 'And you?'

'Calming down a bit.'

The pathologist patted her hands on the desk, then eased herself from her chair and crossed to a bookshelf next to Jan.

She pulled a thick tome from the bottom shelf as Mark slumped into the spare visitor seat.

'Checking something?' he said, raising an eyebrow.

In reply, Gillian extracted a bottle of single malt that had been hidden behind the reference book, and grinned.

'You wouldn't believe the places we have to hide this stuff just so the students don't find it.'

'You're full of surprises,' he said, choking out a laugh.

'Jan? You okay to have a small one? I presume it's your car outside.'

'Yes, and thanks – I will.'

Mark waited until Gillian had pulled three glasses from the back of a filing cabinet drawer and poured them each a nip, then clinked his glass against the others.

'To Angela Powell,' he said.

The two women murmured their agreement before taking a sip, and he relished the first smooth burn of liquor in his throat.

'All right,' he said eventually, pointing to the X-ray images fanned out on the desk between them. 'How the hell did Kerridge fuck up so badly? Because believe me, Kennedy is going to want some answers in the morning.'

'Sadly, forensic research into elder abuse isn't as far advanced as that for younger victims. Robert might not have come across something like this before in his career.' Gillian pursed her lips. 'After all, his work has tended to be at the forefront of anthropological breakthroughs relating to younger murder victims.'

'The sexy headline-grabbing work, you mean?' Jan said.

Mark's lips quirked.

As usual, his colleague spoke her mind.

It was why he enjoyed working with her so much.

'Where was he based prior to Nottingham?' he asked.

'Leicester. Again, working with higher-profiled murder investigations. He was lucky from a career point of view – he was employed by one of the leading experts as a post-graduate and hasn't looked back.'

'Perhaps a bit of navel-gazing might be appropriate after this.' Jan took another delicate sip of whisky.

Mark heard the sneer in his colleague's voice and picked up one of the X-rays. 'How did he miss the age, though?'

'Because he was assuming your killer had a predilection for younger women, based on the state of the bones.' Gillian sighed. 'He failed to take into account what the archaeologist was telling us. We're all experts in our field, but we do have to remember to review all of the evidence available to us before forming a conclusion. Same as you do.'

Jan peered at the X-ray Mark handed to her and frowned. 'So, how would you tell if our victims were abused in the days or weeks leading up to their deaths?'

'Typically, we'd look for trauma to the upper part of the body – evidence of fractures to the arms, ribs, even facial fractures. Sometimes those fractures can occur by accident – the frailty of bones that have degenerated, due to osteoporosis for example, could make it very easy to cause injury when lifting a person from a bath. One thing you'd want to look into is that arm fracture.'

'But you don't lift someone out of a bath and then bash them around the head,' said Mark.

Gillian shook her head and took a sip before peering over her glass at them. 'No, you don't.'

Jan finished sifting through the X-ray images and slid them across the desk. 'Did the second victim's remains show signs of potential abuse?'

'Not that I could ascertain.' Gillian slipped the images back into a large paper envelope and placed it on a filing tray beside her elbow. 'But abuse comes in many forms, as you know.'

CHAPTER TWENTY-ONE

An overwhelming sense of déjà vu swept over Mark the next morning as he stood in front of the whiteboard and faced the team.

Despite being a Saturday, a full contingent of officers were in attendance, attentive and keen to progress the investigation.

He'd already been the bearer of bad tidings during this case, and what he was about to share wasn't going to help.

If he wasn't careful, his colleagues would soon have a new nickname for him, and probably a derogatory one at that.

Glancing across to where Kennedy stood with his sleeves rolled up to his elbows, arms across his chest while he stood beside the front row of officers, Mark cleared his throat.

'So, to cut a long prognosis short, Angela Powell told us last night that Kerridge's interpretation of the first victim's skeleton was wrong. She wasn't middle-aged when she was murdered. In fact, both of our victims are well over fifty.'

'What do you mean by that?' Caroline asked, her laptop open while she listened. 'How much older are they?'

'Dr Powell reckons both victims were in their seventies when they died. We've got two pensioners in the morgue. Not middle-aged women.'

'If she's right, then we've been looking for the wrong missing persons, haven't we?'

Mark nodded. 'I'm afraid so. Gillian has spoken with the archaeologist to get his opinion about what Dr Powell suggested contributed to Kerridge's error – the environmental side of things – and Hayden Bridges backed her up.'

Kennedy groaned, glanced down at his coffee as if wishing it were something stronger, then glared at Mark. 'When I speak to Kerridge, I'll—'

'After me, guv. As it is, we're going to have to restart the interviews. Start from scratch, as it were.'

'And our esteemed expert can bloody well pay for it. He'd better not send me a fucking invoice…' The DI shook his head and sighed. 'All right – what else have you got? Does Powell think it's the same killer, given the location of the two graves?'

'She does, guv. Both victims suffered head trauma – a blow to the back of the skull, just behind the ear.'

Mark didn't look at his notes. He recalled Angela's findings all too well, having spent most of the night awake, thinking about them.

He took a sip of water to ease the scratching sensation at the back of this throat, then continued.

'The victim that was retrieved from the second grave didn't die instantly, not according to Dr Powell. Instead, she thinks she was still breathing after falling to the ground, and was then strangled. The hyoid bone showed signs of damage.'

Alex ran his finger under his collar, then raised his hand. 'Maybe the killer was in a hurry with that one, then? That was the grave that was rough around the edges, wasn't it?'

'That's a good point,' said Kennedy. 'What about timings between the two murders, Mark? Did Dr Powell have any opinions about that?'

'The deterioration in that soil really screwed with what she was able to ascertain from the remains, guv. She and Gillian are sending off samples to another lab but probably won't get the results for a week or more. What she did say was that these women were buried no more than two years ago – and perhaps less. The first skeleton that was found was in slightly better condition, so when I asked for something off the record, Dr Powell said she thought that one had probably been buried three to four months after the other. That's not going in the report she's sending to you this afternoon, though.'

'Understood. At least that's something for us to bear in mind once we're going through the bloody missing persons information again.' Kennedy slurped the last of his coffee, and then placed the empty mug on the desk beside him. 'Anything else?'

'That's it, guv.'

'All right, thanks – and to you too, Jan. I'll give Gillian a call after this. I appreciate that was a late night for all of you.'

Mark wandered over to a spare seat beside Jan and opened his notebook as Kennedy continued with the briefing.

'Based on that bombshell, we'll abandon the remaining interviews that were planned for today,' the DI said. 'Caroline, Alex – sorry, but it's going to fall to you to work with Tracy to collate a new list of local missing persons based on the new age parameters. You can have four from uniform to get you started but I want a preliminary list by this afternoon's briefing.'

'Understood, guv.' The DC gave a slight shrug, and closed her laptop, resigned to the new assignment.

'Mark, Jan – while they're doing that, start phoning doctors' surgeries in the vicinity of the two graves, and work your way outwards. A lot of them are open this morning so do what you can. Find out if they're aware of any missing persons from their patient lists, or patients they haven't heard from for a while where they haven't moved from the area. Keep your ears open for anything that gives you cause for concern, and again be ready to present your findings this afternoon.' Kennedy tugged at his tie and lifted his gaze to the back of the assembled officers. 'We've lost a lot of time on this investigation thanks to Dr Kerridge, and we're going to have to put in long hours to make up for that. I'll clear the overtime with Kidlington, but in return I need you all to give this your complete focus, is that understood?'

A murmur of acquiescence carried through the room.

'Delegate what you can from other cases, and let me know about anything you can't pass along. I also want to know about any court appearances that can't be ignored so we can have new rosters drawn up this afternoon.' Kennedy gave a grim smile. 'I won't go as far as to cancel any leave already booked but I won't be approving any more until we've got some answers. If you have a problem with that, come and see me after this meeting.'

Mark swallowed, the tension in the room palpable.

He was sure if Kerridge walked through the door right then, there would be a scuffle in the haste to land the first blow.

'Right, that's it until four-thirty,' said the DI, checking his watch. 'Dismissed.'

CHAPTER TWENTY-TWO

Jan wiped crumbs from her fingers with a paper tissue before squinting at her computer screen once more.

She and Turpin had started an internet search for local doctors' surgeries following the briefing, and now sat opposite each other while they worked through an initial list of ten, all covering the area south-west of Didcot.

Phoning the first two that appeared on the list, she was partly relieved and partly frustrated that no one from those GP practices had gone missing within the past two and a half years, and that the only known missing person one receptionist had found on her patient list had been located within two days – staying at a nephew's house after falling out with her husband for the third time last year.

'Regular as clockwork, that one,' the receptionist chuckled. 'But she wouldn't divorce him.'

'Was he abusing her?' said Jan, shocked.

'Not at all – she'd just walk out if she got annoyed with him. That last time, it was because he wouldn't pay someone to decorate the downstairs bathroom, even though they could well afford it.'

Jan shook her head, wondering if people like that realised how much time they wasted – both that of her colleagues, and the local charities that would have organised a search, expecting the worst. 'And now?'

'She died three months ago – and got her own back on her husband. Her will stated he had to rent a horse and carriage to take her coffin to the church. He had no idea she'd changed her will last year – he assumed she wanted to be cremated because it was cheaper. We all thought he was going to have a heart attack when he found out.'

Battening down a fit of inappropriate giggles, Jan fought to keep her voice stern. 'Well, if you do hear about anything that might help us with our enquiries…'

She gave the chatty receptionist her direct number before hanging up and eyed the next surgery on the list.

'Have you finished that already? I thought we were saving these for lunch.'

She peered over at Turpin's desk as he ended another call and pointed at the empty sandwich wrapper abandoned next to her elbow.

In response, she swept it into the bin. 'I'll eat yours as well in a minute if you don't hurry up. You forget – I didn't get any dinner last night.'

'Nor did I.'

Jan cocked an eyebrow at him in reply.

'All right, maybe I managed to eat some of mine before the dog finished it.' He grinned, unwrapped the food and sank his teeth into the bread.

'Any luck with yours yet?' he said between mouthfuls.

'No.' She scowled at the computer screen. 'We've got six more to go.'

He swallowed, then wiped his mouth with a paper napkin she passed across to him. 'I reckon if we have no luck with these, we ought to speak to care homes in that vicinity as well.'

'That's a good point. I hadn't thought of those.'

Scrunching up the sandwich wrapper, Turpin chucked it and the napkin into the bin beside their desks and rubbed his hands together. 'All right, you take the top three on this list, I'll take the others and we'll see if we can wrap this up in the next hour.'

Jan stabbed the next GP surgery number into her desk phone and pushed back her chair, stretching her legs while she listened to the dial tone.

After three rings, she listened to a recorded message that informed her that she was currently number four in the queue.

She eyed the next number on the list, and was wondering whether to hang up and call that instead when a perky female voice answered.

'Crescent Wood Practice, how may I help you?'

'Morning. My name's Detective Constable Jan West, and I was wondering if you could...'

Jan repeated what she had told the other GP surgeries, that they were seeking information about any missing persons on the doctors' registers over the age of fifty and female, and then paused as the woman interrupted.

'Who did you say you were?'

'DC Jan West, Thames Valley Police.'

'Look, I've only been here for two weeks but I'm sure I've seen something on our system like that. Can you hang on?'

She didn't wait for a response.

Jan sighed as a dreary version of *Greensleeves* started playing, and held her phone away from her ear.

'Got something?' said Turpin, lowering his phone.

Spinning her chair back and forth while she resisted the urge to hum along to the tune, Jan gave a slight shrug.

'I don't know,' she said. 'Maybe. She's checking with someone else.'

She held up a hand to him as a different voice came on the line.

'Hello? Is that DC West?'

'It is, yes.'

'This is Marion Stephens. I'm the practice manager. I understand you're after information concerning a missing woman aged fifty or over?'

'I am. Your colleague mentioned she thought you might have a patient on your system who fitted the description.'

'We do, I'm sorry to say. Hold on – I'll just close the office door.'

There was a rustling at the other end of the line, then the soft slap of a door shutting before the practice manager returned.

'That's better. Right, I've found the details on our system.'

'You have?' Jan pulled her notebook closer, unable to keep the excitement from her voice. 'What can you tell me?'

'It was nine months ago, back in early November,' said Marion. 'Annabelle Studley. Seventy-two years old when she went missing – her birthday was in October. Her husband John and daughter Elizabeth were the ones who let us know. I'll never forget the morning they walked in here. Shell-shocked, they were.'

Jan craned her neck until she could see past Turpin to where Caroline sat, and waved her hand until she caught the woman's attention. Beckoning her over, she pointed to her notebook when she neared, and underscored Annabelle's name, adding a question mark.

Caroline nodded before dashing back to her computer.

'... and we haven't heard anything since,' Marion continued.

'I'm sorry – I was just speaking to a colleague,' said Jan, contrite. 'Could you repeat that?'

'I said, with Annabelle's condition, we've become increasingly concerned with the lack of news. John's own health has deteriorated since she went missing. Have you found her?'

Jan bit her lip before replying. 'I'm unable to say at this time, I'm sorry. We're just retrieving our own records about the missing persons report, but what do you mean by her condition?'

'She had dementia. Quite severe, too. John was waiting to hear whether there was room at a specialist care facility close by, but the waiting times are horrendous—'

'Would you mind giving me his phone number?' Jan asked. 'We really would like to speak with him today.'

There was a moment's silence, and then, 'I'm not supposed to give out personal details just like that, but I suppose in the circumstances…'

'I'd appreciate it if you could.'

Jan crossed her fingers, hoping her desperation wasn't too obvious.

'Look, all right. Here you go. This is the phone number for the daughter, Elizabeth. Like I said, John's own health has gone downhill this past year so it's probably best if you call her in the first instance.'

Scrawling the mobile number across the page, Jan exhaled when she finished. 'Thanks. Would it be possible to speak with Mrs Studley's doctor this morning as well?'

She heard the other woman hiss through her teeth before she replied.

'We tend to keep Saturday mornings free for walk-ins, emergencies, things like that.'

'We can be there within the hour.'

'I don't know, he doesn't really like—'

'This isn't about what he likes,' Jan snapped, then rubbed at her temples. 'Look, sorry. But it's urgent that we speak with him as soon as possible.'

Marion fell silent, and all Jan could hear was the sound of fingernails on a computer keyboard at the other end of the line. Eventually, the woman spoke.

'I can squeeze you in at ten past eleven. Will that do?'

'Perfect, thanks. We'll be there.'

Ending the call, Jan turned as Caroline hurried back over, a freshly printed report in her hand and a determined expression in her eyes.

'Found her?'

'Yes, but you're not going to like it.'

CHAPTER TWENTY-THREE

'What does it say?'

Mark slid his hand around the steering wheel, flicking the indicator stalk and eased onto the exit slip road of the dual carriageway.

Beside him, Jan kept her head bowed while she reread the missing persons report Caroline had found, her jaw set.

'The PC who filed this suspected he was abusing her.'

'The husband?'

'Yeah.'

'What about the statements taken from the family?'

'The daughter clearly didn't suspect anything, and the husband was frantic by then – they could hardly get a straight word out of him. When I phoned the GP's surgery to get this meeting brought forward after reading this, I mentioned the abuse to the practice manager. She took a quick look at the records they've got and said the doctor who saw her last noted bruising to her upper arm.'

'Did he tell her to go to the police?'

'She didn't want to, apparently. She was pretty insistent.'

'When was that?'

'Two weeks before she went missing.'

'Shit.' He sighed, then eased to a standstill at a set of traffic lights. 'Did Caroline check, just in case?'

'Yeah. Nothing on the system. John Studley was formally reinterviewed as a matter of course when he and the daughter reported Annabelle missing, but wasn't considered a suspect at the time.'

'Where was he when she went missing?'

'Out buying cigarettes. Reckons he was only gone fifteen minutes. When he came back, the front door was open and she'd vanished. Caroline's pulled together a transcript of the triple nine call the daughter made when she got there.'

'The husband didn't call?'

'No – he phoned Elizabeth, the daughter, and they drove around trying to find Annabelle themselves before calling.'

The lights turned green, and Mark sped away from the junction.

Soon, the road narrowed and after a steady incline, the hedgerows gave way to grass verges that allowed a panoramic view across the barley and wheat fields that stretched in each direction.

Ramrod straight, the asphalt dipped and rolled under the

car's tyres while he mulled over the questions he wanted to ask.

'Was Annabelle's GP interviewed at the time?' he asked eventually, changing gear as the road descended through a series of twisting bends, then braked at a staggered crossroads.

'Yes. Only to clarify what medication she was on, and whether he had any concerns about her welfare prior to her going missing.'

'Did he mention the abuse when he was interviewed?'

'It doesn't say anything here in the notes. He wasn't asked to provide a statement.'

'Bloody hell. Okay – which way from here?' Mark checked his rear-view mirror as another car approached. 'Left or right?'

'Go right – the surgery's off the main road after we reach the speed limit signs for the next village.'

Five minutes later, he pulled into a gravel car park outside a modern-looking doctor's surgery.

Sunlight glinted off the darkened privacy glass that covered the lower windows and baked the red brick façade, while well-tended flowerbeds bordered the parking area.

When Mark climbed out, he could hear water running and peered beyond a privet hedgerow beside the car to see an older man with a hosepipe tending to a bed of rosebushes.

'They smell amazing,' said Jan, her nose in the air while they walked towards the entrance. 'Reminds me of my grandad's garden.'

Double doors slid open as they drew near, and a large man

wearing a faded T-shirt with an official-looking badge pinned to it helped an elderly woman negotiate the sloping kerb and into a waiting car. The pair were laughing, and Mark smiled at the cheeky banter between the two as the man ensured the woman was comfortable before fastening her seatbelt and closing the passenger door, whistling under his breath while he filled in a document on a clipboard.

A welcome blast of cool air greeted Mark when he followed Jan into the reception area, the doors swishing closed behind them.

The scent of roses was immediately replaced with the pungent smell of antiseptic cleaning materials, while classical music playing in the background gave an ambience of calm.

Three people – a man and two women – sat in a waiting area off to his left, either looking at their phones or flicking through magazines, all wearing bored expressions as a clock above their heads noisily ticked off the minutes.

Two women worked behind a high reception desk to his right, a transparent plastic panel separating them from the public, and one looked up from her work as Jan approached.

'Good afternoon,' the DC began, and opened the leather wallet containing her warrant card. 'I called earlier...'

'Ah, Detective West, yes – it was me you spoke to. I'm Marion Stephens.' The woman stood and gestured to a side door. 'Dr Hamilton is finishing his phone calls but come on through.'

She disappeared for a moment, and then Mark heard the familiar buzz of a security mechanism being released moments before the door swung inwards, the woman standing to one side to let them pass before closing it again.

'I'll pop you in one of the treatment rooms,' she said over her shoulder while leading them along a short brightly-lit corridor. 'None of the patients out there will need it as they're just waiting to see Dr Hazlitt and he's running twenty minutes behind schedule.'

Moments later, she'd deposited them in a room that looked as if it had been polished to within an inch of its life, told them Dr Hamilton would join them shortly, and closed the door.

While Jan eased into one of the padded chairs beside a blank computer screen and placed her bag next to her feet, Mark paced the room and eyed the shelves full of various sealed packets of dressings and antiseptic swabs.

All of the equipment and supplies had been labelled and filed away for ease of access, a system necessitated by efficiency and budgetary constraints while ensuring whoever was administering the treatment had everything they needed within arm's reach.

The door latch clicked, and he spun around as a burly man in his late fifties entered the room, his sleeves rolled up and carrying a thick wedge of paperwork.

He thrust out his right hand to Jan. 'Detective West, I presume. Dr Hamilton.'

After shaking hands, he took the chair beside her and waved Mark to a spare chair beside a locked cabinet with glass doors, various boxes of drugs and needle supplies crammed into the space.

That suited Mark – Jan had initiated the interview, and he wanted to observe the GP while they spoke, so he pulled out his notebook and gave her a slight nod.

'Doctor, thank you for seeing us at short notice,' she began. 'I'm going to give you the standard caution for an interview, simply because we'd like to make a formal record of our conversation. Is that all right?'

Hamilton's bushy eyebrows shot upwards. 'Of course. Yes, if you think that's necessary.'

'Before I begin, we have to ask that everything we discuss here today is kept confidential,' she said, after reciting the caution. 'Even from your staff.'

'I understand.' Hamilton glanced across to Mark, then back to Jan, his expression perplexed for a moment, and then realisation dawned. 'Oh. Oh my. You've found Annabelle, haven't you?'

'That's yet to be determined,' Jan continued. 'Five days ago, the remains of a woman were discovered in a copse of woodland about two miles from here. At first, due to the environmental degradation to the skeleton, it was thought the bones were of a middle-aged woman. We obtained a second opinion from an anthropologist yesterday who confirms that in fact, our victim was much older than that.'

She paused, reached into her bag and drew out a slim file. Angling it to face the doctor, she flipped open the cover. 'This is a satellite image showing where the body was found. It had been buried in a shallow grave. Timing-wise, our experts believe she was buried between six and twenty-four months ago. You'll appreciate how many missing people we have on our system, not to mention the ones on the national missing persons database, but Annabelle's name was the first to come up while we were searching those this morning and phoning around local surgeries.'

Mark watched as Hamilton sagged against the small desk and pushed the computer keyboard out of his way.

The doctor rested his elbow on the arm of the chair and ran a hand over his jawline. 'I always believed she would've come home, somehow.'

'We understand from your practice manager that Annabelle was here, two weeks before her death,' said Jan. 'What can you tell us about that?'

In reply, Hamilton handed over the sheaf of paperwork. 'I'm not supposed to give you copies of a patient's medical records until I've got the appropriate request forms from you, but in the circumstances...'

'Thank you.'

'Just make sure you get them to me on Monday.' He jabbed a finger towards the paperwork. 'You'll find that appointment noted on the last page.'

Jan flicked through, skimmed the printed words, then leaned over and passed the whole lot to Mark.

He found the page Hamilton referred to, and pursed his lips.

'Was she being abused, then?'

Before answering, the doctor rose from his seat and wandered over to a square window, its darkened glass looking out over the privet hedge that surrounded the back of the building.

'It's hard for me to say for definite,' he said over his shoulder. 'It was the first time in about three years I'd seen Annabelle, you see.' He sighed, staring at the pale tiled floor. 'Like many surgeries, we depend on temporary staff – locum doctors and the like – to help us on a day-to-day basis. It's hard to attract new full-time staff into the profession. It's long hours, stressful…'

He drifted off, and Mark waited as the man gathered his thoughts.

'I sound like I'm making excuses, and I suppose I am.' Hamilton turned back to them, his hands shoved into his pockets. 'The problem is, and what you'll see from those notes, is that some of the temporary and junior doctors we've had through here over the past three or four years haven't been as thorough in their notes as I would have liked.'

'Did something get missed?' Mark flicked through the pages, running his gaze over the succinct and hurriedly typed entries for previous appointments. 'Didn't they spot it?'

'You need to understand – like I said, we're incredibly short-staffed here… We don't often get the opportunity to discuss patients from one appointment to the next – it's almost like a production line out there in reception sometimes.' The doctor removed his hands from his pockets, clasping them in front of him, eyes pleading. 'Elder abuse is… it's hard to spot, if you don't know what to look for, and sometimes even then. Unless you actually witness the abuse taking place, a bruise or even a more serious injury such as a broken arm can be easily attributed to an accident. Osteoporosis, general bone mass degradation… they all contribute to bones breaking more easily at that age. In addition, we have to consider Annabelle's deteriorating mental health.'

'Oh?' Jan sat back. 'The dementia, you mean?'

'Yes,' said Hamilton, nodding vigorously. 'She might have completely forgotten that she'd knocked her arm against something, for instance, and instead blamed John for the bruising.'

'Did you ever meet Annabelle's husband in the weeks before she went missing?' said Jan.

'John? No, I didn't – but I can see if any of my colleagues did.'

Hamilton dropped into the chair beside her, signing in to the computer system with a flourish that suggested he was relieved to no longer be the focus of her questioning.

'Here we go. Yes, he was here the week before.' He frowned and peered closer at the screen. 'Hmm. It says here that he was struggling to sleep and was requesting some stronger painkillers for back pain. Dr Salah – the GP who saw him that day – noted that he was worried John wasn't coping with looking after Annabelle on his own, even though they were getting a carer to come in three times a week to help.'

'What sort of help were they receiving?' said Mark, looking up from the medical records.

'Mostly it was to assist with bathing Annabelle, making sure John was able to administer her insulin injections – she was diabetic, you know – and keeping an eye on her for a few hours so John could rest,' said Hamilton, his eyes troubled when he turned away from the screen to face him. 'Both Dr Salah and I were of the view that it was time Annabelle was moved to a permanent care facility – her illness was taking its toll on John, evidenced by his own health deteriorating, but there's such a tremendous lack of staffing available in most care homes at the moment that the waiting lists are horrendous. The in-care help was as much as they could get.'

'Was that provided by a district nurse?' Jan asked. 'Someone from this practice, or a local hospital?'

'God, no.' The GP gave a despondent chuckle. 'There's a deficit in available NHS services, and no one to fill the vacancies. We're having to advise families to contact private companies more often than not these days, and that's certainly what we did in John and Annabelle's case. We had no other choice, unfortunately.'

Mark closed the folder containing the medical records and recapped his pen as Jan rose to her feet.

'Thanks for your time, doctor. We'll be in touch if we have any further questions.

'Not at all. And remember – get that official request paperwork emailed to me as soon as possible, or else staff shortages will be the least of my worries.'

CHAPTER TWENTY-FOUR

The next day, still weary from the doctor's words and the revelations about the effect Annabelle Studley's illness had had on her family, Mark turned the pool car towards Harwell and rolled his shoulders.

Leaving the junction off the dual carriageway, he cursed under his breath when a slow-moving tractor pulled out from a road ahead of them, towing an enormous trailer. As it heaved its way up the hill, diesel fumes blooming from the exhaust pipe, he glanced at his watch.

They were meant to be meeting John Studley and his daughter in twenty minutes, and he had yet to read through their original statements.

After Dr Hamilton's revelations, he wanted to make sure he was prepared, ready to hear anything that might give him a clue as to why Annabelle went missing in the first place, and why her remains might have been found in a shallow grave outside Didcot, some three miles from where she lived.

Finally, the tractor indicated left and turned into a field, the trailer bumping across a rut-strewn track before disappearing from view, and Mark floored the accelerator.

As the dry countryside shot past the window, he turned down the air con and peered at the clouds forming on the horizon.

'Could be a storm tonight, I reckon.'

'Thank God for that.' Jan pulled a small bottle of water from her handbag and took a sip before handing it to him. 'Want some?'

'I'm okay. Thanks.'

They fell to silence once more while she returned her attention to the documentation Caroline had printed out, and Mark's thoughts drifted to his own family.

His parents still lived on the outskirts of Cirencester, having downsized six years ago and moved into a thriving retirement community well before their health dictated so. His father had accepted the move with a stoical shrug, accepting it was better than waiting for the inevitable and finding themselves living somewhere they hated.

Now, Mark realised just how vulnerable his parents had become, and wondered what decisions faced him when they could no longer make those choices for themselves.

Ten minutes later, he braked in front of a low-set home that had been clad with a sandy-coloured stone reflecting the sun's rays.

Underneath the front window, an array of stone flowerpots were arranged with begonias and geraniums fighting for space amongst stubby magnolias. The lawn had been recently mowed, with dry blades of grass sticking up in defiance of the lack of water.

A single silver two-door car was parked in the driveway, and as he walked past he could hear the engine ticking as it cooled.

'Looks like we weren't the only ones who had to hurry to get here on time,' he said when Jan pressed the doorbell.

Movement behind the fuzzy glass panel caught his eye, and then the door was pulled open to reveal a woman in her early fifties with short dark brown hair, her cheeks flushed.

She raised her chin to look at Jan, then him, and stepped back. 'I presume you're the police? Come in. I was just making Dad a coffee. D'you want one?'

'Thanks, but no.' Jan led the way in, and presented her warrant card. 'Are you Elizabeth?'

'Yes.' She closed the door behind Mark and held out her hand. 'Liz Moorlock.'

Introductions made, they followed the woman along a hallway before she led them through a door to the right at the far end.

Mark blinked, surprised at the size of the well-appointed kitchen and the airy space created by a small conservatory leading from it.

The room smelled of a lemon-scented cleaning product,

and he noticed that both the refrigerator and oven doors were gleaming along with the worktops.

'I only just got here,' said Liz, pouring hot water into two mugs and adding a splash of milk in each. She nodded towards the conservatory. 'Dad's in there. Go on through – I won't be a minute.'

A man in his early eighties eased himself from an overstuffed and worn sofa when Mark and Jan wandered into the conservatory, his tanned forearms set off by a white cotton polo shirt and grey trousers.

He stooped slightly and met Mark with a watery gaze as he held out his hand.

'John Studley,' he said, his voice wavering. He turned to Jan. 'I presume you're DC West.'

'Thanks for seeing us so late in the day,' said Jan.

'I'm going to presume that as there's two of you and you're not in uniform, this isn't going to be good news.' His voice was resigned, as if he was used to false hope and disappointment. 'I think I've always known my Annabelle was gone forever. It's the not knowing that hurts…'

'I'm sorry,' said Mark. 'We have nothing definitive to report yet, but we do need to run through some formalities. Would that be all right?'

Studley shrugged. 'I suppose so. Have a seat.'

He gestured to two wicker chairs opposite the sofa and eased himself back against the cushions as his daughter appeared. Taking the cup she held out, he raised it to his lips, then winced.

'Leave it a few minutes, Dad,' she scolded. 'You'll burn your mouth.'

'Just like her mother, this one,' Studley said as Mark settled into one of the chairs. 'Always fussing.'

Mark looked through the open double doors leading out to a paved patio and a neat garden. A gentle breeze carried into the conservatory and a twinge of sadness clutched at his chest as he turned back to Studley.

'Tell me about your wife,' he said.

The man lowered the coffee cup to his knee with a shaking hand. 'She was the best thing that ever happened to me,' he said wistfully as he peered at the floor. 'We met at a dance at the local village hall, and that was that. There was no one else for me, as far as I was concerned. We were married the next year.'

Mark listened as Studley went on to describe the driving holidays around the UK and Ireland, then the birth of two daughters – Liz, and an older one who lived in Edinburgh. When Studley retired from working as a bank manager in Wallingford, he and Annabelle had bought this house in the village, spending most of their time in the garden.

The only sound apart from the man's voice was the scratching of Jan's pen across her notebook while Studley continued to tell them about the hours his and his wife put into the garden before her health deteriorated.

'It's very pretty out there,' Mark noted.

Studley blinked as he looked at the immaculate lawn and flower beds. 'Sometimes, when I'm out there, I think I can feel her standing next to me. I almost expect her to tell me I'm pruning the roses the wrong way.'

'We understand from her doctor that she was suffering from dementia?'

'It was the little things at first,' said Studley. He paused to drain half the contents of his cup, then sighed. 'I had my suspicions, but after six months, when I found Annabelle standing in the middle of the garden in her nightie one evening, the winter before she went missing, I insisted we go to the doctor.'

'The tests took forever,' Liz added, her voice breaking. 'Mum got bounced around from specialist to specialist for a while. Poor Dad was exhausted by the time the diagnosis came through.'

'That was in the June,' Studley said. 'Annabelle went downhill fast after that, almost as if she knew there was no going back to what we had. I used to see snippets of her old self now and again, but it changed her forever.'

'Your wife's doctor mentioned you were trying to find a place in a care home for her,' said Jan gently. 'I can't imagine that was an easy decision to take.'

The man shook his head, then sniffed. 'I felt like I was letting her down.'

'You weren't, Dad.' Liz leaned forward and wrapped her fingers around Studley's hand. 'It was affecting your health, too remember. Both me and Julie were worried sick about you.'

She paused and turned to Mark and Jan. 'It was why we

suggested the at-home care. Just while we were waiting for a place for Mum, to take some of the pressure off of Dad.'

'What happened the night she went missing?'

Studley squeezed his daughter's hand, then gave her the now empty coffee cup. 'She'd done it before, you know. Twice. That's why I didn't phone the police straight away. I didn't want to waste your time. The time before that last disappearance, we found her outside the village post office, didn't we, love?'

'She was wondering why it wasn't open,' said Liz. 'Never mind that it was half past eight at night.'

'I'd only gone outside to water the garden,' said Studley. 'Next thing I knew, Mrs Jennings from one of the cottages near the post office phoned me to tell me Annabelle was wandering along the street looking lost.'

Mark shook his head in wonder, hearing the anguish in the other man's words. 'And the last time?'

Studley gave a shuddering gasp as if he was terrified to let the memory pass his lips.

'She'd started to complain about my smoking,' he said eventually. 'I'd always smoked, mind. Only four or so a day, but I liked it. Anyway, when Annabelle's dementia set in, she started hiding my cigarettes or throwing them away. She'd had a particularly bad day that Wednesday, and I'd got her into bed a bit early. I-I thought she was asleep... I thought she'd be okay for a little while...'

He paused and pulled a cotton handkerchief from his pocket, blowing his nose before returning it. 'I couldn't find my cigarettes anywhere, and honest to God if I knew I was never going to see her again, I'd have quit there and then, I swear it.'

'You went out?' Jan prompted.

Studley nodded. 'I popped out down to the garage to buy cigarettes – the one just outside the village. You'd have passed it on the way here. It's only a five minute drive away. I still had the car back then. I was gone for perhaps ten, fifteen minutes,' he said, fat tears rolling over his veiny cheeks. 'When I got back, the front door was open and she was gone...'

His daughter wiped at her own tears and reached out for his hand once more. 'Dad phoned me straight away, and I called the police after we'd had a quick drive around the village. None of the neighbours had seen her, either,' she said. 'Mum was diabetic too and although she'd had her insulin that evening, we were terrified what might happen if she was out overnight. It was blowing a gale and freezing cold.'

'We never found her...' Studley's mouth worked, but no other words escaped.

Mark gave them both a few moments to compose themselves while he let the man's words sink in.

He couldn't imagine the guilt the man must have been living with ever since, wondering if his wife would still be alive if not for a nicotine habit that had proved too tempting because of the stress from caring for her.

'Had anything different happened in Annabelle's daily routine before she went missing?' he said eventually.

'No, not at all.' Studley wiped his eyes with the back of his hand. 'The carer had been in that day – Sonia was her name. Bloody marvellous, she was – especially when Annabelle was having a difficult day. Sonia was good at calming her down, and it was because of her I could rest in the afternoons if I needed to.'

'What time did she leave that day?'

Studley bit his lip, staring out through the open doors for a moment. 'About half five. Yes, half five. I remember because I had to give Annabelle her insulin injection at six, which I did. Then she had a light supper before I helped her into bed.'

Mark listened as Jan guided Studley and his daughter through the list of places they had looked for Annabelle before calling the police, and then cleared his throat.

'Part of the reason for our visit today was to ask you, Liz, if you'd mind letting us take a swab for DNA testing,' he explained, keeping his voice neutral. 'Would that be okay?'

The woman straightened in her chair, casting a sideways glance at her father. 'You have found a body, then. Do you think it's her?'

'I'm really sorry – we can't say for certain at this time,' he replied. 'But a DNA sample would go a long way to help us discount your mother from our enquiries.'

'Or confirm it's her that you've found.' Studley blew his nose again. 'I think you should, Liz. I want to know if it's her. The not knowing is too much to bear.'

'In that case,' said Liz, turning to them, 'what do you need me to do?'

'It's really simple – do you want to show DC West into the kitchen and she can take the swab there?'

He waited until the two women had wandered off, and then rose from the wicker chair and crossed to the double doors.

Movement out of the corner of his eye caught his attention, and he glanced over as Studley joined him.

'Thank you for your time this afternoon, Mr Studley. We appreciate it. I realise we've brought up painful memories.'

'Just make sure you find the bastard that killed her, Detective Turpin.' The other man's jaw clenched. 'Because if I do, I'm not sure what I'll do to him.'

CHAPTER TWENTY-FIVE

Liz Moorlock walked them to the front door once Jan had administered the swab.

As Mark pulled the door to the kitchen closed and followed the two women, he caught a glimpse of Studley's thinning white hair catching the sunlight, halo-like, and squared his shoulders.

'Liz? Before we go...'

She stopped at his words, resting her hand on a table set against the hall wall. Above it, a series of framed family photographs were displayed, and she leaned forward to wipe an imaginary speck of dust away from one of them.

'What do you want to ask me that you couldn't in front of my father?' she said, finally turning to face him, and crossed her arms over her ample chest.

'There's no easy way to approach this,' he said, 'but it's a standard question that has to be asked. Did you ever suspect that your dad might be struggling to cope, perhaps taking out his frustration on your mother?'

She visibly staggered at his words.

'No,' she said vehemently. She shook her head as if to clear the thought. 'No, they doted on each other. You heard him yourself. They've been married for sixty years. Dad was devastated by Mum's dementia – we all were. If anyone was suffering abuse, it was Dad, not her.'

'What do you mean?' said Jan, keeping her voice low.

'Towards the end… I mean, in the weeks before Mum disappeared, her dementia was getting worse. She was getting more and more confused, and with it she got angry. Frustrated. She would take it out on both of us.'

'Did she ever suffer a fracture to her arm?' Mark asked.

Liz's eyes widened. 'You *have* found her, haven't you?'

'Please, just answer the question.'

'Y-yes. She did. About a year before she went missing. She slipped on an icy puddle out there on the patio. We were paranoid after that – Dad said he didn't know what he'd do if she did it again. It broke his heart to see how much pain she was in, and by then they were both at their wits' end, even with the help they were receiving from Sonia.'

'Could you let us have her contact details?' said Mark.

'Why would you—' Liz threw up her hands. 'Sorry. I know you're just doing your jobs. Hang on, I've still got her number in my phone. 'Scuse me.'

She brushed past him, went back to the kitchen, and

returned with a mobile phone before reciting the carer's name and number. 'That's the main phone number. It goes through to a call centre at the head office. I think they're based out on one of the industrial estates on the other side of Didcot. If you ask for her, they should be able to put you in touch.'

'Have you seen her since your mother went missing?'

'No. No need to.' Liz jerked her chin towards the back of the house. 'Dad's holding up all right – he's got his health, he gets most of his meals delivered, and I stop by on the way home from work every day to check up on him. We have insisted on him getting one of those help necklaces though, just in case.' She gave them a rueful smile. 'He hates wearing it, but at least it means we know he can get someone here if there's an emergency.'

Mark moved towards the front door. 'Thanks for your time this afternoon. And please thank your father for us, too. We'll be in touch when we have something further to report.'

As he climbed behind the wheel of the pool car, he glanced back at the house to see Liz Moorlock standing on the doorstep, her expression forlorn.

'I hate not being able to give them an answer,' he murmured.

Once Jan had fastened her seatbelt, he pulled away from the kerb and saw the time displayed on the dashboard.

'Do you want to give that care company a quick call?' he said. 'Find out if that Sonia is on shift first thing tomorrow, and if so whether we can speak to her?'

'On it.' Jan already had her phone to her ear, and he

listened while she was first put on hold, and then put through to someone who, by the clipped response Jan gave, was as efficient as his colleague.

He risked glancing over to her when she finished the call. 'Well?'

'Good news,' she said. 'Sonia Adams still works for the company.'

'That's something, at least. Is she around today, or out looking after patients?'

'Oh, she's around all right.' Jan grinned. 'She was promoted six months ago. She's now running the in-home care department.'

CHAPTER TWENTY-SIX

A distinct tang of ozone clutched at the air when Mark climbed from the car outside a modern office block the next morning.

The building overlooked a wide flat plain that once housed the old power station's maintenance sheds and now provided an expansive view across to the back of warehouses and other large buildings that took up the length of another road within the spider-like network of the industrial estate.

Beside him, Jan removed her sunglasses and peered up at the glossy signage and gleaming windows.

'They're doing all right for themselves, then.'

'An ageing population probably helps.' Mark heard the sarcasm in his own voice and smiled. 'Either that, or effective advertising.'

'And a health service on its last legs,' replied Jan, then led the way towards the signposted reception doors. 'I was talking to my mum last week, and they've just got a quote from a place like this.'

'They're okay though, your folks?'

'Yes – just being practical, I suppose.' She paused to let the automatic doors swing inwards, then crossed to a reception desk in the middle of a wide room lit by spotlights and a skylight that poured in sunshine from the ceiling three floors above.

'Hello, can I help you?' The middle-aged man at the desk wore a dark green polo shirt with the company's logo embossed across his heart, and a headset that was connected to a central console.

'We've got an appointment with Sonia Adams,' said Jan. 'I'm Detective Constable Jan West, and this is my colleague, Detective Sergeant Mark Turpin.'

The man pushed a clipboard across the desk to them. 'Sign in, please, and I'll let her know you're here. Feel free to take a seat while you're waiting.'

Mark scrawled his signature underneath Jan's, then followed her to a set of three small oak tables surrounded by six chairs.

Jan used her notebook to fan her face while Mark peered out of the floor-to-ceiling window at the car park as a white van pulled into a space beside the reception doors, its panelled sides covered in the care company's livery.

While he watched, a woman in her twenties got out and

then slid back the side door, revealing an interior well-stocked with cleaning paraphernalia.

'That's just one of the services we provide to our clients.'

He turned at the voice to see Jan shaking hands with another woman who wore a light blue blouse and navy trousers. 'I'm sorry, I was miles away there.'

Giving her a sheepish smile, he introduced himself.

'I'm Sonia Adams.' The woman glanced at Jan, tucking a wayward strand of blonde hair behind her ear. 'I understand you needed to speak with me urgently about Annabelle Studley? Has she been found?'

'Is there somewhere private we could talk, Ms Adams?' Mark asked, his gaze falling on the man at the reception desk who was feigning interest in the contents of his desk drawer while watching them out of the corner of his eye.

'Of course. Come up to my office. And call me Sonia, please.'

She set off with long strides towards a steel staircase that wound up the left-hand side of the reception area, then crossed a landing to a door at the rear and stood to one side. 'I'm afraid the view isn't as interesting as the front, but then I don't get a lot of time to appreciate it.'

Once settled into one of two visitor chairs opposite Sonia's desk, Mark looked around at the various certificates on the walls filling every available space between bookshelves crammed with lever arch files and medical tomes while the care manager tidied away a leather-bound notebook and her computer keyboard, sliding both under a screen to the left of her desk.

'As I said on the phone, Detective West, I've been in this role for less than a year but I'll do everything I can to help you. I understand this is about one of the patients I used to care for?'

'It is,' said Jan. 'We'd like to clarify what your role was at the time, and get your view on Mrs Studley's home situation in the form of a witness statement, if we may?'

'Of course. As I said, anything I can do to help.'

Jan recited the formal caution.

The woman clasped her hands on her desk after confirming she understood the wording, then cocked her head to one side. 'I can't help feeling this isn't going to be good news, detectives.'

'In the strictest confidence, we can confirm that the remains of two women believed to be upwards of fifty years old were discovered south of the town a few days ago,' Mark began. 'The DNA testing is pending, but for the moment, we'd like to talk to you about Annabelle Studley.'

'Two women?' Sonia paled, her fingers travelling to a silver St Christopher medal at her neck. 'Oh my god. Do you… do you know what happened to them?'

'We're unable to divulge that information at the moment,' said Mark. 'We were hoping you could tell us more about your time caring for Annabelle though. When did you start going around to the Studley's house?'

'It must've been three months before she went missing,'

said Sonia, running the silver chain between her fingers. 'I stayed on for a couple of days while the search was underway to keep John company when his daughter couldn't be with him more than anything else. I was worried about him.'

'Did he ever give you any cause for concern with regard to his wife's welfare?'

'No, never.' Sonia dropped her hand to her lap, her eyes wistful. 'He loved her, Detective Turpin. That much was very clear. He was struggling with her health, though – it was so sad to see. That's why I stayed on. I never told my manager at the time – I just took some annual leave so I could be there for him. And Liz.'

'Did the company ever find out?' said Jan. 'Didn't they mind?'

'Yes, and no.' She gave a slight smile. 'A lot of us go out of our way to help our patients, above and beyond what's in the small print in the service contracts they or their families sign. I don't think we could stop ourselves if we tried. We just become so attached to them, I suppose.'

'When did you start working as a carer?'

'In my early twenties. I'd started a nursing degree but then changed my mind about that when I spent a day on a geriatric ward.' Sonia sighed. 'It was depressing to be honest, and all I could think about was wouldn't it be better if those people could live out their lives in their own surroundings, on their own terms? I quit a week later and took on a junior role in an aged care facility on the outskirts of Oxford for about three years, and then side-stepped into the private sector. I joined this company eight years ago.'

'And were you mostly out on the road, or office-based?'

'Always out on the road. I loved it. Each carer is assigned a number of clients, so you're never bored and honestly, it's nice having regular visits.' Sonia smiled. 'I used to look forward to seeing all of mine. You get to know their families if they're close by, and just seeing the extra independence they gain... it's gratifying. It's just a shame what we do can't be offered by the public sector. I'm sure it'd save millions of pounds in the long run.'

'And yet you gave up that for an office-based role,' Mark said. 'Why was that?'

'I was coerced.' Sonia smiled. 'My predecessor changed her mind at the last minute about coming back from maternity leave, and our executive management team leaned heavily on me. I was the longest-serving carer, you see, so I know all the policies and procedures by rote, I knew all of our service level staff, and I could empathise with the problems carers would encounter from time to time. It made sense for them to approach me about this role.'

'I sense some reluctance there.'

'I did take convincing. But the thought of the hassle they'd go through trying to find someone experienced, and who could learn our systems under such pressure... I couldn't do it to them, so I accepted.'

'Do you enjoy the role?' Jan asked.

'I do, yes. It means I have to work a couple of Saturdays

every month in case our weekend care team have any issues, but it's worth it.' A wistful expression crossed the manager's face. 'I miss the people though, I'll be honest. I miss being able to help them.'

'How many people do you have working here?' said Mark.

Sonia exhaled. 'Off the top of my head, about a hundred and fifty.'

'That many?'

'Yes, we're doing well.'

'Is that due to demographics in the area, or—'

'Not really. Our other centres in Bristol and Portsmouth are equally busy, and have been for the past couple of years.' Sonia's mouth twisted. 'We have to use a lot of temporary staff, which is why our overall personnel numbers seem high – we sometimes have three people sharing a day's work in between school runs, university assignments and the like when it isn't the summer holidays. Unfortunately the full-time wages are too low to attract school-leavers, and working with the elderly isn't something for everyone. Since all of the changes to immigration laws and minimum salaries for working visas came into force, there's a huge deficit between service demand and staff availability,' she said. 'Not just here, but countrywide. And, with an ageing population, it's only going to get worse.'

'What sort of services do you provide to your clients?' said Jan.

'A lot of people don't want to give up their independence, detective. Many are happy to stay in their own homes rather than move into a specialised care facility. That in turn creates a problem for the NHS, who don't have the staffing levels to offer at-home care for everyone.' Sonia gave a tight smile. 'There are only so many district nurses available in any one area, and they're overworked as it is. That's where organisations like ours can fill the gaps. We offer a private service to people who want to stay at home, who just need extra support on a weekly or daily basis.'

'So the care you provide isn't full-time?'

'It depends on the needs of the individual. Some people... Often it can be a stepping stone on the way to full-time care but it's been proven time and again that people's mental health is improved if they can remain in their own homes for as long as possible. Going back to your question about Annabelle's home life, we're all trained to look out for any signs of abuse. A lot of our clients are extremely vulnerable, and we take our role very seriously. You have to remember, most of our staff see these people more often than their own GPs so we're almost the first line of defence when it comes to welfare.'

'Tell us about the last time you saw Annabelle,' said Mark. 'When was that?'

Sonia leaned back in her chair. 'It was the day she went missing. Have you spoken to John or Liz yet?'

'Yesterday.'

'Then they probably told you that it had been a particularly trying time for them. Especially John, of course. He was shattered by the time I got there that day.'

'What time was that?'

The woman's brow furrowed. 'That was my afternoon shift pattern, so I would've reached them by about half past two. I stayed until just gone half five.'

'And did you get any indication that Annabelle might wander off?'

'No, none at all. She was argumentative that afternoon, and very confused. It took a little while to calm her down, but I helped her out to the conservatory so she could look out at the garden, and put a blanket around her to keep off the chill.' She gave a small smile. 'John kept saying he was going to get someone around to install a better radiator in there, but he never did. Once she was quieter, I told him to nip upstairs and get his head down for a bit. I could hear him snoring within minutes.'

'And you say you left at five-thirty?' said Mark.

'Yes. I think John must've set his alarm because he came downstairs at five and I made him a cup of tea while I filled out my timesheet for him to sign. I wasn't due to see them again until the Friday afternoon, you see, and the payroll here is done on Friday mornings. If you don't get your timesheet in by nine o'clock on a Thursday you have to wait until the following week.'

'You said you stayed on for a couple of days while the search was initiated,' said Jan, flicking through her notes. 'Did you hear or see anything that gave you cause for concern during that time?'

Sonia's hand returned to the St Christopher's medal while she pondered Jan's question, then she shook her head. 'No.

Nothing that I can think of. Except… I was surprised John left her alone. I mean, it's all hindsight of course, isn't it? But knowing the sort of day she'd had, and how confused it often left her, I do wonder whether he should have gone out and left her on her own. And now you're saying she was murdered?'

'We're not saying anything for certain at the moment,' Mark clarified. 'Only that the remains of two women have been found. We don't know for sure yet that one of them is Annabelle.'

'Of course. My apologies.' She sighed. 'Then I do hope that it isn't. I mean, I know the chances of finding her after all this time are slim, but…'

Mark rose from his seat while Jan dropped her notebook in her handbag, and handed over his business card. 'Thanks for your time this afternoon. We'll be in touch if we have any further questions, but if you do think of anything that could help us, my direct number's on that.'

'Please, let us know what's happened to her when you can,' said Sonia. 'Whatever the outcome. She really is a lovely woman, and we miss her. I miss her.'

'I will, thanks.'

CHAPTER TWENTY-SEVEN

Mark's hand hovered over his computer mouse, his eyes sore from staring at the screen for over an hour.

Beyond his desk, beyond the blinds that covered the windows overlooking the fast food restaurant and the district hospital, the rumble of thunder grew closer.

''Night, Sarge.' Alex passed his desk, backpack slung over a shoulder, then paused. 'Are you staying much longer?'

'Just reading through the last of the statements we took this afternoon, and I'll be out of here.' He pushed the mouse away and stretched his arms above his head. 'Thanks for your help today.'

'No problem.' The young DC forced a smile. 'With any luck, we should have that new list of missing persons finalised sometime in the morning. Hopefully it'll tie in with some of the other information in Gillian's reports.'

'Fingers crossed.'

A brilliant flash of lightning coursed around the fringes of the window blinds, and the building shuddered with the force of the thunder only a mile or so away.

'Best you go – that rain isn't going to be far off.' Mark dropped his hands to his desk, easing a kink from his neck as Alex threw a wave over his shoulder and headed for the door.

Seized by a wide yawn, he glanced up at the open door to Kennedy's office, the inspector's voice audible as he bickered with a media officer from Kidlington about the wording for the formal press statement to be released in the morning.

Rumours were starting to swirl amongst the local journalists, and Jan had already feigned ignorance when a senior editor from an Oxford-based newspaper had called her on their way back to the station.

Five days, no progress to report...

He grimaced, glad not to be in Kennedy's shoes.

Reading through the last paragraphs of Carly Evans' statement about her daughter Tara, he reached out for his mobile and pressed the speed dial.

'Dad!'

'Jeez, Louise.' He wrenched the phone away from his ear and lowered the volume. 'Where are you?'

'Ice rink.' His daughter's voice muffled, then returned. 'Sorry – I was underneath one of the music speakers. Wassup?'

'Nothing. Just wanted to see how you're doing. Is Anna there with you?'

'Yeah. She's not skating though. She says it's dumb. She's over in the café, watching me.'

He rolled his eyes, imagining the argument if his younger daughter could hear her sister's words. 'She's glaring at you now, isn't she?'

Louise laughed. 'How did you know?'

'You're my daughters. I know everything.'

'Yeah, right.'

He moused over the print icon on the screen, then pushed back his chair and wandered across the room as the machine whirred to life. 'How's your mum?'

'Good. Are you still at work?'

'Just finishing for the day.'

There was a pause, then Louise lowered her voice. 'Are you working on a murder case?'

'Uh-huh. Listen, I might have to postpone our catch-up next weekend. I wanted to apologise to you both before I call your mum.'

'Oh.'

Her single word response couldn't mask her disappointment.

'I'm sorry, Lou. I would've said come and stay anyway but Lucy's got an exhibition at a local gallery launching in the next few days too, and I don't think you'd want to hang around on your own all day, would you?'

''S'pose not.'

Mark swore under his breath as the printer juddered to a

halt and a red warning light started to flash on the front display.

'Dad? I've got to go. I—'

'I know, ice skating to do, right?' He smiled. 'And I'm guessing it hasn't gotten any cheaper since we last went together.'

'And someone's glaring daggers at me.'

'Give Anna a hug from me?'

'Laters.'

He lowered the phone, staring at the display, a painful tug at his chest.

His daughters were growing up fast.

Too fast.

Tucking his mobile into his pocket, he tried to fathom the instructions on the inside of the printer's front casing, and wished one of the junior administrative staff were still around.

They'd know how to fix it.

'Still here, Mark?' Kennedy looked at the printer as he passed on the way over to the whiteboard, and grimaced. 'Best leave that for the morning. What was it?'

'The GP's statement from earlier today. It's in HOLMES2, I was printing out a copy for Jan to check when she comes in tomorrow.'

'Did you get to the bottom of the suspected abuse there?'

'John Studley's daughter denies her father would have ever hurt her mother, and the woman we spoke to at the care company reckons she never saw any injuries to give her cause for concern.' Mark rubbed his back while he made his way over to where Kennedy now stood and ran his eyes over the swirling looped handwriting across the whiteboard. 'And we can't follow up the original report that was filed because the officer who wrote it is no longer with us.'

New photographs had been pinned along the top of it, Annabelle Studley's now in the centre with a second photograph beside it showing the grave that had been discovered.

'What the hell connects them, Mark?' Kennedy mused. 'Do you think they could be related?'

'I don't know. I don't think so, not given the adjustment to the ages Gillian's expert gave us. It's got to be something else. If we could get something on the second victim to at least give us an idea of who she might be...'

'Did you speak to the lab when you got back, about the DNA samples?'

'Yes. Unfortunately they're backed up so we're not going to get anything this week.'

'Shit.' The DI removed his reading glasses and pinched the bridge of his nose for a moment.

'How'd your meeting go, guv?' he asked.

Kennedy lifted his head, his gaze tracing the thick black lines drawn around an enlarged map of the crime scene. 'About as good as can be expected. Of course, Andrew Tolley from the media relations team wants to give more information than we're comfortable with at the present time. He says it's in the hope of getting us a breakthrough, but trying to make him understand that there's a difference between a useful lead and a deluge of useless bloody information to wade through…'

'What are we releasing?'

'The basics. Two victims found in shallow graves on a construction site south of Didcot, estimated age above fifty. Thought to have been in the ground for no longer than three years. Call us if you saw something unusual in the vicinity of Hacca's Brook, blah, blah, blah…'

Mark exhaled, looking at each of the crime scene photographs in turn, finally reaching out and straightening the image of the second victim's skeleton. 'We need something, guv. Soon.'

'And instead, we'll be subjected to speculation and desperation the minute the news sites publish our statement in the morning.' The detective inspector gave a weary smile and replaced his glasses. 'So expect the deluge.'

Raising his eyes to the ceiling as a loud thunderclap reverberated around the station, Mark gave a sardonic snort.

'Speaking of which, I'd better head off, guv.'

'I'll see you in the morning. Be prepared – things could get ugly.'

CHAPTER TWENTY-EIGHT

Jan lay with the bedsheet pulled down to her waist, a cotton vest top providing a modicum of modesty in case one of the boys wandered in again.

Beside her, Scott snored once, then rolled over, his breathing settling once more as he fell back into a deep sleep.

Rain roared across the roof tiles, peppering the windows at the foot of their bed while the final remnants of the storm grumbled in the distance.

Eyes gritty from lack of sleep, she twisted her neck to see the alarm clock's digital display on Scott's bedside table.

Half past three.

She exhaled, wishing for sleep, knowing the moment she closed her eyes it would be time to get up, and wondered how many more summers Luke would have to endure his terror of storms.

By the time she left for work, both the twins and Scott would all be emerging bleary-eyed from the effects of his terrified cries waking them an hour ago.

Even Harry was worried about his brother, and she wondered why it was that one of her twins could be so scared and the other his polar opposite when it came to their individual fears.

A flash of lightning escaped past the curtains, illuminating the ceiling and casting shadows around the walls.

Holding her breath, waiting for the anguished cry from the bedroom along the hallway, she counted to five.

The thunder was softer now, retreating.

And Luke slept on.

Soon, the rain subsided to a gentle patter and the curtains billowed as a breeze chased the last of the clouds away, instantly cooling the room.

Jan peered up at the ceiling, her thoughts turning to the missing people on Caroline's list.

How many were now homeless, with nowhere to shelter from the storm?

Why had none of them contacted their families to let them know where they were?

What were they afraid of?

Rolling onto her side, she wiggled the pillow to get it the way she wanted under her neck and closed her eyes, brow furrowed.

She recalled the remains of the two victims laid out in

Gillian's morgue, her nose wrinkling at the memory of the sickly stench filling the room as the pathologist had worked, the list of questions morphing into a worrying range of things she might have missed.

Had she asked the right questions?

What if they didn't find out who was responsible?

Exhaustion seeped through her muscles, and as she lay as still as possible, not wanting to wake Scott, she wondered if Turpin and the rest of the investigative team were as troubled as she was about the cold case they were expected to solve.

Moments later, her phone jerked her from a troubled sleep, vibrating across the bedside table, screen alight as she scrambled to answer it while Scott grumbled under his breath and turned over.

'Hello?' she murmured, reaching out blindly for the lamp cord trailing over the table and switching it on. Raking her hand through her hair, she glanced at the time on the display.

Five o'clock.

'Jan? Sorry to wake you, but Tom Wilcox said you were on call tonight.'

'Jasper?' She swung her legs over the side of the bed then, heart racing from the shock of the phone ringing, and the tremor in the lead CSI's voice. 'What's going on?'

'I need you to come back to the woods, quick as you can.'

'Th-the woods?' She paused with her trousers halfway up her thighs, confusion sweeping over her.

Then she heard shouted voices in the distance, Jasper's

muffled response as he covered his phone's microphone with his hand, then a mumbled apology.

'Are you at Hacca's Brook?' she managed.

'Yes, and you need to get over here now,' came the reply.

'Why?'

'Because we've just discovered a third body.'

CHAPTER TWENTY-NINE

Mark thrust his arms out to his sides, cursing the slippery mud-strewn footpath under his boots.

Bleary-eyed from a late night pondering the case before being woken by his phone ringing, trousers already dirty around the hems and soaking wet, he paused to take a deep breath and refocus on the task at hand.

Up ahead, farther along the familiar path winding its way alongside the now-swollen stream, he could see Jasper and his team gathered beside a new cordon of blue and white tape.

The wooded area had morphed from an idyllic copse to a dank, dark place that reeked of damp rotten undergrowth, dimly lit by a grey sky that tried to penetrate the tree canopy above.

Taking another step forward, his boot easing from the mud with a reluctant squelch, he spotted his colleague amongst a group of uniformed officers, her back to him while she gave orders.

The lead CSI looked up from his tablet computer as Mark drew nearer, excused himself from the impromptu meeting, and met him at the outer line of tape.

'Morning, Mark.'

'Jasper. Jan said on the phone you'd found another body.' He peered around the man's shoulder, past the tape and towards the overflowing stream. 'Where is it?'

'Over there on a tarpaulin, just behind that tree trunk to the right.' Jasper grimaced. 'We had no choice – the water is rising quickly.'

'How quickly?'

'This'll all be under water within a couple of hours.' The CSI wiggled his mask and lowered it to his neck.

'Who found it?'

'I did. I got here a couple of hours ago at first light. I was worried about the effect of flooding on the two grave sites, in case Gillian or yourselves needed more information before we hand the woods back to the construction company. I was chatting to Hayden Bridges the other day, and he said Hacca's Brook – this stream – has a tendency to flood. Back in the villages, the property owners manage flood mitigation and keep the stream clear of debris during the year, but out here…'

'What did you see when you got here?'

'I'll show you. Are you wearing waterproof boots under those?'

Mark glanced down to the protective plastic coverings

over his feet, and nodded. 'Although I think the manufacturer's idea of waterproof is being generous with the description.'

'Come on then, let's go before everything's waterlogged.'

Jasper replaced his mask, waited a moment while Mark did the same and pulled a protective hood over his head, then held up the tape.

Falling into step behind the CSI lead, making sure he placed his feet in the other man's footprints, Mark followed him past the two original graves.

Both were full of dirty coffee-coloured water, with leaf litter and twigs floating on the surface where the rain had washed across the field on the other side of the hedge and towards the stream.

'This way.'

Jasper's voice jerked him to attention, and he hurried to catch up.

The path widened towards the stream, and Mark noticed the waterline seeping over much of the thin sliver of soil that sloped downwards.

The ground here had collapsed, taking with it an old fallen oak trunk that partially blocked the stream's progress.

'We've already had the Environmental Agency onto us,' Jasper said, clinging onto a sapling with a gloved hand to stop himself sliding into the water. 'They want to get in here and remove that tree within the hour, otherwise there'll be flooding farther back by lunchtime.'

'Christ.' Mark swept his gaze back and forth. 'All right – where was the body when you found it?'

'He was about two metres to the right of where you're standing. I only saw him because I wandered along here to see how far up the water was.'

Mark stepped sideways, groaning as his boot sank into the soil and water sloshed up to his knee.

'It wasn't as high as that an hour ago, obviously,' said Jasper without mirth. 'That's why we moved him.'

'Him, not her?'

'That's what Gillian said when she saw the remains. I saw the skull amongst the soil that's at the foot of that tree root over there. The rain must've washed it out or something.'

Mark carefully extracted himself from the water and took Jasper's outstretched hand with a grunt of thanks. 'How bad is it? The skeleton, I mean.'

'In worse condition than the others.' The CSI wrinkled his nose. 'The soil's probably damper down here, even during dry months, so that might be why. As soon as I saw him, I called it in and got three of my team down here so we could rescue what we could before this bank flooded.'

'Jesus.' Mark took one last look at the water lapping at his feet. 'All right, let's have a look at him before he's taken away, shall we?'

'Back this way.'

They found Jan talking to Gillian beside a plastic tarpaulin that Jasper and his team had laid out on a grass verge higher than the waterline and tucked away from the torrents now cascading through the undergrowth from the surrounding fields.

Laid out in a rough approximation of a human form were the broken remains of a skeleton, and at its feet were a motley collection of clothing remnants.

Jan grimaced when she caught his eye. 'Whoever killed him chopped off his ring finger, Sarge.'

Mark looked to where he'd expect to see the skeleton's left hand, and frowned at the jumbled bones. 'How can you tell from that lot?'

The pathologist crouched and pulled a ballpoint pen from her pocket. 'See the bone here? I realise some bone fragments have probably been lost in the flooding, however this one has been broken. Not in the way you'd see from a fracture. It's my belief – and I'll confirm this once we're back at the lab – that this was cut off with a blade.'

Mark grimaced. 'Shit. Before or after…'

'Sorry. I can't tell from this.'

'So we might assume this victim was married, and whoever murdered him couldn't get the wedding ring off.' Mark turned his attention to the skull. 'Same injury, behind the ear?'

'There's damage to the skull, yes. I can't confirm if it's the cause of death until I get him cleaned up though.'

Jan moved until she was standing at his shoulder and gave him a slight nudge. 'Gillian's found something that might help us, Sarge.'

'Really? What?'

In reply, the pathologist raised her gaze to Jasper. 'You did a good job getting what you could, given the circumstances. Especially this.'

She turned the skeleton's left leg until Mark saw a tiny glimmer escape the gloom.

'Is that...'

'Yes.' Gillian looked up and smiled. 'He had knee replacement surgery at some point. We should be able to clean this up and get a serial number from part of this for you.'

Despite everything, despite that they now had a third victim, despite the fact their crime scene was rapidly disappearing under water, Mark smiled.

'Well, it's about bloody time we caught a break, isn't it?'

CHAPTER THIRTY

Mark paused at the threshold to the incident room, his heart sinking at the cacophony of telephones ringing.

'Oh my God,' Jan murmured, slicking wet hair away from her face. She gave him a gentle shove so she could reach her desk and pulled a towel from the bottom drawer. 'The press release went out this morning, didn't it?'

'And we've had Bill McFarlane on the phone twice already,' said Caroline, handing them both a briefing agenda before they could remove their jackets. 'Apparently his managers and the client have started contract negotiations for an extension of time, and it's going to run into the hundreds of thousands.'

'Bugger the contract negotiations.'

Mark turned at the gruff voice to see Kennedy standing at the door to his office, hands on his belt.

'How the hell did the cadaver dogs miss a third body?' he barked.

'Maybe we send in Jasper rather than the dogs in future,' said Alex, then lowered his gaze to his computer screen, his face flaming as the DI glared at the back of his head.

'Very bloody funny, McClellan. Mark, Jan – get yourselves into some dry clothes. Briefing in ten.'

Mark snatched up his backpack from under his desk and raced downstairs to the men's locker room, Jan disappearing into the ladies' seconds before him.

After the fastest shower possible, he fetched a clean shirt and socks from his locker, pulled a pair of jeans from the backpack and padded back to the incident room in his socks.

Jan grinned when she saw him, her wet hair tied back away from her shoulders and the previous day's copy of the *Herald* held in her hand. She tore it in half and handed him the sports section.

'Stuff that in your boots,' she said. 'With any luck, they'll dry in a few hours.'

He did as she suggested, then picked up his notebook and a pen and hurried to join her next to the rest of the investigation team in front of the whiteboard.

Kennedy raised an eyebrow and checked his watch as Mark dropped into a spare chair beside Tracy.

'Not bad. At least you managed to run a comb through your hair, Turpin.'

The rest of the team sniggered, and then the DI's face turned serious.

'First things first,' he said. 'Jan – the photographs on your phone, I need you to upload those into HOLMES2 as soon as we're finished here. Did you take some of the surgical parts Gillian identified?'

'I did, guv. She managed to clean off some of the dirt at the scene and I've got a note of the serial number she located, so I'll try to track down the manufacturer this morning. Hopefully they'll be able to tell us where those parts were used, and we can then get in touch with the relevant hospital.'

Kennedy updated the notes on the whiteboard as she spoke, then nodded. 'Good, thanks. Does anyone have anything useful from the phone calls that have come through so far following this morning's press release?'

'We've managed to remove three people from our list of missing persons,' said Caroline. 'The national helpline received two calls, and we received an anonymous one here from a woman asking us to let her family know she was safe and well – she just wants to avoid contact with them.'

Mark saw some of the stress leave the DI's face.

'Good to have something positive come out of all this,' he said. 'Let's hope for some more like that. Anyone else?'

'I've reworked the missing persons from the database to factor in our latest victim,' Alex said from the back of the group. He got to his feet and raised his voice over the murmured conversations. 'Working within the same parameters as our list of female missing persons over the age of fifty, and keeping to men within the local area to start with, I've narrowed it down to seventy-two names.'

His words were met with a loud groan, and Mark dropped his gaze to the carpet, his heart lurching at the news. When he looked up, even Kennedy looked crestfallen.

'Anyone on that list who stands out?' the DI asked.

'I've skim-read some of the reports that were filed at the time,' Alex replied, keeping his voice upbeat despite his colleagues' despair. 'I think if we cross-reference these with what the national helpline might have by way of information, we might knock some of these off the list – you know, people who don't want to be traced by their families, or those I find in our system who are on remand, again perhaps unknown by their families. I should have a finalised list to share within an hour or so, guv.'

'Okay.' Kennedy turned back to the board and added Alex's update. 'Give me an update as soon as you can. Who's back at the site with Jasper's lot?'

'Grant Wickes and Alice Fields, guv. Now that the press have got a whiff of this, I figured we ought to have a regular presence there – at least until we're absolutely sure this time there're no other remains there.' Mark wiggled his socked toes over the carpet while he ran his eyes across the older notes on the board. 'We need to monitor the water levels there, and as soon as it looks like it's receding Jasper says he'll go back with a team to search the area in case anything's been washed up that was missed before.'

The DI sighed. 'I'd best give Headquarters a call after this and tell them they're going to have to release a bigger budget for this one… Alex, can you keep on top of the lab regarding that DNA analysis? I realise they'll tell you it'll be a week or more, but perhaps they might take pity on us.'

'Will do, guv.'

'Right, then.' Kennedy ran his thumb down his copy of the briefing agenda, and then looked up. 'Priorities for the rest of today – identifying the hospital that received those knee replacement parts and the patient who they used them on, and finalising the rest of the interviews with families of local missing persons who fit our revised profile. Let's get on with it.'

Mark pulled his phone from his shirt pocket as it vibrated, took one look at the screen and then crossed to where Kennedy stood while the rest of the team made their way back to their desks.

'Gillian's messaged me to say she's going to do the post mortem for our third victim this afternoon,' he said. 'She plans to video conference with Angela Powell at the same time. She mentioned this morning that it's the only way she can get an anthropological assessment on the remains at short notice. Angela's unable to get back here for another three days due to teaching commitments but she'll be on call after that if Gillian feels there's a need to have her take a closer look.'

'Okay.' The DI jerked his chin towards the lower-ranked detectives as they huddled around their desks. 'Start phoning around the medical manufacturers. Caroline and Alex can attend the post mortem while you and Jan work your way through the surgical parts and see if you can trace our victim from that serial number.'

'Sounds good, guv.'

'We need to keep this one moving in the right direction, Mark. Especially now that the press have got their teeth into it.'

CHAPTER THIRTY-ONE

Cupping his chin in his hand, Mark blinked to counteract the dryness in his eyes and the glare from his computer screen.

An early morning, another victim, and the terrifying thought that a killer had gone unnoticed for two years, maybe longer, was starting to take its toll on the whole team.

'Here.'

He jumped at the voice beside him, then gave a sheepish smile as Caroline held out a large takeout cup of coffee from the fast food restaurant over the road.

'You looked like you needed it,' she said, carrying the cardboard tray around to Jan's desk and doling out the remainder of the drinks. 'I know I did.'

'I owe you.' Mark eased away the lid and inhaled the aroma.

'How's it going?' Caroline dropped the tray into an empty box they kept for recycling and eyed Jan's screen.

'We're waiting for a call back from the National Joint Registry about the serial number on the part that Gillian found,' said Mark. 'If we knew who the victim was, we could simply ask his GP for the hospital where he had the operation and they'd be able to confirm it via the stickers they remove from the part and add to his hospital record.'

'So this is the back-to-front way of doing things?'

'Yes, in a way. But if the registry can trace the serial number then the same principle should work. They ought to be able to put us in touch with the hospital as well as tell us our victim's name.'

'As long as our victim didn't have that operation done overseas.'

Mark gave a mirthless chuckle. 'Thanks for that.'

'Sorry. A lot of people do though, don't they?'

'Well, keep your fingers crossed our victim isn't one of them. What time is Gillian doing the PM?'

'At one o'clock. They didn't want to hang around moving the remains away from the stream in case they lost more bones, and she says the earlier she gets underway, the more time she's got to phone Angela Powell and consult with her in between her lectures this afternoon.'

'Makes sense. Okay, in the meantime, log back in to your computer and help me and Jan with this list, would you? Alex has widened the database parameters to include men as well as women over fifty, and we're looking for any statements that mention knee surgeries just in case we don't get anything from the joint registry.'

'No problem. How many have you got so far?'

'Four possibles. Jan's phoning around to try to get more information about those.'

'And you can cross off that last one.' His colleague held up her mobile phone. 'Mr Lucas was found six weeks after he went missing. Neither he nor the family let us know, so the record hadn't been updated.'

Mark rolled his eyes. 'Will you let the Missing Persons lot know as well?'

'Just about to send them an email.'

'Thanks. Onwards, eh?'

He gulped half of his coffee, then set the cup next to his in-tray and brought up the next entry on the list.

This time, it was a female in her sixties who went missing from Grove one morning, never to be seen again.

As he skim-read through the original statements taken from family and friends, he tried to ignore the desperation clawing at his insides.

So far, the online news sites were running with the wording of the press release issued that morning, but with three bodies now recovered and no answers, it could only be so long before a journalist ventured to suggest there was a serial killer in the area.

A serial killer who had – somehow – gone undetected until now.

Despite Kennedy's frustration at the cadaver dogs'

progress at the crime scene, he had arranged with Jasper to send them back within the hour.

Mark swallowed.

The thought that a fourth body, or more, could still be buried within the woodland copse would send the local newspapers into a frenzy – and would, in all likelihood, attract attention from the national media.

Exhaling, he scrolled to the next report before his eyes flicked to his desk phone as it rang.

Recognising the displayed number, he snatched it from its cradle before the second ring.

'DS Turpin.'

'Detective, it's Madeline Taylor from the National Joint Registry. I've got the information you requested.'

Mark sat bolt upright in his seat and clicked his fingers at Jan, then pointed at the phone.

'You've got a name?' he said, rising to his feet, unable to keep still.

'I have. That particular part was used in knee surgery for a patient from the Blewbury area. A Mr Roger Parnett. Seventy-two at the time – that was almost two years ago. I've got the surgeon's details here, as well as his GP. Do you have a pen to hand?'

Mark scrawled the details in his notebook, thanked the woman, and then hung up.

Jan smiled. 'Found him?'

'Sounds like it. I'll phone the GP surgery while you phone

the surgeon's office. Once we've confirmed this Roger Parnett is our man, we'll start by interviewing the GP, then family.'

'What do you want me to do?' Caroline asked.

'Tell Gillian we've got a name when you see her, and that we're going to speak to the man's GP. If there's anything she finds during the PM that you think we should know, phone me straight away.'

'Will do, Sarge.'

'Right, Jan – let's go. We can make those phone calls on the way down to the car park.'

CHAPTER THIRTY-TWO

Mark leaned against the car, enjoying the cooling breeze that fluttered the delicate willow branches above his head.

Across the road from where he stood, a paved driveway curled past a privet hedgerow that graced the front garden of a large sandstone-clad house. With tall chimneys at each end of a gabled roof and high windows, the building would have looked imposing if it wasn't for the pretty lilac wisteria that graced the entrance porch and hugged the window frames each side.

Parked on the driveway was a sleek black coupé, its soft roof lowered exposing tan leather seats that oozed comfort.

He sighed and turned away as Jan finished her call, relegating the sight of the car to a wish list that would never eventuate on a sergeant's salary.

'Sorry – had to take that.' She shoved her phone in her bag and hitched the strap over her shoulder.

'Everything all right?'

Huffing her hair from her eyes, she nodded. 'Scott's due to start a new decorating contract tomorrow so we've been waiting to hear whether his mum can have the twins for the next few days.'

'If you need to clock off early after this, I can cover for you,' he said, leading the way towards the house. 'Just so you can sort things out.'

'Thanks, but we're all good. She's going to pop over tomorrow to collect them before I leave for work.' She smiled. 'I think they both thought they were going to be allowed to tag along with me for a minute.'

Mark chuckled. 'Okay, so while you were on the phone I was looking up Dr Wilson—'

'In between eyeing up her car?'

'Very funny.' He glanced at his notes. 'Dr Candice Wilson, GP at Roger Parnett's surgery for thirty years before retiring a short time ago. Holly, the receptionist I spoke to there, said she was diligent, great with the patients, and very much missed.'

'All right, shall we see what she can tell us about Roger, then?'

Mark turned to Jan when they reached the porch and rang the bell. 'I'll lead this one, if that's okay with you.'

'Sure, no problem.'

He automatically reached up to straighten his tie as he

heard a bolt being shot back, and then the door opened and a woman peered through the gap, green eyes keen under a mop of white hair.

'Detective Turpin?'

'And my colleague, DC Jan West.' He held out his warrant card for examination. 'Nice house, Dr Wilson.'

'Thank you. Although it feels quite empty when the grandchildren aren't here, tearing around the place. Come in, please.'

The woman led the way across a flagstone floor, then down a single step into a bright kitchen, a back door open and leading out to a wide garden that gently rolled down towards a riverbank.

Mark ran his gaze across the engineered oak floor and bespoke worktops, and recalled that the doctor's husband had once been a trader in the City. Evidently, retirement suited them both – and their considerable pensions.

'I understand you wanted to talk to me about one of my patients,' said Wilson, gesturing to the back door. 'Shall we sit outside? It's shaded this side of the house for another hour or so, and I've made iced tea.'

Catching the look of desperation that Jan shot his way, Mark acquiesced and followed the two women outside.

The retired doctor walked across the manicured lawn to a round hardwood table and matching chairs that had been set out under a large chestnut tree, the sound of bees humming within the boughs above Mark's head providing a soothing noise that reflected the peacefulness of the expansive surroundings.

'Michael's out for the day – cricket at Edgbaston,' said Wilson, pouring iced tea from a large jug into three glasses and passing them around as they sat. 'Can't abide the game myself, but with him out of the house until later tonight, it gives me time to lose myself in a good book.'

Mark noted the upturned romance novel, recognising the author's name as a local writer. 'Then we're sorry to interrupt your day.'

Wilson held up a hand. 'Don't be silly. You've got a job to do, and I want to help. What do you need to know? It was Roger Parnett you wanted to talk about, wasn't it?'

'Yes.' He paused to take a sip of the cool drink, then settled back into his chair, nestling his spine between two of the hardwood spindles. 'We understand from your old surgery that you were both his and his wife's regular GP. We were hoping to speak to her, but apparently she died six months ago – just before you retired.'

'That's right, yes.' Wilson lowered her glass, her gaze drifting towards the house as she spoke. 'Brenda never did recover from Roger's disappearance. She had a massive stroke in the end, although at the time, one of my colleagues suggested she died from a broken heart. Of course, there's no specific medical condition called that, but I do think the stress was a major contribution to her stroke.'

'As I said on the phone, we're investigating the remains of a man found south of Didcot and traced Roger through the records from his knee replacement surgery,' said Mark. 'I'm hoping you can give us some idea of what he was like while he was your patient.'

Wilson leaned back in her chair. 'Poor Roger. He didn't deserve that.'

'How long had you been his doctor?'

'Oh, gosh – forever.' Wilson gave a fleeting smile as she turned the glass within a pool of condensation forming on the table. 'At least twenty years, maybe a bit more.'

'Did he or his wife ever mention any issues, perhaps any concerns about people around them?'

'No, not that I can recall. They had no close family, no children.' She grimaced. 'Roger's knee replacement didn't go as well as we'd all hoped, and he was in a lot of pain afterwards. Brenda was overweight, and struggled caring for him. They didn't get out much before his operation, and afterwards I tried to coax them into going for short walks to help with his rehabilitation. He was still house-bound weeks after the op, although I do think that was his own fault. He was more reluctant than most to follow the physiotherapy routine.'

'Oh? Why was that do you think?'

'Roger and Brenda kept to themselves, mostly. Any hobbies they had didn't involve other people. It was such a shame to see – they weren't struggling financially, so they could've got out and enjoyed themselves more. They simply chose not to.' Wilson sighed. 'I mean, of course I'm not saying people should have a lot of social interaction to have a better quality of life – some people are simply more introverted than others – but once you got to know Brenda and Roger, they were quite gregarious. I used to end up in fits of giggles whenever Roger came to see me. He had a very sharp wit.'

'When did you find out he'd gone missing?'

'The following morning.' Wilson paused to take a delicate sip of iced tea. 'I seem to remember it was Holly at the surgery who heard the voicemail message on our answering system.'

'Who was the message from?'

'Brenda – she had the police around by that time, and they've got no children so I suppose she didn't know who else to call. As I said, I got on well with them so I presume that's why she phoned the surgery.'

'What time was that, when you received the message?'

'I was reading through my notes prior to us opening, so it must've been about ten to eight when Holly burst into my consulting room to tell me. I phoned Brenda straight away, and then I went around to the house as soon as I could. We were booked solid, so I didn't get there until late afternoon. There was a policewoman with her, and one of the neighbours.'

'Obviously without being able to speak to Brenda ourselves, we're trying to understand as much as possible about Roger's disappearance from interviews such as this,' said Mark. 'Can you remember anything she told you at the time that might help us? Was there any indication that her husband might go missing?'

'No, and that's the thing that's been bothering me ever since,' said Wilson. 'Roger was the one who was reluctant to introduce walking into their routine, not Brenda. A few weeks after his operation, I'd gone around to the house and given them both a bit of a pep talk about their health. I think after that, Brenda realised that without him being mobile, she needed to lose some weight. She said she started the day after I saw them...'

'When was that, in relation to the day he went missing?'

'About a week. Maybe ten days, but no more.'

'Go on.'

'From what I can gather – her next-door neighbour was also one of my patients before I retired – Brenda would wait until it was dark before she left the house. I think she felt a bit self-conscious about it all, to be honest. The neighbour spotted her a couple of times while she was closing the upstairs curtains. Anyway, Brenda told me that she would walk to the end of the street, turn left and follow the main road back around the avenue where they lived, and circle back on herself.'

'How long did it take her to walk around the block?'

'She said thirty minutes. Bear in mind, she was very obese, so she would've been out of breath by the time she was heading home I'd imagine.' Wilson smiled. 'She really was determined to improve her health though, detective. I just wish the pair of them had started something like that a few years before.'

'Back to the night that Roger went missing...'

'Yes, of course. Sorry. Well, she got back from her usual walk, and he wasn't there. He'd just... vanished.'

Mark frowned. 'Did she happen to mention whether the front door was locked, or open?'

'I can't remember, sorry.'

'Okay. What about other health issues? Did Roger seem confused or disoriented the last time you saw him?'

'No, nothing like that. Like I said, he was sharp as a pin, and completely devoted to Brenda. It was totally out of character for him.'

'One last question if I may, Dr Wilson.' Mark waited while Jan pulled a manila folder from her bag and extracted a photograph. 'Could you tell me if you ever met this woman, Annabelle Studley?'

The doctor picked up the reading glasses beside the book and put them on, peering at the image for a moment. 'I can't say I recognise the face or recall the name. Is she...'

As her words faded, she removed her glasses, her face paling a little. 'Oh, no... is she another victim?'

'We're trying to trace her whereabouts at the moment.' He passed the photograph back to Jan. 'But you're sure you never treated her? She lived about three miles from your old surgery.'

'You're welcome to check with Holly, of course but no – I don't remember her. Did she have a regular GP she visited?'

'She did, yes.'

The doctor drained her glass, then looked at him curiously. 'Can I ask you a question? With regard to Roger.'

'Of course.'

'Why on earth would a man who was unable to walk far

on his own and reluctant to leave the house do exactly that, only to be murdered and buried in a shallow grave?'

It was Mark's turn to sigh.

'Doctor, if I knew that, I wouldn't be sat here asking myself exactly the same thing.'

CHAPTER THIRTY-THREE

There was a tangible shift in energy amongst her colleagues when Jan walked into the incident room the next morning.

She spotted Alex standing beside the whiteboard talking to Kennedy and checked her watch.

The briefing was due to start in ten minutes, and she spent a moment reflecting on her notes from the interview with Roger Parnett's doctor. As she flicked back and forth between the pages, she wondered who else they might speak to with regard to the man's disappearance.

They were fast running out of options – after leaving Dr Wilson's house, Turpin drove them to the Parnett's old street where they spent an hour door-knocking and speaking to neighbours who remembered the couple.

Despite recalling them as a quiet pair who kept to

themselves but were friendly enough when encountered, the neighbours provided no new information.

One woman, two doors down from the Parnetts' old house, recalled that Brenda might have had a sister living in Canada, but had no recollection of a name let alone an address.

'Kennedy's about to start,' Turpin said. 'Best get over there if you want a seat.'

Snapping her notebook shut, Jan joined him in front of the whiteboard and took a seat beside Alex.

'How did the post mortem go yesterday?' she murmured.

The younger detective gave a half-hearted shrug. 'As well as it could…'

Before he could say more, Kennedy strode out of his office and across to where they waited and launched straight into the assigned agenda.

'Let's get on with it,' he began. 'Caroline and Alex – findings from the post mortem, please. What've you got?'

'What remained of the skull indicated a similar fracture to the back of it like the others,' said Caroline. 'It was too hard to tell whether strangulation had occurred as well – the bones were too badly damaged by either wild animals getting hold of them, or being washed away before Jasper and his team could retrieve them.'

'Or got lost during the retrieval process.' Kennedy added a note beside the most recent crime scene photograph. 'Any news from the search team on site, or Jasper's lot? How are they getting on?'

'They're struggling with the water levels, guv,' Alex

replied. 'It's slowed them down while they were working farther along the stream. Jasper extended the search quadrant after this morning's find but says they haven't found any more bones.'

'He's sure this time, then?'

'That's what he says, guv.'

'Maybe our murderer stopped at three, then.' The DI drew an arrow across to a small space available amongst the various notes and added Alex's suggestion. 'Does anyone know how often that stream floods?'

'According to the bloke I spoke to at the parish council, about every four to five years,' said Caroline. 'It hasn't flooded in recent years, but they've got a mitigation strategy in place in the villages and amongst landowners since the last big one to make sure the watercourse is kept clear.'

'This latest bottleneck was caused by the land being sold for the project,' Alex added. 'So no one's been keeping an eye on the stream along that stretch since the contracts were signed.'

'Hence the flooding.' Kennedy paced the carpet in front of the seated officers, tapping the end of the pen against his chin. 'What about our second victim? Has anyone been able to identify her yet?'

'Not yet, guv.'

Jan twisted in her seat to see PS Peter Cosley standing at the back of the semi-circle of officers, his eyes harried behind his glasses as he spoke.

'Nothing at all?'

'Unless we find a connection between all three victims, guv, I think it's going to be near impossible. The clothing that was discovered with her was in such a bad state it's proving hard for the lab to get a decent sample for comparison purposes to tell us what it might be.'

Jan turned as her colleague's mobile phone pinged.

Turpin took one look at the text message before raising his voice.

'Guv? Just heard from the lab. They've completed analysing the DNA swab that Liz Moorlock provided. It's a familial match for the first victim.'

Kennedy tapped the photograph of the first victim laid out in her grave, then turned back to the team.

'We have our second confirmation, then. She's Annabelle Studley.'

Jan dropped her gaze to her notebook, recalling the woman's husband and the desperation in his voice when they'd interviewed him. Her chest tightened, and then she heard her name called out.

'Jan, Mark – get yourselves over to the family and let them have the news,' Kennedy instructed. 'Before the media catch wind of it. The rest of you – keep your focus on the second victim now, and any connection between all of them. We'll reconvene in the morning.'

'I'll phone Liz,' Jan murmured as she followed Turpin back to their desks. 'Hopefully she can pop round to be with her dad when we let him know.'

'Good idea.' He checked his watch. 'If she can't, then ask

her if there's someone else – a close friend, or a neighbour who can meet us there, and then we'll…'

Jan's mobile phone started ringing, and she bit back a surprised cry when she saw the number on the screen.

'It's Liz Moorlock,' she said.

'Put it on speakerphone.'

Turpin leaned against his desk while Jan answered the call.

'Ms Moorlock, I was about to call you,' she began. 'We were wondering if you could—'

'Detective West?' The woman sounded frightened, breathless. 'Can you come over? To Dad's house, I mean.'

'Is something the matter? What's wrong?' Alarmed by the woman's tone, Jan pulled her jacket from the back of her chair and eyed the car keys next to her keyboard.

'It's Dad. He's saying things about when Mum went missing… Things he hasn't told me before. I think you need to come over. I don't know what else to do.'

Jan was already moving towards the door, shooting Turpin a grateful look as he swung her handbag over his shoulder and followed. 'We're on our way.'

CHAPTER THIRTY-FOUR

Mark elected to drive and shot down the dual carriageway towards the Harwell turn-off, his colleague burying her head in the original investigation file while he manoeuvred the car into the overtaking lane and accelerated.

Jan lowered the pages in her hand to look out of the passenger window for a moment, then turned to him. 'The original attending officer never asked Liz what her movements were when her mum went missing.'

'What?' Mark blinked, correcting the slight swerve across the dashed lines down the middle of the road, and glanced across at her. 'Why not?'

'It doesn't say. He was a probationer who's since left, according to this old file. Liz was asked about her mother's illness and what happened after her father phoned her, but not what she was doing prior to that.'

Mark frowned. 'I'm not sure I would've thought of that as a probationer, to be honest. I mean, it seems obvious to us in hindsight, but at the time…'

'He would've been more concerned with getting on with the search for Annabelle,' Jan mused, her attention turning to the countryside shooting past the window once more. 'I know…'

'What are you thinking?'

She waited while he negotiated a busy junction and accelerated through an amber traffic light, then sighed. 'I may just be grasping for anything here, given we've got nothing so far, but what are the chances of her phoning me before we've had a chance to tell her about the DNA results?'

'You don't think it's a coincidence?'

'I don't know. I mean, it's convenient she's already been talking to her dad before we can get a chance to break the news to him that one of our victims is his wife, isn't it?'

He frowned, expertly twitching the steering wheel to counteract the uneven camber of the twisting road, then indicated left for the village where John Studley lived.

'She'd have probably seen the news release that went out this morning. Maybe she was worried her dad would hear about it too, and that it'd upset him. I mean, she said herself that she normally calls in on her way home from work to see him, didn't she?'

'I suppose.' Jan closed the folder and placed it in the footwell. 'Mind you, it also gives her ample opportunity to make sure her dad's story is straight before we break the news. If she knew the victim was her mother, I mean.'

The car swerved towards the verge as Mark shot a glance at his colleague, then quickly corrected the vehicle and slowed.

He frowned as a sign depicting the village name appeared. 'Then why the phone call to tell us that he was saying things she hadn't heard before, and that he was frightening her?'

'I don't know.'

Mark pulled to the kerb outside a pretty thatched cottage and wrenched the handbrake. He gazed sightlessly at the narrow street, his thoughts tumbling.

'Do we have anything to suggest that Liz knew Roger Parnett?' he said finally.

'Not that I can recall.'

'What about John?'

'I don't know.'

'Give Caroline a call. Ask her to check. I know Dr Wilson said the Parnetts didn't get out much, but maybe the two families crossed paths at some point.'

While he waited, he tapped his fingers on the steering wheel, his jaw clenched as he listened to Jan's side of the phone call.

After five minutes, she ended it and shook her head. 'There's nothing in any of their statements to suggest a connection.'

Taking a deep breath, Mark released the handbrake and

surged forward. 'All right. We'll see what John and Liz have to say for themselves when we speak to them in a moment, and then we'll take another look at your theory. Sound good?'

'Okay.'

'And let's not give them any indication that they're under suspicion. Not until we have some answers to back that up.'

'Understood.'

He gave her a quick smile as he drew to a standstill outside the house. 'And you can run this one. I want to watch their reactions.'

'Okay.'

Mark heard the nerves in her voice now, the doubt starting to creep in. 'Look, you might be onto something. We won't know for sure until we do this.'

'I know.'

Jan climbed from the car, squared her shoulders, and marched towards the front door.

It opened before she had a chance to ring the bell, and Liz Moorlock peered out, her face pale.

'You didn't say on the phone why you were going to call me,' she said as she ushered them inside. 'I didn't give you a chance, sorry.'

'All in good time,' said Jan smoothly. 'How's your dad?'

'He's calmed down a bit, thank goodness. He's out in the conservatory.' Liz called ahead as she led them into the kitchen. 'Dad? It's the police. The two detectives who were here the other day.'

When Mark saw John Studley, it was almost as if the man had aged another decade.

His hair stuck out in tufts and his cheeks appeared sunken, his blue eyes watery as he turned away from the view of the garden and faced them.

Jan sat in an armchair beside the man. 'Mr Studley, your daughter called me to say you'd remembered some things about the day your wife went missing. Is that right?'

'Yes.' His lips trembled. 'And, no.'

Frowning, Jan leaned towards him. 'Okay... well, why don't you tell me what you told Liz?'

John eyed his daughter for a moment, then gave a slight nod.

'I knew I had cigarettes.'

'Pardon?'

'The night Annabelle went missing.' His brow puckered. 'I don't know... I-I suppose I blamed her for hiding them because she did that from time to time, but they weren't in any of the usual places.'

Mark saw the confusion etched across Jan's features.

'Where did you find them?' she asked.

'That's the thing. I didn't. Ever.' Studley reached out and wrapped his hands around hers. 'I always found them eventually. She had favourite hiding places for things, you see. It was part of the dementia.'

'I'm sorry, Mr Studley, I don't understand. What are you trying to tell me?'

'I'm telling you it wasn't Annabelle who took my

cigarettes. Otherwise I would've found them. Otherwise, I wouldn't have…'

He released her hand and wiped at his eyes.

Mark rocked back on his heels, holding his breath.

'Mr Studley, are you suggesting that someone else hid your cigarettes so that you'd leave the house?'

The man nodded, and then sniffed. 'Exactly, detective.'

'Do you have any idea who?'

'He hasn't been able to think of anyone who would do such a thing,' Liz said, crossing to where her father sat and doling out paper tissues from a scuffed box. 'Have you, Dad?'

In response, Studley shook his head, lowering his gaze to his lap.

'Who else had access to the house apart from yourself and the part-time carer?' asked Jan.

'My sister, Julie, and my husband at the time,' said Liz. Her mouth twisted. 'We got divorced last year.'

'We'll need their contact details.'

The woman walked out to the kitchen and returned with her mobile phone.

Writing down the numbers and addresses, Mark cleared his throat.

'The reason Detective West was going to call you was to let you know that we've received the results from the DNA swab you provided us with.'

'So soon?' Liz tore her gaze away from her phone screen, eyes wide.

'It's unusual, I'll admit.' Mark crossed to where her father dabbed at his cheeks with a scrunched-up tissue and crouched beside him. 'Mr Studley, based on those DNA results I'm very sorry to tell you that it is our belief that the remains discovered earlier this week are those of your wife. I'm so sorry.'

Studley uttered a shuddering sob, and Liz rushed to his side.

Mark moved away as she sat on the arm of the old man's chair and cradled his shoulders, watching as she gently brushed tears away from his cheeks.

Crossing to where Jan sat, he jerked his chin towards the kitchen. 'Let's give them a moment.'

After a few minutes, Liz wandered in to find them and ran a hand through her hair, her eyes distraught.

'I'm sorry, Ms Moorlock,' said Mark. 'It's not the news you were hoping for...'

'But in our hearts we always knew. You're absolutely sure, though?'

'The DNA results were double-checked before our analysts provided their report.'

Liz hugged her arms around her waist and bit her lower lip.

'Ms Moorlock, we have to ask – where were you the night your mother went missing, before you received the call from your father?'

'I was at home.'

'Can anyone vouch for you?'

Liz's eyes narrowed. 'Are you accusing me of killing my mother?'

'It's just a standard question, Ms Moorlock.'

'My ex-husband. We were cooking dinner.'

'And had you been to see your parents that day?'

'Yes. I told you, I always come around here after work.'

'And where is that?'

'I was working for a company in Oxford at the time. I left eighteen months ago to take on an admin role for an engineering company based at the science park in Drayton.' She sniffed, and eyed the man huddled in the conservatory, his head bowed. 'They offer flexible hours, which works better for us. At the last place, I was always having to scrounge time off here and there so I could help look after Mum, and they didn't like it. I couldn't wait to leave.'

'Do you have contact names and numbers for both your employers?' Mark looked up from his notebook to see the woman glaring at him. He held her stare. 'It's customary in investigations like this to speak to everyone.'

Liz raised her phone and pecked at the screen with her forefinger before extracting the details and reciting them.

'Thanks,' said Mark. 'The cigarettes your father mentioned earlier. Do you recall him looking for them while you were here that day?'

'No – Dad was always an evening smoker, you see. It's a habit he's always had. I suppose it's his way of relaxing at the end of the day. When we were kids he'd either sit outside on the patio with a glass of wine, or head down to the pub.' She gave a sad smile. 'When it was still open. I'm sure he could do with somewhere like that to go now that he hasn't got Mum for company.'

'Does he smoke now?'

Liz dropped her gaze to the tiled floor, and lowered her voice.

'He hasn't had a single cigarette since the night Mum went missing.'

CHAPTER THIRTY-FIVE

Mark stabbed a fork at a piece of battered haddock and smiled at the text message on his phone.

Lucy was having dinner with a friend on a narrowboat half a mile down the river from where they lived with Hamish in tow, and she had sent a photograph of the three of them, both women with substantial glasses of red wine in hand.

Texting a quick reply to let her know he'd meet her there and walk home along the towpath with her rather than letting her do so in the dark, he turned his attention back to Ewan Kennedy.

The DI balanced a greaseproof fish and chip packet on his lap, his chair a little closer to the whiteboard than his four junior detectives' seating arrangement, and took a swig from a soft drink can.

Mark noticed the tiredness in the other man's face, the

strain of an active investigation combined with the intricacies of managing both the media interest and that from Headquarters starting to take its toll.

Despite the frustrating pace at which the case was progressing, the afternoon had passed quickly, the whole team processing new information and following up potential leads well past six o'clock.

It was why, once the majority of the admin staff and uniformed officers had left for the day, that Kennedy suggested an early evening strategy session as a way to try and brainstorm the case to date without the usual interruptions.

Before the DI could resume his review, Caroline hurried across from her desk, and Jan pushed the last remaining bundle of food towards her.

'Thanks,' the DC said, tearing the paper open and applying a liberal sprinkling of vinegar.

'Well?' said Kennedy between mouthfuls of fish. 'What did the employers have to say?'

'The personnel manager where Liz works at the moment said there were no problems, and that she was a model employee,' Caroline replied, munching on a chip, 'and I tracked down her boss from the company who employed her when Annabelle went missing before he clocked off for the day. They use a swipe card security system, and he was able to check the records for me – she never left any earlier than three-thirty in the weeks leading up to that time, and that was only on four occasions.'

Jan handed Mark her leftover chips and wiped her fingers

with a paper napkin. 'I spoke to Liz's ex-husband as soon as we left the house this afternoon, and he confirmed her statement that once she was home that day, she didn't return to her parents' house until her father called about Annabelle's disappearance.'

'Bugger.' Kennedy rose to his feet, cupping his chip wrapper in one hand before he licked his fingers and used a whiteboard pen to cross through the woman's name. 'I think we can safely say that Liz Moorlock isn't a suspect – there's nothing linking her to the other two victims either, is there?'

Mark added extra salt to Jan's chips before working his way through them while he listened, aware that he hadn't eaten since the previous night and recalling the way that Lucy had insisted he go on a diet prior to the summer. At least he could finish the leftovers with less guilt, although at the rate he was going, she'd have him on another one before long.

'We're back to square one, guv,' he said.

'Not quite, but I realise it feels like it.' The DI stared at the board. 'Where's the pattern, though? I mean, when it was the two women, we at least had that link. Now with Roger Parnett's body being discovered, that profile has changed. And we still don't know who our second victim is.'

Mark wrapped up the last of the chips, conceding defeat as he threw the lot in a nearby bin, and held out his hand for the pen. 'May I?'

'Be my guest.' Kennedy returned to his seat and continued eating.

Turning to a second whiteboard that had been wheeled to

the front of the room earlier that week, Mark drew a line down the middle to section off a clean space beside the other notes and then added three circles, each containing one of the victims' names.

'I hated maths at school,' he said ruefully, 'but let's try a Venn diagram. Maybe we can do this visually instead of going around in circles in our heads.'

Kennedy mumbled his approval.

'Support groups, perhaps?' Caroline looked up from her fried scampi as all eyes turned to her, and shrugged. 'Both Annabelle and Roger suffered from different ailments, but perhaps there's a common link in any local support they might have been receiving – or things like food delivery companies.'

'Good one.' Mark drew a larger circle in the middle of the smaller three linking them all together, wrote Caroline's suggestion inside that, then waggled the pen in the air as he paced back and forth.

Alex cleared his throat. 'We can discount the GP surgeries. I've gone through the statements you've taken and I've spoken to the reception staff at both, and neither Annabelle or Roger attended each other's surgeries prior to their disappearances.'

'Okay.' Mark added a cross in the top right-hand corner of the board and wrote "GPs" underneath it. 'What else haven't we covered yet? What have we overlooked?'

He paused, realising Jan had been quiet for a while and turned around to see her staring into space somewhere above the whiteboard. 'Are you okay?'

His colleague's attention snapped back to him, and she blinked.

'Sorry, miles away there.'

'What're you thinking?'

'Just what Caroline was saying, about local support,' she said. 'We never asked Dr Wilson if Roger Parnett and his wife received anything like that. She said she dropped by when she could to help them out but given how badly those two were coping, I wonder whether they had a district nurse popping in.'

Mark looked across to the DI as he rose to his feet.

'Get over to Dr Wilson's old surgery first thing tomorrow and ask them,' said Kennedy, scrunching up the greasy paper and tossing it into the nearest bin. 'And make sure you give me an update by lunchtime, latest.'

CHAPTER THIRTY-SIX

A bright fresh morning greeted Mark as he stepped over the narrowboat's gunwale and made his way across the meadow.

Bleary-eyed, and cursing himself for acquiescing to the glass of red Lucy's friend had thrust at him when he'd turned up last night, he ruefully conceded that sinking into bed after midnight midweek wasn't the best idea during an active investigation.

He was still yawning when he reached the pool car parked next to the metal five-bar gate, envious of Lucy who was back at the boat and still buried under a thin blanket and snoring gently.

'Morning, sunshine,' Jan chirped. She lifted a takeout coffee from the cup holders between the seats. 'Here.'

'You're an angel.'

'So I keep telling my kids.' She smirked as he fastened his

seatbelt, then eased into the traffic. 'Thought we'd take the back road through Sutton Courtenay to save fighting our way through town to get there.'

'You're in charge.' He sipped the coffee and eyed her handbag in the footwell. 'Have you got any painkillers in there?'

'Inside pocket. Help yourself.'

'Thanks.'

Swallowing two with a gulp of coffee, he reclined the seat a little and closed his eyes.

'Good night, was it?'

'I only had one glass,' he protested. 'Must've been cheap or something.'

'How big was the glass?'

'Big enough.'

Half an hour later, and too soon for Mark's liking, Jan braked outside Dr Wilson's old surgery and killed the engine.

'Want another ten minutes?'

Opening his eyes, he sat upright. 'Did I fall asleep?'

His colleague grinned in reply.

'Oh, God. Don't tell the others.' He flipped down the vanity mirror, ran a hand through unruly hair and grimaced. 'Shit, that'll have to do. Let's go.'

Jan had placed the empty coffee cup back in the holder while he was dozing so he snatched it up and tossed it into a wastepaper basket in the surgery car park before following her to the front door.

Airy and light, the waiting room was packed full with

people of various ages, some looking more worse for wear than others.

As Mark walked over to the reception desk that took up the whole far end, he saw three women working the busy switchboard with efficiency and purpose.

Waiting patiently beside Jan, he kept his gaze on a skeleton beside the desk. Someone had put a tie around its neck, and he smiled.

Somehow, despite the fraught atmosphere of the early-morning appointments, it seemed the staff managed to keep a sense of humour.

'Can I help you?'

He turned at the voice to see the younger of the three women peering over the counter at Jan.

His colleague kept her voice low while showing her warrant card, and asked for Holly.

'That's me,' the woman replied, her eyes widening.

'Can we have a quick word? Somewhere quiet,' said Jan.

Holly nodded, and pointed to a side door. 'It really will have to be quick. We're flat out this morning and one of our GPs has phoned in sick.'

'That's ironic,' Mark murmured.

Jan glared at him, her lips quirking.

Moments later, Holly showed them into a small back office the size of a store cupboard and folded her arms across her chest.

'What's this about?'

'Just some follow-up questions regarding Roger Parnett,' Jan explained.

'Did you speak to Dr Wilson?'

'We did, yes. Can you tell me from your patient records whether Roger and his wife were ever visited by a district nurse after his operation?'

'Hang on.' Holly leaned over a laptop computer on a desk beside the window and logged in. She wrinkled her nose. 'They definitely didn't have a district nurse attend the house, but then that's not unusual.'

'What about private care?'

Holly straightened. 'No need for them to pay out for that. Dr Wilson used to pop by on her way home to check in on them.'

'She mentioned she'd done that, and tried to coerce them into getting out more to help with Roger's recovery,' said Jan. 'What we want to know is whether they received any help with things like housework, cooking—'

'Yes, I know. But that's what I meant. They didn't need to,' said Holly and smiled. 'Dr Wilson did that while she was there. She'd run around with the vacuum cleaner once a week and make sure they had enough food in the fridge. She always said it'd be just until Roger got back on his feet and they could cope, but we all knew what she could be like. The Parnetts weren't the only patients we had that she'd help out like that.'

'Oh?'

'It's just how she was. Always going the extra mile for people.'

Mark reached into his pocket and pulled out his notebook.

'We're going to need the names and details of the other people she helped please, Holly.'

CHAPTER THIRTY-SEVEN

There was no answer when Jan rang the bell to Dr Wilson's house, or any response when Turpin hammered against the solid oak door.

'Do you think they're both out?' she said, stepping away and peering up at the windows, her shoes crunching on the gravel driveway. 'There aren't any cars here, after all.'

In reply, her colleague held up his hand. 'Can you hear that?'

'What?' She froze, straining her ears, then: 'Music?'

'It's coming from the back. Someone's in. Come on. There must be a gate or something.'

Turpin spun on his heel and marched towards the side of the house.

Jan hitched her bag up her shoulder and sighed, hurrying

to catch up with him while her heels sank between the small stones.

A footpath had been laid between the house and a barn-sized garage, wide enough for them to walk side-by-side towards a wooden gate at the end.

The music grew louder as they progressed, and she recognised a concerto the twins had tried murdering last term.

With his extra height, Turpin was able to snake his arm over the gate to reach the latch.

'Wait.'

'What?' He glanced over his shoulder.

'What if they have a dog?'

'Didn't see one last time.'

'That doesn't mean…'

He grinned, opened the gate, and held it open. 'Ladies first.'

Narrowing her eyes at him, Jan squeezed past.

She spotted Candice Wilson straight away.

The doctor was at the far end of the garden with her back to the gate, shears in hand while she attacked a privet hedge with gusto.

The back doors to the house were wide open, the music loud enough that the retired doctor could listen while she worked.

A small white West Highland terrier lay on the patio pavers.

The dog's head swivelled when Turpin let the gate snap

back into place, whereupon it immediately climbed to its feet and started barking.

Jan stepped back.

'I told you,' she hissed under her breath.

'Harmless, I'll bet.' Turpin reached into a pocket, then held out his hand. 'C'mere, boy.'

The terrier shot across the lawn towards them as Dr Wilson placed her shears in a nearby wheelbarrow and removed gardening gloves.

'He's friendly, don't worry,' she called.

Jan decided to reserve judgement for the moment, but Turpin crouched to his haunches and held out his hand as the dog approached.

'Biscuit,' he said.

The dog stopped short and promptly sat, tongue lolling.

'Good boy.' Turpin handed over the treat.

'I'll tell Hamish,' Jan hissed. 'I thought those were his.'

'I always carry spares.' Her colleague winked, then rose and turned his attention to the dog's owner. 'Sorry to disturb you, Dr Wilson. We tried the front door.'

'I presume you have more questions.' The woman pointed to the table and chairs under the willow. 'Come and have a seat in the shade. I could do with a break anyway.'

She didn't offer iced tea this time.

Instead, she settled into one of the chairs and placed her hands in her lap, patiently waiting while they walked over. She raised her chin to Turpin as he sat.

'An unannounced arrival. This must be urgent.'

'And formal,' he replied before reciting the caution.

Dr Wilson's composure slipped a little, and Jan noticed a tic begin under her left eye.

'Is this still about Roger?' she managed, then ran her tongue over her lips as if her mouth was dry.

'You didn't mention when we last spoke to you that you were spending so much time at the Parnetts prior to his disappearance,' said Turpin. 'Why was that?'

'Well, I – I suppose I didn't think it was relevant.'

'This is a murder enquiry, Dr Wilson. Everything is relevant. Answer the question, please.'

'As I said to you before, they were struggling. I liked to keep an eye on them, when I could.'

'When we last spoke, you said you went to their house after his operation to try to convince them to start exercising. What else did you do?'

'I felt sorry for them. Like I said, I'd known them for twenty years or so, and they had no family to help them. I visited them a few days after Roger came home from hospital, just as a courtesy on the way home. Brenda wasn't coping at all well – the place was a state. There were at least three days' worth of dirty dishes covering the worktops, I could see dirt on the carpets…' The doctor sighed. 'I did what I could that afternoon, then started popping back every two days. I made it clear to them it wasn't a permanent arrangement – I have my own house and husband to look after. But it was just a way to give them time to adjust to the way things were, that's all.'

'Were you still doing that when Roger went missing?'

Wilson shook her head. 'No. That's why I didn't think to mention it when you were here yesterday. By then, Roger could get about all right in the house, and Brenda could keep on top of the cooking and cleaning with a bit of effort.' She smiled. 'Besides, Michael was starting to feel neglected.'

'Did you ever help out any other patients like that?'

'Not as much. The Parnetts were special, I suppose. Besides, I was starting to make plans for my own retirement by then, and becoming their full-time carer wasn't something I was prepared to do. That's why I gave them some brochures.'

Jan's heart slammed against her ribs, and she looked at Turpin.

He had the same surprised look she was sure she wore.

'What brochures?' he asked.

'For part-time carers,' said Dr Wilson. 'For all their issues, the Parnetts lived comfortably, and so I suggested to them that they have someone come in once or twice a week who could make sure they were eating healthily but who could also help with some basic housework.'

'Which company did you recommend?'

'Oh, I didn't recommend one – that would have been outside of my professional remit. I simply gave them some brochures to take a look at.' Her face fell. 'Sadly, Roger went missing shortly after that, and Brenda never did recover enough to consider it.'

'Can you remember the names of the companies whose brochures you gave to them?' said Jan, unable to keep the excitement from her voice.

'No, sorry…'

Turpin sighed.

'… but the surgery should be able to. They keep a display in the reception area, you see. You know, a rack of brochures with all the private services available to patients.'

CHAPTER THIRTY-EIGHT

Mark fanned the coloured brochures across a spare desk outside Kennedy's office and loosened the top button of his shirt.

His colleagues crowded around the table, Jan nibbling at a ragged thumbnail.

A palpable expectation clung to the air, and he willed his thoughts into a coherent order before he began.

After leaving Dr Wilson's house, Jan had raced back to the surgery, braking so hard outside the reception doors that Mark was thrown against his seatbelt.

Twenty minutes later, they emerged with a paper dispensary bag laden with glossy leaflets.

'All right,' said Kennedy, emerging from his office and shoving his phone in his pocket. 'What've you got for me?'

'There are thirty different companies here all providing

services ranging from in-home care to walking aids,' Mark began. 'These include older brochures that were shoved into the back of a cupboard, not just the recent ones.'

'Holly – the woman at the surgery – said they don't always keep old leaflets, so there might be some missing,' said Jan.

'Glass half-full, Jan. Glass half-full,' said the DI. 'Which ones can we eliminate?'

Mark pointed to five that were laid out on the far left. 'Those ones. Prosthetics, hearing aids, and furniture such as recliner chairs. Items, rather than person-to-person services. We've done that on the basis it doesn't involve so much contact with individuals, unlike the others we've got here.'

'That makes sense.' Kennedy nodded. 'Next?'

'Jan and I divided the rest into four different groups. This first one, with eight companies in, is for companies who provide mobility aids – equipment to assist around the home with day-to-day things like using the toilet. One-off items that probably don't require repeat visits, but do involve at least one visit to the person's home to assess their needs. The second group over there nearest to Alex, is for companies who provide counselling, physiotherapy and suchlike – some of those have clinics, others provide in-home services.' He reached across and tapped the next selection to his right. 'These ones are companies who Holly says are no longer in business, but were when Roger Parnett went missing.'

'And these?' Kennedy picked up the three remaining brochures closest to him.

Mark smiled. 'In-home care services. Exactly the same ones that Dr Wilson gave to Roger and Brenda Parnett.'

'Okay, good work. How do you want to proceed?'

'I'm proposing that Caroline track down as much information as she can about the companies no longer in business. There should be a list of directors on the Companies House website to start with, and I'm assuming some of those will have moved on to other roles. With any luck, if we can trace one from each company they'll be able to provide the other names, and might even be able to recall staff names too.'

'Sort of like a domino effect,' ventured Alex.

'Exactly.' Mark nodded at the young DC. 'I'd like you to follow up with the counselling and physiotherapy companies you've got in front of you. Same process, except you've got it slightly easier because they're still in business.'

'I'll take the mobility aids companies, too,' said Alex, sweeping up the brochures and splaying them in his hands like oversized playing cards. 'That frees up you and Jan to focus on the in-home care brochures, given that you've already spoken to the one who John and Annabelle Studley used. It seems the more likely candidate at the moment, doesn't it?'

'Until we know otherwise, yes. However, it's equally important that you investigate the others so we can rule them out. That all okay with you, guv?' Mark glanced at Kennedy.

'I'll be in my office if you need me,' said the DI, and gave a wry smile. 'Sounds like you've got it all under control.'

'Okay, so how do you want to do this?' Jan asked as they

walked back to their desks. 'Go straight back to the company that cared for Annabelle Studley, or look at the other two?'

'Let's speak to the others first,' said Mark, holding out his hand for the car keys. 'But let's do it in person rather than over the phone. Phoning them will only delay us.'

CHAPTER THIRTY-NINE

Half an hour later, after fighting his way through traffic, Mark pulled into the car park of a medium-sized industrial unit on the outskirts of Wallingford.

In place of the usual roll-down doors on the front of it were darkened privacy windows that reflected the heat from the afternoon sun and gave no hint as to the business carrying on behind them.

Mark cupped his hand against his brow to ward off the glare from the windows and peered up at the top floor.

Four more windows faced the car park, similarly glazed.

'Looks as if they knocked two units into one,' said Jan.

'Doing all right, then.'

Entering the building through a single door to the right of the lower windows, Mark took in the minimalist decoration and furniture similar to that back at the station before turning his attention to the woman at the reception desk.

Her name badge said her name was Linda, and – as with the care company the day before – she wore a polo shirt with the company's branding across the left-hand side. The material was blue this time, not green.

After making the introductions, Linda directed them to four newly upholstered seats in the same branded colour as her shirt that had been placed along the left-hand wall, and said they would have to wait – the person they needed to speak to was currently in a video conference call for another fifteen minutes.

Mark eyed the brochures spread out across an oak-effect table beside the chairs, then at the landscape photograph adorning the wall, recognising it as a mass-produced item with a motivational phrase printed in the white space underneath, before sitting beside Jan to wait.

He peered at the display of brochures, all extolling the company's services.

The staged photographs on the front page of each showing a uniformed care worker standing on the doorstep beside an elderly couple, wearing an identical shirt to the receptionist's and a bright smile.

He nudged Jan's arm, and lowered his voice, passing one of the brochures to her. 'Here, take that home and show Scott. Tell him you're researching for his old age.'

She spluttered, then glared at him as a door opened opposite.

A man in his late twenties strode towards them, his hand outstretched, whitened teeth glaring.

'Detectives, I'm Dan Nelson, sales manager. Would you like to come through to the conference room?'

Without waiting for a response, he winked at Linda, turned on his heel and marched back through the door from which he'd appeared.

Mark followed him and Jan along a wide carpeted corridor then into a room on the right that faced the car park through two of the darkened windows.

An array of empty coffee cups and discarded pens littered the polished oval table in the middle, and the aroma of a long meeting lingered in the artificial air.

A laptop computer remained open at the far end of the table, its motor running hot as if it too was gasping for breath.

'Sorry to keep you,' said Nelson, waving them to two seats at the far end away from the door. 'Our monthly sales review went on for longer than expected. And apologies for the mess – I've asked the admin team to wait until we've finished before they tidy up.'

'Not at all.' Mark waited until the other man sat at the head of the table.

The sales manager seemed at ease, resting his left elbow on the polished surface and swivelling his chair at an angle to face them before crossing his legs, his posture one of confidence.

'How can I help you?' he asked.

'We're investigating the murders of three elderly people

whose remains were found south-west of Didcot,' Mark began. 'As part of that, we're looking into common factors that linked them, including their relationship to service providers.'

Nelson's mouth dropped open. 'Were they clients of ours?'

'That's what we're here to find out.'

Any pretence of controlling the conversation faded as the sales manager swivelled around to face his laptop. 'I can soon tell you. What were the names?'

'We've only got two at the moment.' Mark told him, then waited while the man pecked away at the keyboard. 'Anything?'

'No, look.' He pushed the screen across to where they sat, then trundled his chair nearer in its wake. 'This is our customer system, and I've filtered the search to show anyone who we've lost contact with.'

'Does that happen often?' said Jan.

Nelson shrugged. 'Sometimes, as you can see here, yes. Sometimes the family might change their arrangements to look after a family member themselves, or the client might go into a full-time care facility if their health deteriorates. Or, sadly, they might die. With all of that going on, it's quite natural for people to forget to tell us – we'll get a call to cancel the services in amongst all of that, but we don't pry. Not straight away, of course. We'll make a courtesy call three months later to see if we can help but after that, the record is marked like this.'

'What about missing persons?' said Mark.

Nelson grinned, flashing his sparkly teeth. 'I don't think we've ever lost anyone.'

'This isn't a joke, Mr Nelson.'

The smile went as fast as it arrived. 'Sorry. I didn't mean to be insensitive. No, I don't think any of our clients have been reported as missing.'

'Any problems with any of your staff in the past three to four years?'

'Not that I can recall. If there was, we have procedures in place to carry out a thorough enquiry – the personnel department manage all of that. But if someone was causing problems, the name would be passed to us in sales so we didn't send them anywhere until the enquiry was complete.'

'And would they abide by that?'

'If they wanted to keep their job, yes.'

CHAPTER FORTY

'Just because the man's an asshole doesn't necessarily mean he killed off other companies' clients.'

Mark heard Ewan Kennedy fumble his phone while he closed his office door, then the DI's voice came back.

'What did the other company's sales manager have to say when you spoke to him?'

'It was more or less a repeat of what we heard from Dan Nelson, guv,' said Mark. 'And he denied all knowledge of his company having any dealings with Roger Parnett or Annabelle Studley.'

'Think he's telling the truth?'

'Without us suggesting we'd come back with a search warrant, he showed us the sales records for the two periods when they went missing. There was no contact with either family.'

'And nothing else to connect those two companies to the victims, apart from the brochures?'

'No, guv. We checked with the company Sonia Adams works at too, and they confirmed that Roger Parnett was never a client of theirs either.'

'Fuck it.' Kennedy's chair creaked as he leaned back. 'I thought we were onto something there.'

'Me too.' Mark heard the disappointment in his own voice.

'All right, well there's no need to attend the briefing – you won't get back in time now anyway,' said the DI. 'I'll see you both tomorrow morning. Eight o'clock start, mind. The briefing will be at ten – I've got a phone conference with Headquarters first thing.'

'Thanks, guv.'

He ended the call and clasped the phone between his hands, staring sightlessly through the windscreen.

'Shall I pick you up at seven thirty tomorrow, then?' Jan asked.

'Is that all right?'

'Sure.' She raised a finger off the steering wheel as the road curled through the village and pointed at a blackboard placed on the grass verge as they got nearer, its surface covered in swirling chalk writing.

'Drink?' she said.

'Thought you'd never ask.'

She grinned in reply, and slowed the car.

———

Mark stepped aside to let a young couple enter the pub, then carried two fresh pints of bitter out to a table at the far end of a rectangular garden overlooking the village green.

Established lavender and buddleia grew in pots that had been lined up to create a border between the pub garden and the gravel driveway that swept up against it, the heady scent mixing with a whiff of cigarette smoke that drifted on the breeze from the smokers' area several metres away.

Jan looked up from her phone as he approached. 'Are you going to be okay sitting here, or do you want to head around the back if that's going to aggravate your throat?'

He shook his head and handed her one of the pints. 'I'll be fine. Besides, it's busy there. Quieter here.'

'Okay. Cheers.' She clinked her glass against his, took a gulp and sighed with contentment. 'Bloody hell, I needed that.'

Mark grinned, savouring the hoppy flavour of his ale while he took in the view.

The pub had been built several centuries ago on a sweeping curve that wound through the village between Didcot and Abingdon, set back on a wide grassy expanse that acted as a natural buffer between the building and the main road.

A steady stream of traffic passed as the offices and shops in both towns emptied and people commuted home – or to work, if they were on shift.

Jan waited until a couple had passed them by, gently bickering about which table they wanted to sit at, then turned to Mark as they disappeared towards the expansive garden at the back. 'So, what now?'

'I don't know.' He ran a hand over his jaw, blinking back exhaustion.

Every waking moment this past week had been spent thinking about the case, and at night his sleep was restless, unfulfilling as his mind wrestled with all the unanswered questions the team faced.

He checked over his shoulder for any nearby patrons who might overhear their conversation, then pulled out his notebook and started flicking through the pages.

'Something's got to give,' he muttered. 'We've missed it, somewhere along the way, surely.'

Jan took another sip of beer, then unzipped her bag and did the same with her notebook, thumbing back and forth.

After a moment's silence, she paused. 'The first care company – Sonia Adams I mean, not the two we spoke to today…'

'What about her?'

'Well, just because Roger Parnett wasn't an actual client, it doesn't mean that her sales team wasn't aware of him, does it? She only knew Annabelle because she looked after her. What if someone else there knew about Roger? Dr Wilson said that she gave him and his wife a selection of leaflets. We've got nowhere with the other two companies – they didn't even have Annabelle in their system…'

'But we didn't ask Sonia about sales leads because we didn't have the information at the time.' Mark checked his watch. 'Too late to ask her now – she'll have left for the day.'

Jan sighed. 'Well, I don't fancy turning up at tomorrow's briefing empty-handed. What if we reinterview Sonia first thing, and then let Kennedy have a full update?'

Mark picked up his half-empty pint glass and clinked it against hers.

'Sounds like a plan.'

CHAPTER FORTY-ONE

Mark leaned against the passenger door of the pool car the next morning and watched while the care company's staff car park filled.

Quarter to eight, only twelve spaces remaining, and there was no sign of Sonia Adams.

'What if she's got a day off?' said Jan, tying her hair into a knot at the nape of her neck while he juggled the car keys from hand to hand.

'Then we'll just have to speak to someone else. Got the search warrant in your bag?'

Jan tapped the pocket on the side. 'In here. Reckon we'll need it?'

'Probably. We want to look at personnel and patient records if we find something, after all. Better safe than sorry.'

'How did you manage to find a magistrate to sign this off so late last night?'

Mark grinned. 'She and her husband drink in the same pub as we do. Figured I'd find her there. After she got over the shock of me interrupting their evening meal, she was fine.'

'Rather you than me.'

'I don't think I'd want to try it twice. You should've seen her husband's face. Turns out, it was their anniversary.'

Jan's laugh carried across the car park, and then she turned at the sound of a car approaching.

A shiny SUV slowed on the road beyond the fence, its indicator flashing before the vehicle swept under the raised barrier and straight into a space in front of the building.

'That's her.' Mark straightened and crossed to where Sonia Adams was getting out, her movements brisk as she swung a leather tote bag over one shoulder and then lifted a briefcase from the back seat. 'Morning, Ms Adams.'

The woman did a double-take when she saw the two detectives approaching, but then forced a smile.

'How long have you been waiting?'

'Not long. We'd like an urgent word.' Mark unfolded the warrant and handed it over.

'What's this?'

'Like I said, it's urgent.'

Her jaw dropped. 'But... but I have a meeting at eight o'clock. It's important.'

'It'll have to be cancelled.'

'I can't, I...'

'Ms Adams, this is a murder investigation,' said Mark patiently. 'I'm sure whoever you're meeting with will understand when you tell them.'

'Tell them?' She paled, holding out the warrant to him as if it were diseased. 'I can't tell a client that, I—'

'Tell them whatever you need to. But we need to talk to you. Now.' He jerked his chin at the document in her hand. 'And you can hang onto that. We've got a copy.'

Sonia's shoulders drooped, and then she aimed her key fob at her car, the indicators flashing once. 'Follow me.'

Leading the way through the front door without acknowledging the receptionist's attempts to have Mark and Jan sign in, the care manager walked up the stairs and into her office without breaking stride.

She swung her briefcase onto her desk, placed her handbag underneath it and begrudgingly waved them to the two seats they'd occupied four days ago.

Mark shut the door, ignoring the offer.

'Tell me about Roger Parnett.'

'Who's he?' Sonia's gaze moved to Jan, then back to Mark. 'Is he another missing person?'

'Mr Parnett's GP gave him a selection of care providers' brochures. Given that your company is based in the near vicinity of where he and his wife used to live before he also went missing, it's probable that one of those brochures came from here.'

'I'm sorry – I don't recognise the name.'

'How do you record sales enquiries?'

Sonia reached out and switched on her computer, wrestling her arms from her jacket and placing it over the back of her chair while she waited for it to start. 'If someone phones the number or uses the email address on the brochure then that initial contact is logged into our sales lead software for the team to progress.'

'Same as a lot of companies.'

'Yes, we probably even use the same software, detective.'

'Please take a look to see if Roger or Brenda Parnett contacted you.'

He moved around the corner of the desk while she worked so he could see the screen, Jan watching curiously.

'They did. Here.' Sonia beckoned him closer.

'What would this have been for?' asked Mark, tapping the screen.

'The code next to the address confirms that they contacted us after reading a brochure,' she said, squinting at the text. 'Typically, the sales team would allocate someone to make an appointment to visit the person to discuss our services and find out more about their needs before providing a quote.'

'How do I find out if that appointment was made?'

'Hang on.'

Mark waited while her fingers flew across the keyboard.

'Have you experienced any problems with competitors in the area?' he said, flexing the window blind behind her and peering through at the other buildings that peppered the large industrial park.

'In what way?'

'Poaching clients, perhaps. Underhand methods…'

He turned in time to see a dimple forming in her right cheek as she bit back a smile.

'Now what would make you ask that?' She looked up at him as he returned to her side. 'Ah, let me guess. You've spoken to Daniel Nelson.'

'Well?'

'Nothing we can prove.'

'But you do suspect it happens.'

'Put it this way, the company Daniel works for isn't the biggest in the area, detective, but it *is* the most ambitious.'

Her attention returned to her screen as a new window popped up.

'Okay, so this is where the sales team record the progress of a new lead,' Sonia explained, 'so that they can trace it from first contact through to a successful pitch and a new sign-up.'

'There's nothing here.'

'That means the contact was never followed up.'

Mark frowned. 'Is that unusual?'

'It can happen from time to time.' Sonia sighed. 'It's like I said to you the other day, we've been so busy – these past two years especially – that one or two can fall through the net. They don't get picked up until the six-monthly reviews, and by then often it's too late to follow up because the potential client would've already gone to someone else.'

'And the system has always worked this way?'

'Pretty much, I would think, give or take the occasional

upgrade. It's a logical process, which is why the software is so popular with companies like ours.'

'What about the sales people who progressed the lead to this point? The part where the potential client phoned in via the details on the brochure? We'll need to speak to them.'

Sonia paused.

'It's all in the search warrant, Ms Adams.'

Sighing, she moused across to another tab on the screen, clicked the button, and then glanced up again. 'It was Gary Levine.'

'Is he in today?'

'I'm afraid he left the company early last year.'

'We'll need his address.'

'I thought you might say that.'

CHAPTER FORTY-TWO

'Gary Levine lives in rented accommodation on the Broadway in Didcot. There's nothing on the system about him, apart from a speeding fine from three years ago. He was caught by a camera on the A34.'

Caroline's voice carried through the car speakers while Jan weaved the vehicle through a myriad of roads leading out from the industrial estate.

'What time of day was that?' Mark asked, looking up from his notes.

'One-twenty in the afternoon. He didn't contest the fine – I checked with the magistrates' court and he paid it well before the deadline date too.'

'Squeaky clean,' Jan said.

'No one's that clean. Where does he work now, Caroline?'

'According to his social media, he's currently unemployed. After he left the care company, he worked part-time from home for one of those companies who sell mobility aids we've already interviewed, but he left there six months ago.'

Mark's stomach tumbled. 'Huh. Didn't last long. Got a photo?'

'Sending it to you now.'

'Thanks. Can you find out who his manager was at the mobility aid place while we interview Gary?'

'Will do. Talk in a bit.'

Caroline hung up, and a split second later his phone pinged as a new text message came through.

Jan braked at a set of lights at a railway crossing as the red-and-white barrier started to descend and glanced over at the screen while he opened the file and enlarged the photograph.

A train rumbled past, the vibrations from its weight rocking the car as it gathered speed.

The photo had been taken at some sort of outdoor gathering, a barbecue perhaps, or a picnic. In it, Gary Levine had a bottle of beer in his hand and stood beside a smiling couple in their forties, his mouth set in a fine line.

He was a big man. His short-sleeved shirt stretched across large biceps and he towered above the couple. He looked awkward and out of place.

Mark jumped in his seat at the sound of a car horn, and realised the traffic was moving once more.

'Shit.' Jan shoved the car into gear, raised her hand to the driver behind them, and accelerated forward.

'Are you okay?' said Mark after a moment. 'You were lost in thought there.'

Her brow puckered. 'I recognise him from somewhere. Recently, I mean.'

'Where?'

'That's just it. I can't put my finger on it.'

Mark pursed his lips. 'Let me know when you do.'

His colleague circled a roundabout before taking the spur for the Broadway, and he turned his attention to the houses crowding the left-hand side.

After passing a builders' merchants and a Royal Mail delivery office on the right, the residential side of the street fared little better with the view.

Many of the shopfronts wore whitewashed windows, some boarded up as if taking a longer view of the situation and lack of commercial enterprise, whereas others had been turned into temporary charity shops. Here and there, a small business thrived – an essential service, a specialist shop, a hopeful real estate agent.

The houses themselves were older, in keeping with the town's railway and army history, and in varying states of repair.

It was easy to spot the rental accommodation.

'There's nowhere to park along here, so we'll find out where he lives, and then walk back once we've found a space elsewhere,' he said, keeping his eyes on the passing house numbers.

'Sounds good. There're plenty of streets leading off this.'

He spotted the house as Jan braked to let a glazier's van pull out from a side street.

A tumbledown stone wall separated the terrace from the pavement, behind which he could see a gravelled front garden – no doubt installed by the landlord as a low-maintenance option, given the height of the grass in the neighbouring property. The two houses were joined by an upper level above an opening leading through to more housing.

To the right of a battered green front door, a single window was obscured by yellowing thick net curtains. The upstairs window faced across the road towards the empty shops.

'Take the next left turn,' said Mark.

Two minutes later, they returned on foot, and he wrinkled his nose at the discarded food wrappers and cigarette butts that had been thrown over the broken wall while climbing the three low steps from street level up to the gravelled area.

Taking one look at the wires protruding from the door frame, the plastic bell cover hanging off, he rapped his knuckles against the door instead.

Jan craned her neck to peer up at the window, then side-stepped and checked along the passageway.

'Do you want me to see if there's a back door along here?' she asked.

'Wait here. I'll check. We don't know how he's going to react.'

He recoiled at the overwhelming stench in the short alley, realising it was probably used for convenience by many a passing drunk at night, blinking as he emerged into a brightly lit shared yard bordered by overflowing wheelie bins.

To his right, a door matching the state of the front one remained closed, a glass panel in the top of it cracked and secured from the inside with black electrical tape. He raised his eyes to the two upper windows facing the yard.

Nothing.

No one peered out.

No curtains twitched.

After checking there was no way out of the yard through a back gate, he returned along the alleyway, holding his breath.

Jan was peering through the front window. 'Any luck?'

'I don't think he's home.'

'He's gone out.'

They spun around to see a woman in her twenties on the doorstep of the property next door, a cigarette hanging from her mouth and a mobile phone in her hand.

'And you are?'

'Charmaine.'

'Do you know where he's gone, Charmaine?' Mark flashed his warrant card as he walked over, seeing the wariness in her eyes.

'What d'you want with him?'

'Just hoping he can help us with some questions, that's all.'

She grinned, exposing blackened teeth. 'Liar.'

'Do you know him well?'

'Nah. I just see him now and again. Usually when I put the bins out. Sometimes he helps me. That's all.'

'Do you know where he's gone?'

'No. Like I said, we don't talk much. Just hello, that sort of thing.' She paused and took a drag on the cigarette, her eyes narrowing.

'Does he go out much?'

Charmaine shrugged. 'I suppose. Not regular, like. I don't think he's got a job.'

'What makes you say that?'

'I heard him arguing the other day. With another bloke who turned up here.'

'About what?'

'Rent payments. I think the other bloke owns the place.'

'Does he own this one too?'

'Nah – I rent from the agent up the road.'

'You said Gary doesn't keep regular hours. What did you mean?'

Another shrug.

Another drag on the cigarette.

She exhaled, spewing smoke into his face.

Deliberate.

Daring.

Mark blinked, bit back the cough. 'You were saying?'

'He's in and out all hours. Late, early. Not on the same days.'

'Not like working shifts then?'

'No.'

'Any idea when he'll be back today?'

She glared at him. 'Which part of what I said don't you get? I don't know him, all right? I just live next door.'

With that, she stepped back inside and slammed the door shut.

'That went well,' said Jan, leading the way back along the short path to the pavement.

Mark waited until they were a few metres away from the house, then started coughing. An uncontrollable expelling of dirty air that hurt his throat and made his eyes water.

'Are you okay?' His colleague stopped walking, unzipped her bag and handed over a small bottle of water. 'Here.'

'Thanks,' he croaked.

'At least you made it this far.'

He managed a small smile, took another sip and set off once more towards the car. 'I'll buy you another bottle on the way back.'

He reached the pool vehicle before her, reached out for the passenger door handle, then frowned.

It was still locked.

Mark looked over his shoulder.

Jan was standing a few paces away, stock-still, a look of utter surprise on her face.

'What is it?' he said.

'I remember where I saw him now.'

'Who, Gary?'

'Yes.'

'Where?'

'At Annabelle Studley's old doctor's surgery, the first time we went there. He was the volunteer driver helping that woman into the car that was parked outside.'

CHAPTER FORTY-THREE

The late-morning briefing was already underway by the time Jan walked into the incident room.

Her cheeks burned as she hurried towards the gathered officers, Turpin at her heels.

Alex was mid-update when Kennedy spotted them, the DI's glare boring into her as she quietly slipped into a seat on the far end and lowered her gaze to her notes, while Turpin attempted nonchalance and leaned against a desk beside her.

'Nice of you to join us, you two,' said Kennedy when the young DC had finished speaking. 'What time do you call this?'

Jan blushed even more and avoided looking at her watch.

They were twenty minutes late, thanks to getting caught in slow-moving traffic all the way from Didcot.

'I take it there were more pressing matters than my

briefing?' Kennedy continued, sweeping his gaze across the other officers while he paced the carpet. He paused and looked over his shoulder. 'Or...?'

'We've got a suspect,' Jan blurted.

Kennedy froze, then turned to face her. 'You have?'

'Yes, guv. Gary Levine.' She held up her notes. 'He used to work in the sales team for the same in-home care company as Sonia Adams, but lost his job. He then went on to sell mobility aids for a while before being made redundant six months ago. During all that time, he's been a volunteer driver. You know – taking patients to hospital or doctor's appointments, things like that.'

'Have you spoken to him?'

'We found out from Sonia Adams where he lives, guv,' Turpin said. 'He wasn't in this morning, and the neighbour we spoke to doesn't know where he is.'

'Has he done a runner, do you think?'

'It's too hard to tell because the house he's renting is in such a state. The neighbour didn't give us the impression he'd gone though, just that he was out.'

'What else can you tell me about him?' Kennedy crossed to the whiteboard and wrote down the name.

'I recognised him from when we went to Annabelle Studley's old surgery,' said Jan. 'Roger and Brenda Parnett didn't have a car according to DVLA records, and when we phoned Dr Wilson on the way here, she confirmed that Roger stopped driving a couple of years before his death, so how did they get to and from hospital and doctor's appointments?

Same as Annabelle and John Studley. I double-checked – their neighbours worked full-time back when Annabelle disappeared, and so couldn't help with the appointments. If their daughter Liz couldn't drive them, they had to rely on someone else.'

'Same volunteer service?'

'Same volunteer, guv.' Jan crossed her legs and shifted in her seat, more comfortable now that she was the centre of attention for the right reasons, not for being late to the briefing. 'Gary isn't with one of the organised services from around here. He just offers free transport to help out those who can't get rides elsewhere.'

'When we spoke to Dr Hamilton, he confirmed that Gary was known to them because of his previous roles with the in-home care company and then the mobility aid one so when he approached them about helping out, they took up his offer,' Turpin added. 'He passed all the DBS checks, and there aren't enough drivers to go around these days. We spoke to three of the local volunteer services who confirmed that they're always on the lookout for new drivers – they can't keep up with demand.'

'And he's definitely not registered with those?'

'He's not registered with any services covering the whole of Oxfordshire, guv.'

'Does he have previous?'

'Nothing at all,' said Jan. 'No convictions, not even ones that have been acknowledged by the DBS checks. Just the speeding fine that Caroline found from three years ago.'

Kennedy tapped the end of the pen against his chin. 'Which means, if he's our man, he's been very careful.'

'If he's our man, then he could very well still be active, too,' said Turpin. 'Just because we haven't found any more victims buried near Hacca's Brook doesn't mean he hasn't found another site.'

Jan's stomach flipped at his words, dread crawling in her belly as she recalled the list of missing persons they'd compiled.

How many more were never going to go home?

Kennedy signalled to two constables. 'Get a patrol over to Levine's house now. I want him brought in for questioning the minute he turns up.'

'Guv.'

The uniformed officers pushed back their chairs and hurried from the incident room, the door slamming shut in their wake.

'Mark, Jan – good work,' the DI continued. 'I want you to lead the interview when we've got him in custody. In the meantime, I need you to sort out a warrant so that we can search his car as well. If he is our killer, then there might still be trace evidence in that vehicle.'

Alex's hand shot up. 'Guv? Surely there'll be traces of Annabelle and Roger in his car anyway if he's driven them to appointments and things before they went missing?'

Kennedy gave the young DC a patient stare before answering.

'Not if we find that evidence anywhere other than the seats, Alex. The boot, for example.'

Jan bit back a smile as Alex's eyes widened, the detective realising his error.

'Guv, what about Gary's current clients?' she said. 'Should we interview them to see if there are any concerns?'

'Good thinking. Caroline and Alex – give the two GP surgeries a call and find out from them which of their patients use Levine's free car service. Split up the interviews between yourselves and uniform. I want anything of concern flagged for Mark and Jan before they interview Levine.'

He clapped his hands together once, a loud report bouncing off the low ceiling tiles.

'Let's go, people. Time to stop a killer.'

CHAPTER FORTY-FOUR

Gary Levine was a shrunken version of the man in the photograph Caroline had found.

When Mark opened the door to interview room two, he reared back at the stench of unwashed skin and nicotine.

Jan bumped against him with the manila folder she carried before squeezing past and busied herself setting up the recording equipment while he crossed his arms and stared at their suspect.

Beside him, a second man glanced up at the two detectives, then returned to his note-taking, his slight frame swamped by a cheap black suit that was creased in all the wrong places as if he had spent the day travelling from one custody suite to another.

He shoved a business card across the chipped and pitted table towards Mark as he sat.

'Justin White, duty solicitor.'

His current client, Levine, wore a grubby dark blue T-shirt with a sports logo embossed over the front, but it hung loosely off his frame as if he'd lost a lot of weight within a short amount of time. His jowls were flabby, with sunburnt skin peeling at his brow while he chewed a thick lower lip, his gaze downcast.

When he did look up, pale blue eyes glared at Mark before turning to Jan while she recited the formal caution.

'I'm going to be late for work,' he growled in response.

'Please confirm you understand the caution I've provided,' she said.

His top lip curled. 'I understand.'

'Tell me about Roger Parnett,' said Mark. 'How did you meet him?'

Levine frowned. 'Did you find him?'

'Answer the question, please.'

'I was put in touch with him via his doctor's surgery after his knee operation. Neither him or his wife could drive so I used to help out.'

Jan sighed, reached into the folder and extracted a copy of the sales data that Sonia Adams had provided. 'It says here you spoke to them before that. While you were still working at the in-home care company. You never progressed their request for assistance. Why?'

The man blinked, then ran his tongue over his lips. 'I don't remember that. I lost my job there early last year. I liked chatting with the oldies, so that's why I thought I'd continue with the volunteer driving while I was looking for a new job.'

'Why didn't you approach one of the registered volunteer services?'

Levine shrugged. 'I knew the GP surgeries. I had contacts there from my time working for the care company, so I just figured I'd approach them direct. Easy enough.'

'The car you're driving now – how long have you had that?'

'About six years.' He grimaced. 'God, when I think I used to turn up my nose at people who drove cars that old. I used to try to change it every two to three years, just so I could make sure I had all the manufacturers' warranties and stuff.' He clasped his hands on the table, rubbing his thumbs together. 'Now I'm just glad if I can afford a tank of petrol.'

'And yet, you still volunteer to drive other people around.'

A shrug this time, no words.

'Back to Roger – when was the last time you saw him?'

'The day I dropped him home after his operation.'

'How can you be so sure?'

'He was a nice bloke, all right? Him and his wife. Hard to forget.' He shook his head. 'Hell of a shock when he went missing.'

'Do you know what happened to him?'

'No. Why would I?' Confused, Levine looked from Mark to Jan, then back. 'What's going on?'

'What about Annabelle Studley?' said Mark, ignoring the

question and flicking across a photograph of the woman. 'Where did you meet her?'

'I don't recognise her.'

'She lived out near West Hagbourne and went missing late last year. Only eight months or so after Roger.' Jan slid another photograph across, and Mark watched Levine's reaction as he took in the shallow grave and crime scene tape. 'Her remains were found here. Alongside another woman and Roger Parnett.'

Levine's face turned grey, tearing his gaze away from the photograph. 'Jesus Christ, and you think I killed them?'

'Did you?'

'Of course I bloody didn't!'

'Who's the second woman buried here, Gary?'

'I don't know – I've got nothing to do with this. Who told you I did this?'

In response, Mark passed across copies of the original missing persons reports and tapped the date at the top of each. 'Where were you on these dates?'

Levine snatched the documents from him, and stared at the pages for a moment. When he looked up, his eyes were triumphant.

'I was away, detective. Out of the country.'

'Three times?'

'That's right.'

'Doing what?'

'I don't have to tell you.'

He tossed the pages back across the desk.

'There's nothing on your social media for those dates to support that statement.'

'I don't use it that much. I don't like everyone knowing what I'm up to.'

'Oh? Something to hide?'

'Of course not. I just like my privacy, that's all.'

'Got someone who can provide an alibi for you on those dates, then?' said Jan.

Levine turned his attention to her. 'Speak to Aidan Barclay. He'll back me up.'

'Who's he?'

'A mate of mine – I've known him since school.'

Mark gave Jan a slight nod, then spoke for the purposes of the recording.

'Interview paused at four thirty-two.'

CHAPTER FORTY-FIVE

'What do you think, Mark?'

Kennedy closed his office door and waved him to one of the visitor's chairs. 'You look…'

'Frustrated? I am.'

Mark ignored the offer of a seat and looked at the various certificates and commendations on the back wall of the DI's office before rubbing a hand over tired eyes.

'Having second thoughts about Levine?'

'Possibly.' Dropping his hand, Mark exhaled and faced him. 'It depends what this friend of his says – if we can locate him.'

'Got an address?'

'Yes. Uniform went over, but there's no one in. According to a neighbour, he might be at a local gym before they close at ten so they've gone there. We're just waiting to hear now.'

'And if his alibi holds up…'

'Then we're screwed. Sorry, guv.'

Kennedy shoved his hands in his pockets and leaned against a filing cabinet before staring at the carpet. After a while, he sighed. 'Cold cases are never easy, Mark. We might never have the answers.'

'I have to try, guv.' Mark peered through the blinds across the interior window at the whiteboard, at all the notes and scrawled theories covering its surface. 'We owe it to those three victims, and I need to know that whoever did that to them isn't out there still, getting away with murder.'

He saw the shiver that wracked Kennedy, and knew then that the DI wouldn't give up either.

'Can you authorise us holding Levine for another twelve hours if we need it, guv?' he ventured. 'Just in case this alibi of his is no good?'

'Of course. Do the paperwork and I'll sign it off. Do you plan on being here all night?'

'If I have to. I'm going to send Jan home before it gets too late.'

'Tell her I'll pay for a taxi for her if she hasn't been allocated a car.'

'Thanks, guv.'

The DI was silent for a moment, and Mark watched as the man's gaze turned to the officers milling about beyond his office.

'If we don't get some results soon, something else will crop up and we'll lose the resources we've got,' he said eventually. 'And there's only so much stalling I can do when it comes to orders from Kidlington.'

'I know.'

Kennedy nodded in response.

Mark squared his shoulders and gave him a wry smile. 'Back to it, then.'

The DI reached out and opened the door for him. 'You know where to find me.'

'Thanks, guv.'

He strode across to his desk, peeled off two sticky notes from the middle of his computer screen, and sank into his chair.

Neither message was urgent, and he stuck them on top of a growing pile of varying colours beside his phone.

He would deal with them when there were less pressing matters to contend with.

In the meantime, there was the paperwork to draft for Kennedy to sign off, and a new strategy to discuss with Jan once they restarted their interview with Levine.

'Scott's ordered takeaway pizza for the kids, so I'm good through to half nine at least,' said Jan, breaking into his thoughts.

'Okay, thanks.'

'Sarge?'

He looked up from his screen to see Alex hurrying towards him, out of breath.

'What's up?'

'Just had a call from Tom Wilcox – they've brought

Levine's alibi in. Aidan Barclay's downstairs in interview room three when you're ready.'

Mark shoved back his chair as Jan started to gather her notes and files. 'We're on our way.'

———

Mark held open the door to the interview room for Jan, then followed her across to the table in the middle and introduced himself to the bronzed giant that rose from his seat and held out an enormous hand.

'I'm Aidan Barclay,' he said, his grip surprisingly gentle. 'What's going on? Why is Gary here?'

'All in good time, Mr Barclay.' Mark held up his hand while Jan started the recording and provided the formal introductions and caution, then checked his notes.

'Mr Levine is currently helping us with our enquiries, and asserts that he was on holiday with you on some dates we're interested in.'

'Which dates were they?'

Mark told him, and then waited while the man retrieved his mobile phone from his pocket and opened a social media app.

'Hang on. I think I've got some photos here.'

Biting back a rising sense of impending disappointment, Mark glanced at Jan.

She looked as if she'd stopped breathing, her gaze fixed on Barclay's phone.

'Yeah. Here you go. That first date, we were in Magaluf for a week, and then that second one we headed off to Croatia for a couple of weeks.'

'Doing what?' said Mark.

'Bodybuilding contests. Amateur ones, of course. The prize money paid for the holiday. We'd go hiking afterwards, or cycling.' Barclay shot Mark a sheepish grin. 'Or we'd just hang about in town and go clubbing, meet girls.'

'Gary's a bodybuilder?' Mark couldn't keep the surprise from his voice, recalling the state of the man they'd arrested earlier that day.

Barclay sighed. 'Well, I'll be honest – he's let himself go a bit this past year but that's only because he can't afford the gym membership or the supplements he used to take.'

'And you can verify the dates?'

'Yeah. Definitely. Look.' He turned the screen to face Mark and Jan. 'I've got the posts here. Gary was always a bit more shy about it so didn't share them. I think he thought his workmates would take the piss if they found out. Now he doesn't like talking about it. He hasn't been able to afford the competitions and holidays since losing that sales job at the care company last year.'

Mark snatched the phone from him, his gaze falling on the first date while Barclay tapped his foot impatiently.

Sure enough, both he and Gary were in the photograph, grinning from ear to ear while clutching small trophies in their hands.

Scrolling to the earlier date, seeing a similarly posed image, he closed his eyes.

'Shit.'

'See what I mean?' said Barclay, his tone urgent. 'Gary couldn't have done whatever it is you think he did. He wasn't even in the country. You can check his passport records or something to confirm it, can't you?'

Mark opened his eyes and looked at Jan.

Disappointment radiated from her as she slapped shut the manila folder and ended the interview.

'Thanks for your time, Mr Barclay,' she said.

'No problem. Can I have my phone back now?'

CHAPTER FORTY-SIX

It was past midnight by the time Mark made his way back downstairs to the custody suite.

Kennedy had left the station twenty minutes ago with frustration etched across his features and a promise to do what he could with regard to reporting to Headquarters.

Mark wasn't holding his breath.

Soon, the LPA's management team would decide personnel were required elsewhere, and the investigation would enter the next phase.

He'd be little more than a caretaker, desperate for snippets of information to be unearthed by chance, and he couldn't let that happen.

He didn't want to let it go.

Not yet.

He owed it to Annabelle, to Roger, and to the unknown second woman who lay in Gillian's morgue.

Justin White, Levine's solicitor, waited in the corridor outside interview room two while his client was brought from the cells and studiously ignored Mark when he joined him.

Instead, the man made a point of checking his watch, checking his phone, and then huffing under his breath in a perpetual cycle while Mark stared at one of the health and safety posters on the brick wall.

He turned at heavy footsteps to see Levine being escorted towards them by Tom Wilcox, and opened the door to let them in.

Levine scowled at him as he passed, then crossed to one of the seats beside the table and slouched in it while his solicitor fussed about with pens and notepads.

'Thanks, Tom.' Mark restarted the recording equipment as the sergeant left the room and leaned back in his seat. 'Aidan Barclay confirmed your statement, Gary. You're free to go once we're finished here.'

The smile that cracked Levine's sour features was both triumphant and relieved. 'What did I tell you, eh? Told you I was innocent.'

'And we have that on record.' He opened the file before him and spun the paperwork around to face the other man. 'If you could sign this, we'll get your belongings back to you straight away.'

He watched while Levine scrawled a hasty signature across the documents.

'Why were you made redundant from the care company, Gary?' Mark tidied the papers now littering the desk and stacked them into a neat pile, his gaze never leaving the other man.

Levine's shoulders sagged. 'Someone made a complaint against me. It was all lies, of course. It was just easier for me to leave quietly than try to fight it – discrimination tends to work one way these days, detective. I might not look much now, but I was a big bloke. Who'd have believed me if I told them I was the one being bullied and harassed?'

'What were you being bullied about?'

'I was trying to work my way up in the company. I liked it there. I liked the customers I spoke to. There was an internal promotion available for a supervisor role, and I fancied my chances so I applied for it.' A sad smile crossed his face. 'I'd have been good at it, too.'

'What happened?'

'About a week or so after my application went in and the first interview had taken place, I found something in the system. An anomaly.'

'What sort of anomaly?'

'Someone had been removing data about potential customers. Changing phone numbers, deleting notes we used to identify potential clients rather than time-wasters, that sort of thing.'

'Any proof?'

Levine sneered. 'That's what they asked me when I mentioned it. I didn't have any proof, I just had a feeling.

Like, when people would phone up for a quote, it'd be logged in the system with a reminder for one of us to give them a call back. We'd have sales scripts to follow, up-selling techniques to use, things like that. I'd cast my eye over the next day's list before leaving for the night, and that's when I started noticing that some of the details were disappearing, or the numbers had changed. When I phoned them, I kept getting automatic messages saying the numbers were wrong. Or, if I'd spoken to someone and they were keen to get some help, I'd set a diary appointment for one of the senior carers to go round and assess their needs. Those entries would disappear too.'

'Do you mean that someone was deleting them?'

'Yeah, exactly.' Levine's face became more animated. 'I mean, everyone's got access to the system so they can look up customers' details, appointments, home care schedules, that sort of thing. I don't know whether it was random or what, but it was definitely happening.'

'How could you be so sure about the phone numbers? I mean, there must've been hundreds going through that system on a monthly basis.'

'Like I said, I used to check each night for the next day's calls. I liked to be prepared, go through in my head how I was going to speak to each of them. Some of the ends of the phone numbers were easy to remember – 737, 113, stuff like that. And they'd be different the next day. Or gone.'

'What happened when you reported it?'

'Nothing. I told my manager, and she took it upstairs, and then nothing happened. I even spoke to some of the managers in the other departments to see if they'd noticed it.' Levine's face fell. 'And that's when I started to get accused of harassment.'

Mark took a deep breath, trying to calm his racing heart rate. 'Who lodged the complaint, Gary?'

'It's too late now. It doesn't help me, does it? I'm still out of work, and I can't get a reference from there.'

'Who was it?'

Levine's gaze flickered to Mark's as he let out a shaking sigh.

'Sonia Adams.'

CHAPTER FORTY-SEVEN

Mark tapped his fingers on the steering wheel and stared at the sun-baked sandstone cladding of the house across the street.

He bit back a yawn, sipped at a takeout coffee he'd bought at the drive-through fast food restaurant on the way, and wondered for the nth time whether he should have taken up Tom's offer of one of the empty bunks in the custody suite rather than sit all night at his desk after releasing Gary Levine.

The front door opened, and then Jan hurried down the block-paved driveway towards the car balancing a travel cup, handbag and a small package wrapped in aluminium foil.

She thrust the package through the open window to him. 'Bacon sandwich. Reckoned you hadn't gone home last night.'

His stomach rumbled in response while she went around to the passenger side and climbed in.

'I take it Lucy texted you, then,' he said between mouthfuls.

'She's worried about you.' Jan adjusted her seatbelt over her chest as he shoved the last crust into his mouth, then handed him a paper tissue.

'Thanks.'

'You're welcome.'

'I'll buy her some flowers on the way home tonight.'

'You probably should. All right, what's going on? What did I miss?'

Mark turned the car around and aimed it towards the ring road, battening down his impatience as the traffic crawled towards the dual carriageway while he told her what Gary Levine had divulged earlier that morning.

'What do you think?' said Jan when he'd finished.

'When Gary was telling me all of this, I think he thought he'd uncovered a case of industrial espionage,' Mark explained. He paused to overtake an articulated truck with Polish licence plates, then planted his foot firmly on the accelerator, mindful of the minutes ticking away on the dashboard clock. 'I think Sonia was covering her tracks.'

Jan shuffled in her seat to face him. 'Do you think she was using her access to the system to hide the fact some of the people she was coming into contact with were going missing?'

He glanced at her, then back to the road. Enough time to see the incredulous expression in her eyes.

'It makes sense,' he said. 'What if she killed Annabelle, and then realised how risky that was, given that she was her carer? What if she then decided to go after victims who weren't yet clients?'

'But she stayed with John for two days after Annabelle went missing. That was hell of a risk to take if she was responsible for her murder.'

'Or extremely clever. She placed herself above suspicion by being there.'

'Back to the potential clients, then – how was she targeting them?'

'She could have done what Gary suggested – remove their details from the database so no one was any the wiser. They couldn't be traced back to her.'

'Did Gary suspect she was doing that?'

'No – it's something that's been going around in my head since I released him earlier today. He said he backed off the minute she put in a formal complaint in the hope he'd keep his job – he said he wouldn't be able to find anything that paid that well.'

'Didn't do him much good, did it? He was asked to leave anyway.'

'And on that point, he reckons he was bullied out of the job, rather than being formally told he was out because of any harassment on his part. The whole process was dragged out over weeks, with insinuations and the like. He said his health was starting to suffer.'

Mark slowed back to the speed limit as he saw the sign for Didcot flash past. 'Apparently, their contracts all state they can't go and work for a competitor for six months, which is why he was unemployed for a while afterwards.'

Jan sat back and stared through the windscreen in silence, nibbling a thumbnail while he exited at the next junction and powered towards the industrial estate.

He realised he was holding his breath, waiting for her next reaction.

'Well? What do you think?'

She shook her head. 'I don't know, Sarge. I mean, why? What's the motive?'

'I don't know yet.' He checked his rear-view mirror, then indicated and slewed the car into a lay-by beside the railway tracks. 'Run me through Sonia's background again. What did Caroline come up with before we first spoke to her?'

Paging through her notebook, Jan muttered under her breath until she found the details. 'No criminal record, DBS checks are clear, and we know from Sonia herself that she started out as a trainee nurse before switching careers. She went from that to working in a care home.'

'Did anyone speak to her manager at the care home?'

Jan bit her lip. 'I don't think so.'

'Got a number?'

'I'll get one. Hang on.'

With that, she pressed the speed dial on her phone and activated the speaker as Alex answered.

'Caroline's in a meeting at the moment,' he said. 'Can I help?'

Mark leaned closer. 'We need to talk to Sonia Adams'

manager at the care home she used to work at. Have you got a number on the system?'

There was a clatter as Alex put his phone on the desk before the sound of fingers on a keyboard carried through to where they sat. Then—

'Here it is.'

Jan wrote down the number. 'Thanks, Alex.'

She didn't wait for his reply, and instead ended the call and immediately dialled the new number.

A man's voice answered after three rings, and Jan angled the phone towards Mark.

'Is that Ian Allenson?'

'It is. Who's this?'

'My name's Detective Sergeant Mark Turpin. You're on speakerphone with my colleague, DC Jan West. We'd like to ask you some questions about Sonia Adams.'

'Right…' The man's voice was hesitant, confused. 'Is something the matter?'

'Were there any issues at the care home while Sonia worked for you there?'

'What sort of issues?'

Mark swallowed.

Now or never.

'Any signs of abuse, or misconduct?'

'Sonia?' Allenson spluttered. 'Absolutely not. She loved the residents. They adored her. We were sorry to see her go.'

'So, no complaints, or—'

'No. Nothing. Detective, what's going on?'

'Thanks for your time, Mr Allenson. If you could keep this conversation to yourself for the moment.'

He reached out and ended the call, then leaned back in his seat with a sigh.

'Bugger. That's that theory out the window.'

'Not necessarily.' Jan put her phone and notebook in her bag. 'Maybe she didn't start there. Maybe it all started once she changed jobs and moved to the in-home care company. But again, why?'

Mark blew out his cheeks and released the handbrake. 'Only one way to find out.'

Five minutes later, he parked in a spare space outside the company's building and peered up at the corner office window as he pocketed the keys.

'Her car's not here,' said Jan, jerking her chin towards the other vehicles dotted around the car park.

Mark said nothing, eyeing the panel vans parked beside the reception doors, and recalling the way in which the carers kept the vehicles well-stocked in between visits.

A nudge to his arm brought his attention back to Jan, who was frowning.

'What are you thinking, Sarge?'

'One of those would be perfect for hiding and transporting a body, wouldn't it?' he said.

She cocked an eyebrow at him. 'Let's go and find out where she is.'

She set off towards the front doors at a brisk trot, shoved her way past a delivery driver coming the other way, then stood to one side while Mark advanced towards the lone man behind the reception desk.

'Back again, detectives?' he said cheerily, gesturing to the visitor log and holding out a pen.

'Where's Sonia Adams?' Mark asked. 'Her car isn't outside. Is she in today?'

'Oh, she's out and about catching up with some of her old patients,' said the receptionist. 'She does that some mornings. She loves staying in touch with them.'

Mark's eyes narrowed. 'Where *exactly* is she?'

'Hang on. I think I might have their details somewhere.' The man turned to his computer, pressed a few buttons, then looked up from his screen. 'Here we go.'

Jan wrote down the name and address, then headed towards the doors.

Mark paused. 'If she's the care manager now, why does she visit your clients?'

'She can't help herself,' said the receptionist with a shrug and a benevolent smile. 'She says she misses them, and can't bear to think that they're struggling on their own when our staff can't be there to help.'

CHAPTER FORTY-EIGHT

'There's her car.'

Jan pointed through the windscreen at a black SUV parked across a driveway farther into the leafy cul-de-sac, then hissed as Mark braked the car inches away from the other vehicle's bumper.

'At least she can't go anywhere now,' he said, jerking his chin at the motorbike parked squarely across the SUV's back end. 'She's boxed in.'

'How do you want to do this?' said Jan.

'Fast. I want her out of there and under arrest before we start questioning the couple she's visiting.' He checked his door mirror as blue flashing lights caught his attention, the patrol car shooting past their position before turning around at the end of the road and returning. 'Right, let's go.'

By the time he slammed shut the car door and joined Jan

on the pavement, a net curtain covering the lower front window had twitched back into place. Casting his gaze to the neighbouring property, the sound of a pair of uniformed constables' footsteps hurrying towards him, he saw a pale face emerge from behind a gap in the front door.

He could feel eyes on him from the homes across the road while he led the way up the driveway to the front door, realising that the area wasn't the sort of place where a police car was seen unless there was a break-in.

Not affluent, by any means, but what his mother would call "well-to-do".

Easy pickings, his former DI would've said.

Jan's face was grim when she rang the doorbell and turned to him. 'I'll deal with them, you take her. Sound all right, Sarge?'

He nodded in response.

No doubt the old couple who lived here were oblivious to their visitor's ulterior motives for being present.

Had she already picked her next victim?

Was another disappearance already being planned?

Would she—

'What's going on?'

He turned back to the house at the sound of an elderly voice to see a man in his eighties glaring at them, his pockmarked hands resting on an aluminium walking frame.

'Mr Russell Gregory?'

'Who are you?'

'Detective Sergeant Mark Turpin. This is my colleague, DC Jan West. Is everything all right?'

'Why shouldn't it be? Why are you here?'

'We'd like a word with Sonia Adams, please.'

Confusion grazed the man's features, and then he took a wobbling step backward, dragging the frame with him.

'You... you'd best come in.'

'Thank you.' Mark signalled to the two uniformed constables to wait on the doorstep, then followed Jan and Gregory through the hallway to a rectangular-shaped living room that ran the length of the house.

A tiny woman sat in an armchair, her frame bundled up in a thick cardigan despite the weather outside, her feet swaddled within fluffy slippers.

Sonia Adams stood beside her, a hand resting casually on the woman's shoulder. 'Detective Turpin. What's going on? Why are you here?'

The old woman's eyes widened when she saw the two detectives behind her husband, and she let out a mumbled wail.

'It's all right, love.' Gregory hurried over, his walking frame scuffing across the carpet. He reached out for his wife's hand. 'It's nothing to worry about, I'm sure.'

He looked over his shoulder at Mark, as if seeking reassurance.

Moving closer to Sonia but wary of her reaction, he recited the formal caution, and gestured to the door.

'This is preposterous,' she blurted, looking at the Gregorys, then back to him, her face grey. 'On what basis—'

'Everything will be explained during the interview process,' said Mark. 'Now, if you could come with us?'

'I'll sue you,' Sonia spat. 'You'll never get away with this.'

'I'll remind you, Ms Adams, you're under caution. Anything you say—'

'Oh, fuck off.'

Gregory's jaw dropped, his hands shaking as he steadied himself against the frame. 'Sonia?'

'Everything all right in here, Sarge?'

Grant Wickes appeared at the door, his bulk taking up the remaining space between the furniture and the window while he pulled a pair of handcuffs from his utility vest.

'If you could take Ms Adams into custody, constable.' Mark gave what he hoped was a reassuring smile at Gregory. 'I'd like to speak to Mr Gregory before we leave.'

Mark looked back to face Sonia's steady gaze, her jaw clenched in defiance.

Pale green eyes flashed steel at him before her chin dropped and she held out her wrists to be cuffed.

He heard Jan exhale while they watched Sonia being led away to the waiting patrol car, and then she moved across to where Gregory's wife stared up at them, utter confusion in her eyes.

'Mrs Gregory, can I make you a cup of tea perhaps?' she said.

Her words were met with a jumble of speech, vowels and consonants tripping over each other as the woman reached out and clutched her hand.

'She had a stroke three months ago,' said Gregory. 'But I'll show you where to find everything. Don't make it too hot for her, though.'

Mark's heart ached as the older man led Jan out of the living room and along the hallway to the kitchen, relief clutching at his chest.

A bleat from the armchair caught his attention, and he turned to see Mrs Gregory beckoning to him.

He crouched beside her as her husband had done, and patted her hand.

'It's all right. You're safe now,' he murmured.

In reply, she pushed away the blanket and pulled up her cardigan sleeve.

Mark rocked back on his heels at the sight of the purple and yellow bruises.

When he recovered, he reached out and gently turned her arm. 'Did she do this?'

A nod.

'She won't any more, I promise.'

His words were met with a toothy smile, tears forming in the woman's eyes.

She extracted her arm, pulled down her sleeve, then patted her chest. 'Mary.'

'It's lovely to meet you, Mary.'

'Well, isn't that something?'

Mark straightened at the sound of Gregory's voice to see him and Jan at the doorway.

The old man was beaming at his wife. 'I was right, see? That speech therapist said it was only a matter of time, love. As long as we keep practising.'

'Mr Gregory, we won't take up much more of your time. I apologise for any stress this has caused you both.'

'It's been a shock, I won't lie.' The man eased himself into the armchair beside his wife. 'Your colleague here explained what's going on.'

'Good. In that case I just have a few more questions I'd like to ask before we leave you in peace. Is that all right?'

Gregory waved his hand in the air. 'Go on.'

'When did you start using the company Sonia works for?'

'Just after Mary had her stroke. As you can see, I'm not much use on my own. Charlotte comes in every morning to help her wash and dress, and makes sure I know where to find the ready meals in the freezer. She helps when the delivery driver turns up every week with those as well.'

'Who's Charlotte?'

'She's the lady they send from the care company.'

'If Charlotte is your carer, how did Sonia get to know you?'

'She popped by for the first time about six weeks ago. Said it was usual, just a quality thing to make sure we were happy with the service her carers were providing.' Gregory smiled. 'She's been ever so good to us. We can only afford for Charlotte to do so much, so when Sonia learned that, she offered to help us out. In her own time sometimes, too. Now that's what I call customer service.'

'The bruises on your wife's arm, Mr Gregory. How did she get those?'

The man's face softened. 'Mary's always bumping into things, aren't you love? It's the stroke you see. It's affected her coordination skills.'

'Do you ever leave your wife alone with Sonia?'

Gregory shot a guilty look at his wife. 'You didn't mind, do you love? It's only a couple of times a week so that I can have a nap and not worry.'

Mary glared at him in response.

'Do they stay here, or go somewhere?' said Mark.

'Oh, Sonia's brilliant,' Gregory replied. He jerked his chin towards the black SUV still parked at the kerb. 'She sometimes takes Mary out for the afternoon.'

'Do you know what they do?'

The old man nodded. 'Sonia said she loves the countryside so she goes for short walks with her to help with her rehabilitation. She says it's good for Mary to get some fresh air and a change of scenery.'

'Did she tell you where they go exactly?'

Gregory's brow furrowed. 'Not exactly, but I can probably work it out from a map.'

CHAPTER FORTY-NINE

'Where is she now?'

Kennedy hovered at Mark's shoulder, pacing back and forth while he hurriedly filled out the relevant forms on screen for the remainder of the morning's planned activities.

'Downstairs, being processed. Her solicitor is on his way. Someone from Oxford.'

'And the couple she was visiting when you arrested her – are they okay?'

'I've left a constable with them, taking a statement from the husband and working with the wife's speech therapist to interview her. It could take a while.'

The DI pulled out a chair beside him, glanced across at Jan, then at the printer as Mark finished typing. 'You're absolutely sure about this? It's not a case of Gary Levine being vindictive?'

'I think he was telling the truth, guv.' Mark spun his chair around to face him. 'And it makes sense. He told me this morning that Sonia got Roger Parnett's details from him and said she'd follow up in a week or so, just to see if she could help in any way. By then, it was rumoured Sonia was going to be covering for the care manager's role while they looked for a replacement so Gary didn't feel like he could argue with her. Besides, he believed her. He might've been an aggressive salesperson once – that's encouraged by the company – but he's a compassionate man at heart. It's why he still helps with the volunteer driving. He can't help it – he has to feel that he's contributing in some way.'

'And you think Sonia Adams used the company's system to pick out her next victims?'

'I do, yes.'

'Based on what evidence?'

'On the way back here, I spoke to Dan Nelson from the other care company on the pretence of a follow-up enquiry. I asked him how easily it would be to manipulate the computer system they use to delete or change patient contact details,' said Mark, rising to his feet and gathering together the notes and documents he needed for the formal interview. 'Sonia's company uses the same one. Nelson told me it's relatively simple – mistakes have to be corrected from time to time, after all. The thing is, guv, those changes don't leave a trace.'

Kennedy looked up at him. 'But surely that sort of access is only available to people at a certain level within the company?'

'It is, guv. And it's why Sonia couldn't start changing the records until she was promoted to the manager role.'

'If she deleted all the information from the initial sales enquiry, then how are you going to prove that?'

'She could only delete the instruction for someone to go to the Parnetts, not the original entry with their details on it. Those are kept in the system in case a potential client's circumstances change. I was going to ask you if you could sign off on a warrant so we can get someone from digital forensics over to the care company. Sonia's system access was only as an administrator level – whatever she deleted must still be in the historical records.' Mark swallowed. 'Somewhere.'

'Jesus.' The DI shook his head. 'I leave you lot alone for a morning, and I come back to this. What else have I missed?'

'I took the liberty of organising a search team – with cadaver dogs – and sent them over to the location Russell Gregory told us Sonia takes his wife to.'

'There goes the rest of my budget this quarter. How far from our original crime scene is this place you've sent the search team?'

'I'll show you.'

Mark led the way out into the incident room and paused at a table set up beside the whiteboard, a large map unfolded and spread out across its surface.

It had already been covered in sticky notes and red pen scrawl, so Mark picked up a black marker pen and circled the woodland north of the stream.

'This is where we found the three bodies,' he said, then

stretched out and drew a small cross beside a narrow lane. 'And this is where we've worked out Sonia's taking Mary every week. It's a small wood along a track about halfway between Blewbury and East Ilsley. We took a look at it on the way back here.'

Opening the photos app on his phone, he scrolled through them, Kennedy at his shoulder. 'See? She can park the car off the road behind this hedgerow and access the woods along here. It's only about fifty metres, but the track twists so you can't see it from the road. Anyway, there's very little passing traffic, and the chalky soil means it wouldn't be too difficult to push a wheelchair.'

'Not if you were determined,' Kennedy said, his face grim. 'I take it you've got Gillian and Jasper on standby?'

'They're already there, guv.'

'What? Isn't that a bit too pre-emptive?'

'I'm sure about this, guv. Sorry – bear with me.' Mark held up his hand as Caroline hurried past, the DC making a beeline for Jan's desk. 'Any news?'

Jan looked up from her computer, her mobile phone to her ear. 'Not yet. They've only just started.'

Turning back to Kennedy, Mark opened his mouth to speak but the DI got there first.

'How sure are you about this?'

'I think Sonia picked a new location after she found out that Hacca's Brook can flood. I think she was taking Mary there every week so that when she decided to kill her, she wouldn't struggle.'

'A practice run, you mean?'

'Exactly. The whole routine would be familiar to her.'

'Why wait? You said yourself, she's been visiting them for the past six weeks. Why not kill her straight away?'

'I don't know, guv, but remember she's got to make it look as if Mary went missing. So maybe she had to wait until an opportunity came along to do that.'

'It's a long shot.'

'With respect, guv, you didn't see the bruises on Mary's arm.' Mark's throat ached. 'I did. And she's been non-responsive and unable to ask for help since her stroke.'

Kennedy rubbed his jaw, glanced at the whiteboard and then back to the map. 'You'd better go and find out what Sonia's got to say for herself, then.'

CHAPTER FIFTY

Sonia Adams glared at Mark with indignation when he stepped into the interview room.

She opened her mouth to speak but was silenced by her solicitor resting his hand casually on her forearm, the man focusing on Jan while she started the recording equipment and repeated the formal caution.

'We've been waiting here for two hours,' he said indignantly. 'We don't appreciate being kept locked up while—'

Mark raised an eyebrow. 'Tough.'

'My client denies everything,' he said, straightening the red silk tie at his collar.

'Of course she does,' Mark replied.

He dropped a pile of folders onto the table between them,

placed his mobile phone beside those, and eased into the seat next to Jan.

Kennedy had signed off on the warrant, and there were currently two of the LPA's best IT experts at the care company's offices with Alex.

There was still no word from the search team.

After gathering his thoughts, Mark raised his gaze to the woman in front of him and saw a sneer graze her lips for a brief moment.

Then it was gone, her gaze flickering to the folders next to his elbow.

'Please state your full name for the recording,' he said.

She turned towards the machine and raised her voice. 'Sonia Penelope Adams.'

'Thank you, Ms Adams.'

'I don't understand why I'm here,' she said. 'I haven't done anything wrong.'

'We'll see.' Mark flipped open the first folder and spun around a photograph to face her. 'Tell me why you abused Mary Gregory.'

A hand fluttered to her throat. 'What on earth makes you think I would do such a thing?'

'Mrs Gregory has alleged that you caused injury to her arm.' Mark flipped over a copy of a photograph taken on his phone. 'These bruises were made by you, weren't they?'

'Don't be ridiculous,' Sonia spluttered. 'The woman can hardly manage to string together two words, let alone accuse me of hurting her.'

'Her speech is much better than she would have you believe. We're working with her speech therapist to provide a formal statement.'

There was a flicker of a reaction then, a brief flash in her eye that almost gave way to something altogether more sinister.

'Tell me about Annabelle Studley,' Mark prompted. 'Did you abuse her? Did you break her arm weeks before deciding to kill her too?'

'I don't know what you're talking about,' Sonia replied. 'Annabelle went missing. Nobody knows where she went, or what happened to her.'

'Why did you kill her, and then bury her body next to Hacca's Brook?'

'I didn't. I used to love caring for her and John.'

'What about Roger Parnett?'

'What about him?'

'Why did you decide that he had to die? He wasn't even a client of yours. Did you delete the diary appointment that was made for his assessment?'

'It wasn't necessary for anyone to go and see him. Anyone could see that he was a lost cause.'

'And so you kidnapped and then murdered him, is that right?'

'I don't know what you're talking about.'

'What did you do when you realised the original sales lead hadn't been deleted from the system? Is that why you had to bully Gary Levine out of his job? Is that why you tried to implicate him in the murders?'

Sonia stared back at him, but said nothing.

'Bet you got one hell of a shock when you found out Hacca's Brook was liable to flood. Did you panic?'

The woman reared back in her chair, her eyes widening, and Mark knew he'd hit a nerve.

'How long did it take you to find the new location? Oh – and we know where that is, by the way. Mary Gregory told us. There's currently a search team there. With dogs. Do you know how good those dogs are at locating bodies?'

Jan shifted in her seat beside him, and he hoped the fact that the same dogs had missed Roger Parnett's remains didn't show on his face while he eyed Sonia.

The moment was broken by a short sharp rap on the door, and then Caroline peered in.

'Sarge? A quick word?'

'Pause the tape please, DC West.' Mark pushed back his chair while Jan recited the formalities, and then they both hustled from the interview room, closing the door.

'What have you got for me?' he said.

Caroline handed him her phone in response. 'It's one of the IT lot, over at the care company.'

'Thanks.' He wandered farther along the corridor, away from the interview room and put the call on speakerphone. 'This is Turpin. I've got DCs West and Roberts with me.'

'Sarge, it's Will Trelawny from digital forensics. I've got that update you were after.'

'Go on. Brief, mind – we're in the middle of interviewing the suspect.'

'Right, so we worked with the IT guys here and accessed the customer database at a higher level than Sonia Adams was able. That means we can see every single update to a contact listing, not just the ones shown on the user's display. A step-by-step historical account, if you like.'

'And?' Mark held his breath, eyeing Jan who was staring intently at the phone screen.

'We've got documentary evidence here that Ms Adams deleted evidence on file about the patients she was responsible for. Dates of home visits that had been booked in, as well as allocating other carers' names to historical timesheets.'

Exhaling, Mark closed his eyes for a moment, relieved. Then—

'Will, can you email everything you've got to Caroline? Immediately.'

'It'll be with you in five.'

'Thanks.' He handed back the phone to the younger DC. 'We'll wait out here for you. As soon as that information comes through, I need it printed out, all right?'

Caroline was already running by the time he finished speaking.

He spent the next ten minutes pacing the corridor, intermittently glaring at the ceiling tiles, and then the worn and scuffed carpet while Jan leaned against the wall, hugging the pile of folders to her chest.

Mark checked his watch.

Fifteen minutes.

His gaze locked with Jan, and then he looked away, battening down the nerves that nipped at him, clouding his conviction with doubt.

Neither of them spoke, each lost in their own thoughts.

'Sarge.'

He spun around at the sound of Caroline's voice to see her hurrying towards him.

'What took so long?'

She thrust a stapled document at him, another copy for Jan and then pointed out what Will had told her.

'There's something else, Sarge,' she said, unable to contain the excitement in her voice. 'I got another call as I was about to come back. Jasper said the search team has found two bodies at the new location Russell Gregory gave us.'

Mark staggered and reached out for the wall, a sigh escaping. 'Okay, that's great. Thanks, Caroline.'

Jan wore a grim smile as she started reading through Will's information. 'Sarge, this is perfect.'

CHAPTER FIFTY-ONE

Half an hour later, Mark squared his shoulders and followed Jan back into the interview room.

Sonia and her solicitor had their heads bowed together when the door opened, breaking away as his colleague crossed to the table, their murmured conversation sputtering to a hastened silence.

Sonia's shoulders were relaxed, her whole pose one of someone used to being in control.

She didn't fidget, didn't flinch, when Jan pulled out a chair, the legs scraping painfully across the tiled floor.

Mark didn't bother to sit.

Instead, he moved to the wall behind Jan, leaning against it while he contemplated the charged atmosphere in the confined space.

As soon as Jan restarted the recording, he took the sheaf of paperwork from her and slapped it on the table in front of Sonia.

'Our digital forensics team have been busy,' he said. 'And they've uncovered all the records you thought you'd deleted.'

The woman paled, then looked to her solicitor who gave a slight shrug, not yet convinced.

Mark flicked to the second page, tapping his forefinger on the second entry. 'A meeting was arranged for a salesperson from your care company to visit Roger Parnett and his wife, but you deleted it and went instead. Why?'

No answer.

'I think you went there to find out if he made a suitable candidate for your next victim,' Mark continued. 'And I think you inveigled yourself into their home in the three weeks between this visit and the date of Roger's disappearance. When you murdered him.'

Sonia leaned back and crossed her arms. 'Anybody could have accessed those records.'

'They could, if they had the correct access. But we've got proof the changes were made with your login details.'

The woman reached out, running a finger across the table, then peered at it as if checking for dust.

She dropped her hand and glared at him. 'Someone must have signed in as me to cover their tracks. I told you. I loved my patients, and their families.'

'Did you love the families more than the people you were employed to care for? We've found your new burial ground,

Sonia. Two victims so far. How many more are we going to find, do you think?'

Jan handed him a page from one of the folders, and he slipped it over the table to the other woman.

'This is our missing persons list, Sonia. Hundreds of elderly men and women who disappeared without a trace. Hundreds of families unable to grieve. How many people have you murdered, Sonia? How many families have you destroyed?'

Sonia's expression changed in an instant.

Mark watched, holding his breath as her eyes narrowed, and any remnant of pretence slipped away.

Her mouth twisted into a sneer as she leaned forward.

'Eleven,' she spat.

A shocked silence filled the room, broken only by the sound of Sonia's solicitor dropping his pen.

It bounced off of his legal pad, rolled across the table and tumbled to the tiled floor.

All the time, Sonia never broke eye contact with Mark.

Unnerved, he finally looked away as the solicitor scrambled under the table.

Once the man was seated, his demeanour that of a defeated man, Mark pulled out his chair and collapsed into it.

'Tell me about Roger.'

'What about him?'

'Why murder him?'

'Nothing much to say, really. I went there to see if I could help.'

'By help, you mean kill.'

She shrugged, a nonchalance to the gesture that set his flesh crawling. 'It was obvious to me that Brenda couldn't cope on her own with him, and the man had no intention of even trying to get better. He was too used to being waited on hand and foot. He was slowly killing her. Something had to be done.'

'If he could hardly walk, how did you manage it?'

Her eyes sparkled. 'Easy. Despite all his failings, he really did love Brenda. All I had to do, after agreeing with their doctor's advice that they both needed to exercise, was to wait until Brenda had gone on one of her nightly walks.'

'Why would Roger go with you? Annabelle Studley was confused, Roger wasn't.'

'Easy. I rang the doorbell and told him I'd just got a call from the hospital because Brenda had tripped and fallen while out on her walk. The timing was exquisite,' she said, her gaze unfocused as she stared at a point above Mark's head. 'Five minutes too early, and he wouldn't have believed me. She hadn't been gone long enough. Five minutes too late, and she would've seen me with him.'

Mark hoped the shock didn't show on his face. Instead, he waited while Jan pulled a photograph from the stack of folders.

'Who is this? We found three bodies near Hacca's Brook. Annabelle Studley, Roger Parnett, and…?'

'That would be Gladys Towers.' Sonia's nose wrinkled. 'Dreadful woman. Dementia and incontinence. I had to scrub the car twice after she was in it. Wait until you meet her husband, Gareth. The man's had a new lease of life thanks to me.'

Mark stared at her, realising that before him sat a psychopath.

'Why?' he managed.

Sonia shrugged. 'They were in pain, or causing pain to those around them. Something had to be done.'

'And if they hadn't been, would you have left them alone?'

'Of course.' Sonia's eyes widened and she rocked back in her chair. 'Despite what you might think of me, detective, what I do frees families from a life of servitude. I'm not a monster.'

CHAPTER FIFTY-TWO

Late the next day, Mark flipped down the windscreen visor and squinted into a low afternoon sun as he steered the pool car into the forecourt of the county's morgue.

A weariness clung to his shoulders despite the deep sleep he'd fallen into upon returning to the narrowboat eight hours ago, but it was one of relief rather than stress.

Lucy had taken one look at his exhausted features when he'd emerged from their bed that morning, handed him a large mug of coffee, and made him promise to request the rest of the week off when he returned to the police station.

Kennedy had compromised, telling both Mark and Jan to report back for duty the following Monday as long as they kept their phones on so the team could check facts and provide progress reports to the Crown Prosecution Service, who were now waiting impatiently.

The after-effects of Sonia Adams' shocking admission had reverberated around the incident room, and now the team were tasked with cross-referencing the in-care company's contact database with the missing persons list.

Dread mixed with determination amongst his colleagues, and Mark knew they wouldn't give up until they had names for all of the victims' remains that had been discovered.

He pulled the key from the ignition and got out.

There was one more task to complete before he clocked off.

Striding across the asphalt, he raised a hand in greeting as the door opened and Gillian appeared.

'Thought I recognised the car,' she said as she led him towards the mortuary end of the building. 'Congratulations, by the way.'

'Thanks.'

She paused, her hand on the inner door. 'You sound disappointed.'

'Just thinking about eleven families who now have to be informed that their loved ones were taken by a serial killer.'

Gillian sighed, wrapped a hand around his arm and pulled him into the laboratory. 'Come on. The results were emailed to me twenty minutes ago.'

Mark noticed that the usually bright spotlights above the gurneys had been dimmed, and while the pathologist tugged on a pair of protective gloves, he wandered across to the rows of square-shaped drawers at the far end. 'How did you manage to get the DNA results so fast?'

She joined him, and opened one of the drawers in the middle, resting her hand on top of it. 'Kennedy reckoned with the result you just delivered, his budget could stretch this far. Plus, I think he pulled in a couple of favours.'

With that, she slid out the metal shelf inside, exposing the remains of their second victim.

'Gladys Towers,' Mark murmured.

'It's definitely her.' Gillian ran her gaze down the skeleton, then sighed. 'Her daughter's DNA was a match.'

'I'll ask Caroline to pop round to see her in the morning.' Mark stepped back while the drawer was shut, then looked at the others. 'How many have been recovered from the new site so far?'

'The top row.' Gillian snapped off her gloves. 'It's going to be a busy few weeks. Luckily I've got an extra pair of hands to help me – Angela Powell has offered to assist, and I've borrowed a junior pathologist from the hospital who's worked with me before.'

'Not Kerridge this time?' Mark smiled.

'No, thank goodness. I heard he was considering quitting in favour of touring the lecture circuit instead.'

'God help them.'

'Indeed. What about your killer? Any more progress from your end of things?'

'The team that went to Sonia's house last night found all of the jewellery she'd removed from her victims in a box in her wardrobe – all of her mementos,' said Mark. 'Kennedy's got a couple of constables working through the lost property files to return it all to the victims' families.'

'They'll take DNA swabs this week?'

'Yes. I'm not sure Kennedy's influence will be able to get those results to you much before month end though.'

'The main thing is, we'll get there.' Gillian's gaze hardened. 'And you stopped her, Mark. She can't do this to anyone else.'

'Yeah, there's that. Would you excuse me for a minute? I need to let Kennedy know it's Gladys so he can start processing the paperwork.'

'Sure. I'll tidy up in here and meet you in reception.'

He hit the speed dial on his mobile as the mortuary doors swished closed behind him, the DI's gruff voice answering within seconds.

'Is it her?'

'Yes. Gillian says the results came through just before I got here.'

'Okay, thanks.'

'Everything okay, guv? You sound a bit...'

'Pissed off? I am. The CPS have informed me they want a psychological evaluation conducted before they proceed. Apparently Ms Adams' solicitor has demanded it, telling them she's not fit to face trial.'

Mark groaned. 'That's ridiculous. She knew what she was doing, guv.'

'I know, I've watched the interview recording. Anyway,

we'll do our best. Give my regards to Gillian – and thank her for her work these past two weeks.'

'Will do. Talk later.'

He ended the call as Gillian appeared. 'Kennedy asked me to pass on his thanks.'

'He's welcome. Hopefully I'll have some more answers for you over the coming days.' She glanced up at the clock above the reception desk. 'Shit, is that the time? You'd better get going – I need to lock up here, and then head home to get changed.'

'See you at the gallery.'

CHAPTER FIFTY-THREE

Mark tugged at the bow tie at his neck, the shine from his black leather shoes gleaming as he walked beside Lucy, her arm looped through his.

'Are you being affectionate, or am I actually here to help you keep your balance?' he said, glancing at the four-inch heels she teetered in.

Dimples creased her cheeks. 'A bit of both. Maybe more of one than the other.'

'You look beautiful.'

Pausing on the bridge, her curls tickling her neck, she pulled him to a standstill. She kissed him, then faced the road snaking away across the river and into town.

'I'm terrified.'

'It's going to be fine. They'll love you. You've earned this.'

The bells from St Nicolas' church tolled the hour, and Mark gave her arm a tug. 'Come on, you can't be late for your own exhibition.'

'Hang on.' She removed her shoes, looped the straps over a finger and grinned. 'We'll get there faster this way. I shouldn't have bothered putting these on once we'd crossed the meadow.'

'I could give you a piggyback.'

'I might need that on the way back. It depends how much champagne I drink.'

Laughing, they hurried the rest of the way along Bridge Street, turning into a pedestrianised side street that led towards the Abbey Gardens.

A sandwich board decorated with the art gallery's logo was propped on the cobblestones, announcing a private function that night.

The door was open, and the sound of voices talking at volume easily carried across the quadrangle of buildings.

Pausing to tuck her feet back into her shoes, Lucy straightened the little black dress she wore, then fiddled with the colourful shawl around her neck.

'You're stalling, Miss O'Brien.'

A guilty look shot across her face, and then she squared her shoulders. 'All right. I'm ready.'

Within seconds of them stepping into the airy space, Lucy was whisked away by the gallery owner to be introduced to a waiting line of local VIPs and dignitaries.

A cacophony filled the gallery while the invited guests

milled about eyeing her sketches and watercolours that adorned the walls, and Mark was soon lost amongst the throng as more people arrived.

One of the hired caterers walked past with a tray of canapés and champagne, and, after helping himself to a salmon and cream cheese vol-au-vent, he joined a small group at the far end who were discussing Lucy's artwork.

'Exquisite,' opined one woman.

'Such a unique touch with the brushstrokes,' agreed another. 'I shall be asking Heather to let me put a deposit on the one over there of the swans.'

Mark smiled, took a sip of champagne and made his way along the row of framed paintings, his chest swelling with pride.

He turned and crossed to the other side of the gallery, then saw Detective Inspector Ewan Kennedy in an animated discussion with another man, held up his hand in greeting and moved past.

'No, you're not getting an exclusive,' Kennedy growled. 'I don't care what your editor says. Now f—'

'Found you.'

Mark turned around as Lucy handed him another canapé.

'Cheers,' he said, clinking his drink against hers. 'And congratulations. I'm so proud of you.'

'Thank you.' She kissed him.

'Sounds like you're going to make a few sales tonight.'

'I hope so. Heather says she's had some enquiries, and it'd be good to have some money coming in.' She sipped her drink, then cocked her head to one side. 'What were you grinning at just now, anyway?'

'The journalist over there, trying to get an exclusive out of Kennedy before the media release goes out in the morning.'

Lucy craned her neck to see, then smiled as the reporter slunk from the gathering and out of the door. 'What did Ewan say to him?'

'Trust me,' said Mark, putting his arm around her shoulder and steering her towards a waiting cluster of art aficionados. 'It's not printable.'

THE END

ABOUT THE AUTHOR

Rachel Amphlett is a USA Today bestselling author of crime fiction and spy thrillers, many of which have been translated worldwide.

Her novels are available in eBook, print, and audiobook formats from libraries and retailers as well as her website shop.

A keen traveller, Rachel has both Australian and British citizenship.

Find out more about Rachel's books at: www.rachelamphlett.com.

Milton Keynes UK
Ingram Content Group UK Ltd.
UKHW041550220923
429032UK00002BA/6

9 781915 231581